# The Iron Relic
## Book II: Revelations

Bobby Hundley / James Stevenson

ON THE BOARDS PUBLISHING

Copyright © 2016 Bobby Hundley and James Stevenson

On The Boards Publishing

1005 East Las Tunas Blvd, #236

San Gabriel, CA 91776

Editor: FirstEditing.Com

Copyright © 2016 Illustrations by Bobby Hundley

Copyright © 2016 Cover Art by Bobby Hundley and James Stevenson

ISBN-10: 0-9863006-4-0

ISBN-13: 978-0-9863006-4-6

Library of Congress Control Number: 2014959231
On The Boards Publishing, San Gabriel, CA

Printed in the United States of America.

Visit The Iron Relic Book Series on the World Wide Web at

www.theironrelicbook.com

# DEDICATIONS

I would like to dedicate this book to the mothers in my life;
Anna, Lisa, Isabel, Henrietta, Lupe, Doris
And most of all to my mom,
Virginia aka Jeannie.
The love, support and lives of these tremendous women has and continues
to shape my life for the better. – Bobby Hundley

To Eric, Ethan, Tia and Jessica. – James Stevenson

# ACKNOWLEDGEMENTS

A special thanks to our families, friends and fans. Your encouragement and support has made the writing and success of this book series possible. We are eternally grateful to have you in our lives and sharing in this journey.

# DEDICATIONS

I would like to dedicate this book to the mothers in my life;
Anna, Lisa, Isabel, Henrietta, Lupe, Doris
And most of all to my mom,
Virginia aka Jeannie.
The love, support and lives of these tremendous women has and continues
to shape my life for the better. – Bobby Hundley

To Eric, Ethan, Tia and Jessica. – James Stevenson

# ACKNOWLEDGEMENTS

A special thanks to our families, friends and fans. Your encouragement and support has made the writing and success of this book series possible. We are eternally grateful to have you in our lives and sharing in this journey.

# Chapter 1.

*All will be revealed in thy neighbor's grave.*

The year was 1894; the place was a small village in County Clare, Ireland. Maeve Byrne hollered in pain as she clutched the wooden edge of the bed she was propped up on to deliver her child. She was a young woman of sixteen, nearly seventeen, with dark black, curly hair, bright emerald eyes, and soft facial features that were covered in the grime of a poorer, labor-filled life. Maeve's curly, black hair sank against her neck and shoulders, damp with sweat, and streaks of dirt ran down her cheeks like a mudslide as her face contorted in pain, pushing through another severe contraction. Her voice changed from a helpless scream of pain into a deep guttural yell of determination as she pushed.

The midwife's eyes lit up. She thrust her hands forward, gripped the newborn by the head and shoulders, and carefully but firmly pulled the child into the unfamiliar elements of the world. Maeve's voice exhaled and fell silent, exhausted. A cry broke the silence as the midwife cleaned the newborn's airways and placed the tiny gift of life onto Maeve's chest, skin to skin. Maeve looked upon the child in wonderment and a feeling of unconditional love that can only be understood through the experience of childbirth. Her world would forever be changed, and yet time seemed to hold still. She felt as if her child had always been a part of her life, even though the little boy had been placed in her arms moments earlier. Maeve wept tears of joy as she looked upon the boy's delicate face as he stretched his tiny hands and clasped his fingers to her garments.

"What are you going to call him?" whispered the midwife.

"My little Alroy. Alroy Byrne." Maeve gently kissed the boy's forehead as they rested comfortably. The bond between mother and child was now completely forged between them. Maeve was so infatuated with her little boy and exhausted from the ordeal that she barely noticed the afterbirth pains. Baby Alroy nuzzled his mother's chest as he began to purse his lips and suckle at the air.

"He's hungry," the midwife said with a wistful smile. The wrinkles crinkled across her face in a burst of joy at the beauty of new life.

As Maeve went to nurse the child, there was a sudden pounding coming from the other room. Terror overcame the midwife, who bolted for the window in order to flee the scene. The midwife climbed out of the window and motioned for Maeve to follow suit.

"Come, Maeve. Now. Hurry. It's the Order. They found us," the midwife said as her pupils burst in fright.

The fervor of the pounding on the door grew. The sounds of boots thumped the wooden barrier that shielded her from the hallway. Maeve gathered her son in her arms and strained to push herself off the bed, but it was too late. Maeve froze as the door to the room flew open and wood splinters exploded into the air.

The midwife disappeared from view, leaving Maeve and her baby Alroy to the horrors that awaited them. Several men rushed into the room and took hold of Maeve by her wrists and legs as a nun from the local convent gently but quickly swept up the baby in her arms. Maeve and her innocent child were abducted from their home and hauled off into the darkness toward an unknown future.

The midwife scurried up the backside of the dilapidated two story stone cottage, through the freezing, wet Christmas night air, and onto the thatched roof. The icy roof gnawed at her flesh as she crawled towards the peak. Once there, she stared down to the muddy and partially frozen street below. In the road, she made out the silhouette of a single horse-drawn, covered milk cart with a lone driver seated in the front.

Seconds later, the hunger cries of baby Alroy echoed between the buildings. The nun rushed the baby into the waiting cart, followed by several men who carried Maeve kicking and screaming by her arms and legs. The midwife watched, terrified and helpless, as the men shackled Maeve's wrists and then wrapped a dirty rag tightly around her weeping mouth before lifting her into the cart. With one swift crack of a whip, the horse bolted into action, pulling the covered milk cart down the unpaved road of the village with Maeve, the nun, and the baby stowed away inside.

Maeve tossed her head from side to side, searching for her baby as the cart bumped down the road. The nun leaned over to Maeve, helping her to her side, and placed the baby on Maeve's bosom. The sister slowly draped a tattered wool blanket over the mother and child. Maeve momentarily took comfort that her child was still alive, and even though she couldn't wrap her arms around the child, feeling the baby suckle gave her peace.

"I am Sister Mary Frances," the middle-aged nun said. Her face was worn, resembling a water ripple that extended out from her slender lips and across all the flesh that was visible outside her habit. "You will be under the care of the Order of the Merciful Sisters of Charity."

Maeve had known in her gut that this day might come. She had stayed on the move as much as possible during her unplanned pregnancy—the result of her infatuation with romance and a foolish pipe dream for a better life with an older man. Harold Walsh was ten years her senior. He filled her head with the fantasies of a new life away from Ireland—a new life in New York, a marvelous place, he told her, that knew no starvation or illness—a place where hard work made anything possible. He promised to marry her and whisk her off on the adventure of a lifetime. That all changed once he discovered she was pregnant. That is when Maeve learned that Harold Walsh was Harold Lynch, a merchant and father of two. What she fancied to be her reality was only an illusion brought about by a double-dealing rake who quickly disappeared from her life like an apparition.

Maeve had turned to her parents for guidance, but instead of support she was met with outrage and disdain. Her father threatened to lock her away in a house of ill repute claiming she had fallen to the darkness of prostitution. So Maeve did the only thing she felt she could. She knew her father kept a wooden box containing bank notes buried under a pile of rocks near the well on the family farm. She crept out of the house in the dead of night and, lit only by the glow of a pale blue moon, she stole the box and fled into the countryside.

Maeve intended to journey to the port in Queenstown, where she would use the money to purchase passage on a steamer headed for America. There perhaps her child and she would have the hope for a new life. But on her journey south Maeve contracted influenza. The weak young woman would have likely died with her unborn child if not for the kind and reclusive midwife, who found her starving in a back alley and rescued her. The midwife nursed Maeve back to health and hid her for months. When authorities came searching for Maeve, the midwife fled her home, taking Maeve with her, and headed for the coast.

Maeve was heavy with child, and the labor pains made it impossible for the women to press on. They were forced to stop traveling and take refuge in a small village in County Clare. *Oh, if only her son could have waited a couple more weeks before making his grand entrance to this bitter land*, she thought to herself. Then they would have found sanctuary aboard the steamer. Now she would have to face the harsh law of the land. She knew if she had any wish for a future with her child she must stay strong and survive what lay ahead.

The journey continued through the night and into the next day until shortly after mid-day, when the cart approached the entrance to the asylum for unwed mothers run by the Merciful Sisters of Charity. The entrance was through a single doorway in the center of a thick stone, three-story building that extended north and south. The building was dotted with small, square windows located at an equal distance from one another on both the first and second floors. At the north and south ends of the building a tall stone wall extended back, enclosing the compound and remaining buildings. The driver pulled the reins on the horse, bringing the cart to a slow stop. The man then climbed out of the front and went to assist Sister Mary Frances in unloading Maeve and her baby.

The front building adjoined in the center to a long rectangular building that connected east to west with another building that ran north and south, giving the stone complex an H shape with unpaved courtyards on either side of the center building. The front building housed the administers of the complex, comprised mostly of the nuns of the order, a medical officer, and a Roman Catholic priest. The building at the opposite end of the complex was the dormitories for the women in one wing and the children in the other wing.

Maeve was led into the front building, where she and her baby were processed. Both she and the child were bathed quickly, given a new set of clothes, and then returned to the front where Sister Mary Frances handed Maeve and Alroy off to another nun, Sister Maureen, who didn't appear much older than Maeve. Sister Maureen had an elegant stature to her body but a mousey face. Her skin was freckled and she had soothing crystal blue eyes that gave Maeve a strange sense of peace. *Perhaps Sister Maureen will be a godsend in this asylum, this dank, unforgiving tomb of stone and thatch,* Maeve thought to herself.

Sister Maureen escorted Maeve and her baby past the laundry and into the dining area, where she was given a bowl of broth, accompanied by bread and cheese. The other women of the asylum were all clothed in the same striped dress and smock. They barely took notice of Maeve and Alroy as she sat sheepishly amongst them. Some women had small children at their side, none more than two years old. Others sat quietly side by side, row by row, at the long tables, tearing at their bread and cheese. Maeve took notice of a woman in the row in front of her. The woman must have been all of nineteen or twenty years old, and she was holding a little boy over her shoulder. The little boy could not have been more than a year old. His hands gripped the back of his mother's smock so tightly that you could see where the garment was coming apart. Maeve looked down at Alroy, who was sleeping in her arms.

Sister Maureen stood beside and watched Maeve. "You need to eat," Sister Maureen said quickly. "When the meal hour is up they will clear your meal whether you've finished it or not. Following every meal, we have a prayer service. You are required to stay here."

"I'm allowed to have my son then?" Maeve responded cautiously, keeping her eyes down, staring at her broth.

Sister Maureen peered to each side of her to ensure she was not under the watchful eye of one of her superiors. "For a time," she whispered. "So long as you obey the rules and repent, they will leave your baby with you to nurse. If you try to run away, they will take him from you. Now eat."

Maeve lifted the slightly burnt bread to her mouth and bit into it. She barely had enough saliva to help her chew, and postpartum fatigue had firmly set in, but she forced herself to continue eating. With each bite, her body seemed to burn off the food as fast as she could swallow it, but at least she had her son, and that was reason enough to be thankful.

# Chapter 2.

Present Day

Adam was dumbfounded. He stared at his great-grandfather Henry, who was lying in the bed and said, with a question, just a name. "Alroy Byrne?"

Henry nodded and then lifted his arm steadily, pointing over Adam's shoulder. Henry was pointing at a particular wall in the library that was not only covered in precious works of art but spotted with a number of framed, black and white photographs. The photographs were of old buildings that now housed several of the orphanages that Henry was responsible for funding.

Adam glanced over at the wall. He focused his eyes on the glass of one of the framed photographs. The glass began to vibrate slowly. Then the frame shook, followed by another photograph and another and another until the entire wall trembled. Henry coughed hard, causing Adam to turn his attention back to his great-grandfather, who stared at him with glossed-over eyes. Adam stepped toward Henry and froze in horror. Henry's eyes sunk deep into their sockets, causing his face to shrivel and unfold before morphing into that of a decayed skull.

Adam stared down at the crucifix pendant that rested in his palm, but he was unable to lift his hands. He looked helplessly at the necklace. Suddenly, the skin on Adam's hands began to peel off, layer upon layer, and drift away from the necklace. Adam stood paralyzed by fear while the room rumbled around him. He squeezed his eyes closed until a wisp of lavender and lilac perfumed the air. Adam's eyes sprung awake.

Adam found himself seated in his first-class seat aboard his American Airlines flight headed for Dublin. Sweat had beaded across his forehead and the gentle touch of Rose's fingertips was upon his cheek. The soothing scent of her lavender and lilac hand cream calmed him.

"You were having quite the nightmare," Rose said, concerned. "Do you want me to get you some water?"

Adam nodded and wiped the sweat from his face.

Rose pressed the flight attendant call button. The

yellow light burst on like a beacon in the dark cabin. A few moments later, a pleasant flight attendant stood by their row.

"Would we be able to get a water, please?" Rose said as the flight attendant turned off the call button.

"Absolutely," the woman replied.

"Unopened. In whatever it comes in, please," Adam chimed in.

Rose understood his concern. After all, Adam had recently been drugged by the only relative he trusted.

"Sure thing. I'll be right back," the flight attendant said softly and headed for the galley.

"How are you, Adam?" Rose asked. Her eyes were both loving and concerned.

Adam let out a deep breath and shrugged his shoulders.

"If there was one word to describe how you feel?" She nudged.

"Tricky. That's how everything feels inside: not connected. I suppose a part of me has always felt a bit like a lost child—like an orphan to some extent. I know that must be strange growing up with all the advantages I had and family."

"It's not strange at all. You lost your mother and father at a young age."

Rose knew all too well his feeling. Her existence had been equal parts of trickery and abandonment. She was bred to serve the motherland, yet she had not stepped foot on Russian soil until she was a teenager. Born in the United States, her 'parents' moved and raised her in South America. There they indoctrinated her until she was ten years old when the family was planted back into the suburbs of the heartland of the United States. Rose continued to be homeschooled and tutored by agents living a double life as ordinary Americans. She showed signs of brilliance, scoring an IQ of 160 on not just one but two separate IQ tests. Then it happened.

As a teenager, agents determined Rose was exhibiting "nonconformist" tendencies and she found herself taken from her parents. She was sent to Moscow to complete her private education. It was in Moscow where she became fully initiated in the agency.

Years later, the agency returned Rose to the U.S., where she completed medical school and waited to be activated. Henry Calhoun had been her first and only assignment. Even though she vowed to never return to that life, she was terrified to tell Adam the truth. *He has been through so much, and time has the power to soften things*, she thought or at least was fighting very hard to convince herself of this. So she hid the truth about her origins further and put her focus back on him.

"Tell me more," she asked.

Adam hesitated and looked over her shoulder as the flight attendant stepped up to their row and handed Adam a chilled, sealed can of water.

"Thank you," Adam said, taking the water. Adam popped the tab, opening the can, and took a long sip. The flight attendant smiled and made her way back to the front of the plane.

Adam continued opening up to Rose. "I just feel like there is an empty closet that needs to be filled with knowledge. I'm hoping this trip will fix some of that— connect me to my past...my family's past. I would just like to know what I identify with. And these dreams keep....

"Ah, death sure does play a tricky tap dance on our minds that's for sure. The bits of knowledge that I grew up with has felt like its slowly been dissolving from my memory since my Papa's and Pete's passing. The good thing is that the dreams make me remember the sound of their voices. What a funny thing—the human voice. The sense of comfort the sound of someone's voice can give when it's that of someone close to us."

"I miss his voice as well. I miss hearing Henry's stories," Rose said with a genuine smile. She removed a guidebook on Ireland from the seat back in front of her.

14

The book had several tabs she had placed throughout it. Rose flipped to one of the tabs, showing the Whitefriar Street Church. "Did he ever tell you about this place? I'm sure he must have."

Adam looked over at the book. "Whitefriar Street Church? No, actually."

"Henry said they had the most beautiful stained-glass windows you have ever seen. That you can feel the sunshine that shines through them go straight into your soul. And inside the church are the remains of Saint Valentine."

"Sounds like the perfect date night," Adam joked.

"Yeah, well. I'm going there with or without you." She shot him a look. "So, what's it going to be, buddy?"

"With me." Adam smiled. He was falling deeply in love with this woman. The protective shield he had placed around his heart when Tara died had opened. He was scared, but he felt free to love. "Always, with me." He leaned in to her and kissed her softly.

***

Late Thursday Night, Ohio

Pastor Faith drove his long, Olympic White 1962 Cadillac Eldorado Biarritz convertible into the parking lot of the Mid-City Plaza Motel. After parking in the spot designated for motel registration, he took a moment to check his reflection in the rearview mirror. He wanted to make sure his hair and teeth were perfect for meeting a member of the general public.

Pastor Faith had driven the three hundred miles from Chicago with one thing on his mind: he was going to get the relic. His plan was a simple one. He was to gain an interview with Dr. Adam Calhoun under the guise that he was interested in having the good doctor as a guest on the next "Second Coming" television special. During the fake interview, Pastor Faith would trick the doctor into admitting the existence and revealing the whereabouts of the cross necklace. He would then simply steal the necklace and go back to Chicago, leaving the doctor waiting for a call from the show, not even knowing he had been relieved of ownership of the relic.

After making sure that he looked his best, he took his white suit jacket that had been lying flat on the sandalwood leather passenger seat and flung it over his shoulder as he walked into the motel office to check in.

A thin, pale, white-haired man of about seventy years sat on a high-legged recliner, wrapped in a detailed tapestry design upholstery fabric that looked to be made in the mid nineteen sixties in the lobby of the motel office

16

and watched the television that was mounted high in the corner of the room on a bracket. The man seemed to take no notice of Pastor Faith as he entered the lobby until he shouted, just as the Pastor was about to ring a counter bell in front of the office window.

"Rachel," the old man shouted, "you've got one waiting!"

Just then, a small white-haired woman of about the same age as the man came scurrying from a back room and walked up to the window of the office. She looked at Pastor Faith and for a moment she froze, not moving a muscle. After a second or two, the corners of her mouth began to twitch as they curved up into a warm smile.

"I think I know you," the woman said.

"Do you have a room?" Pastor Faith asked, not paying attention to the woman's gaze.

"You're Pastor Faith." The woman chuckled. "We watch your specials whenever they come on. We never miss a one."

"Well, bless your heart," Pastor Faith replied, flashing the little woman a brilliant smile. "You wouldn't mind letting me stay here for a while, would you?"

"Not at all," the woman said as she slid a room key with the number ten on the fob, "you can stay here for as long as you want. Here's the key to room ten. It's the furthest one down and you'll have the most privacy there. Check out time is eleven am, but don't you worry about that. Is there anything else I can do for you?"

"As a matter of fact, there is. Would you be so kind as to point me toward Hope Hospital?" Pastor Faith asked.

"Oh, you can't miss it," she replied, "Turn left out of the lot and go straight for six blocks. The hospital will be on your left. Do you mind if I ask you one question about your show?"

"Not at all," Pastor Faith replied. He braced himself for the usual questions that he got from people concerning his shows and healing events. Usually the questions came from a place of positive belief. Once in a while, however they came from a place of disbelief. "When did you realize you could heal people?" was one of the questions he usually got from a believer. "How much do you have to pay those people who pretend to pass out after you touch them?" was a question he usually got from a disbeliever.

"Have the ushers ever missed a fainter, Pastor?" The woman asked.

"I'm sorry?" Pastor Faith asked, not understanding what the woman was asking, as he took up the key.

"When you heal someone and they pass out. Have the ushers ever missed and let the person hit the floor? That's what the mister and I are always looking out for whenever we watch one of your TV specials."

"Not yet, but keep watching. You never know." Pastor Faith said with a smile. Then he turned toward the door and on his way out he said, "Thank you so much for the room and the viewership."

Several minutes later, Pastor Faith had set his suitcase on the foot of the bed in the motel room and looked at the flyer on the dresser that listed the local restaurants in the area. The flyer was a disappointing list of fast food burger and pizza places with the exception of one twenty-four-hour diner. Pastor Faith sighed and patted his belly, knowing that the next couple of days would be torture on his ulcers. He dropped the restaurant flyer onto the dresser and laid himself down on the bed without removing the covers. He quickly fell asleep and snored loudly until morning.

***

Adam shifted in his seat as the plane lowered its landing gear. He felt the butterflies of anticipation swell in his stomach before exhaling a deep sigh.

"We made it," Rose remarked as she took Adam's hand in hers. After a few moments, the plane was safely on the ground in Ireland with the fasten seat belt sign off.

Adam stepped into the aisle and proceeded to remove

his suitcase from the overhead bin. As he grasped the underside of the suitcase, his fingers came within inches of touching the paper-thin tracking device that was secretly planted there before he flew out of Ohio.

He set the suitcase on the ground, extended the handle, and rolled it behind him as he followed Rose off the plane. The couple nodded and thanked the flight attendants for a pleasant flight and stepped out of the plane and into the corridor leading to the terminal.

"Phew," Adam exclaimed as he blew out a deep breath. "Solid ground at last."

"And the adventure continues," Rose added before the two set off towards baggage claim and customs.

In the waiting area on the other side of customs, a sharply dressed driver was visible, holding a sign with the name Calhoun printed in bold letters on it.

"There's our ride," Adam pointed out as they worked their way through the custom's line to have their passports checked.

The customs agent took both of their passports and then asked, "Business or pleasure?"

"Pleasure," Rose responded.

"Honeymoon?" the agent said with a curious smile.

"No," Adam interjected.

"Sadly," Rose jested as she held up her ringless finger.

"Well, Doctor, may I give you a bit of advice," the agent said boldly. "I would suggest you remedy that or she might get caught up in the charm of romantic Ireland and stay here forever."

Adam chuckled to himself. "Thanks for the advice."

"Enjoy your vacation."

Adam and Rose collected their passports and made their way towards the waiting driver. As Adam rolled his carry-on suitcase, the hidden tracking device silently began transmitting signals to a nearby relay station where the signal was amplified and transferred across the English Channel and all the way to Russia, where Adam's location appeared as a green blip on the screen of a cell phone resting in the withered palm of Pavel Volkov. The aged man, who was once called the Siberian Tiger, was back on the hunt.

Known for his calculated and ruthless personality, Volkov once survived a trek through artic temperatures during an escape-and-evade maneuver before returning to Mother Russia with a number of classified documents stolen from the U.S. Army. This amazing feat cost him the tips of his pointer and middle fingers on his right hand but earned him the nickname the Siberian Tiger. But like the tiger, he too was now an endangered breed and found himself on the cusp of being phased out of the agency—a habitat in which he thrived during the Cold War. He stared at the little green dot on his cell phone. This simple dot represented a return to glory—a new beginning instead of the slow death of retirement. His eyes flared and his lips creased out into a maniacal grin. *I will soon have my prey*, he thought.

# Chapter 3.

Pastor Faith woke early and eagerly took to his morning routine. He showered, shaved, brushed his teeth, and dressed himself in his favorite all-white suit. After spending a few minutes combing and re-combing his bright red hair to ensure perfection, he got down on his knees at the foot of the motel bed and said his morning prayer.

"Lord, I thank you for this new day. I thank you for your protection, guidance and love. Thank you for the opportunities that you will present to me on this day. And thank you for bringing me one day closer to achieving my goals. Thank you for bringing me one day closer to getting the crucifix and ridding the earth of the vile curse that preys upon it. In your name I pray."

He left the motel and drove his long white Cadillac

toward Hope Hospital. Along the way, he stopped at the diner that was listed on the motel's restaurant list. Pastor Faith thought it looked to be a quaint little place with red vinyl booth seats to offset the black and white checkered floors. He especially liked the old photos of trains and train stations that decorated the walls of the diner.

He was seated, unknown to him, in the same booth where Dr. Adam Calhoun and Peter Calhoun-Mitchell sat the day after Hiram and Horace Grey had attacked Adam in his home looking for the crucifix necklace. He ordered and ate the steak and eggs breakfast from the menu. His eggs were fried, over-easy, and the steak was cooked rare. Blood and egg yolk covered the bottom of the entire platter at the end of his meal, but not a speck of anything tarnished his all white suit. As he paid for his breakfast at the counter, the diner manager asked if he wanted to add a tip for the waitress. Pastor Faith smiled his large and brilliant white smile and replied, "I'll pray for her soul."

Hope Hospital seemed quiet to Pastor Faith as he walked into the main entrance. He was expecting to see nurses and doctors rushing about as paramedics pushed gurneys with patients on them. Instead, what he found was a quiet lobby with a round information desk in the middle. Three hospital volunteers were seated at the information desk. Two were women, in their sixties, who were chatting away with each other, and a man who appeared to be in his late thirties reading a book. Off to the side of them was a small television playing a daytime talk show at a low volume. Suddenly the sound to the talk show cut out and a "Breaking News" bar flashed across the television screen, catching the attention of the two women chatting. The program cut to a live feed where a poised, battle-hardened, female field reporter was on scene, holding a microphone outside the steps of a high-rise building in New York City's financial district. The scene around her was absolute pandemonium, with news reporters rushing on scene and onlookers gawking and taking pictures along the sidewalk. The two women turned their full attention to the breaking news story. One of the ladies tapped the man reading a book on the shoulder and turned up the volume to the television.

The field reporter spoke directly into the camera. "In breaking news: a multi-state raid carried out by the FBI and the Department of Homeland Security led to the arrest of fifteen suspected Russian spies this past week. The raid is the culmination of a secret, year-long operation that uncovered the ring of Russian sleeper spies in New York City, Boston, and Washington, D.C."

The newscast cut away to a stout and bearded man in his late fifties dressed in a dark blue suit being escorted out of one of the high-rise buildings by federal agents. The bearded man turned to the news camera and protested his innocence, shouting in a heavy Baltic accent. "I am no spy. I have been working here for over thirty years! This is absurd!"

The newscast cut back to the field reporter who continued her report. "The spies are believed to have been planted in the U.S. by the Russian Foreign Intelligence Service, also known as the SVR, and were using an intricate network of communication to conduct illegal spying from Wall Street to Washington D.C. A spokesperson for the SVR declined to comment; however, the Kremlin disavowed any agents operating undercover in the U.S. and expressed a willingness to assist the FBI and Homeland Security with their investigation."

Pastor Faith approached the desk, causing the man to break away from the news report.

"Good morning, sir. May I help you?" the man asked.

"I'm here to see Dr. Adam Calhoun," Pastor Faith replied.

"Do you have an appointment?"

"Actually, I do not," Pastor Faith confessed with a smile. "I'm Pastor Faith, from the Second Coming

Ministries. I wanted to speak with Dr. Calhoun concerning—"

"I'm sorry sir," the information desk attendant interrupted, "the hospital does not allow reporters beyond the lobby, and we have a strict policy against—"

"Son, I am no reporter," Pastor Faith said with a slight tinge of agitation in his voice. "I am Pastor Faith. I'm a faith healer, a man of God who has come to discuss the miraculous healing that Dr. Calhoun has performed."

"Again, I'm sorry sir," the information desk attendant began, "but unless you have an appointment, the best I can do is give you the phone number of his office."

"Caleb, do you know who this man is?" one of the older women asked the attendant.

"Um, no Judith, I'm afraid that the pastor is not familiar to me," Caleb said in reply to the interruption.

"This is Pastor Faith. He lays hands on people," Judith said. "Is there something I can help you with?" she asked Pastor Faith, taking over the conversation from Caleb.

"I came to see if I could have a moment with Dr. Calhoun," Pastor Faith said. "I would love to have him as a special guest on my next television special. I just need to interview him in person first."

"Well, I'm sorry," Judith replied after looking at her

computer monitor. "It appears that Dr. Calhoun is scheduled out for quite some time. He probably went on vacation. I would assume he needed one after all of the attention he was getting about the Martinez Miracle. Then his uncle and cousin died. That was tragic, and it happened so soon after his great-grandfather passed. Oh, it's all so sad." She turned her attention back to the computer. "It doesn't say when he'll return, so I would check back in a few days if I were you. You can always call so you don't have to waste the time coming all the way down here. I'll give you Dr. Calhoun's office number. Give me a second to look it up."

As Judith was looking up the phone number, Pastor Faith's mind raced. If the doctor wasn't even in town, then how could he get his hands on the necklace? Should he go back to Chicago and wait for another chance to meet Adam, or should he wait here and hope that the doctor's return would be soon? A brilliant idea came to the pastor as Judith was handing him a small card that she had just written the telephone number for Adam's office on.

"I would like to volunteer to be a servant of the Lord here," Pastor Faith said, having seceded to lie in wait for Adam's return. "I would like to speak with whoever is in charge with the clergy here."

"That would be Father Kellen," Judith said. "He's the

hospital chaplain. He witnessed the Martinez Miracle too. Boy has his schedule gotten busy after that. I'm sure he'd be glad to have you on board, Pastor Faith. Wait just one moment while I see if he's available to see you."

Judith called Father Kellen and told him that Pastor Faith was waiting in the lobby to see him. Father Kellen, the good faith ambassador of the hospital and Catholic Church that he was, told Judith to send Pastor Faith to his office right away. He had been planning to take his lunch, but he put it off for the meeting.

Pastor Faith met with Father Kellen and convinced him to allow him to work out of the hospital chapel as part of a P.R. exchange. Pastor Faith would bring more press to the hospital, volunteering his time praying with the sick that weren't Catholic.

Pastor Faith went back to his motel room and unpacked his suitcase. He would be staying for longer than he initially planned. He would need to shop for a few more clothes, toiletry items, and antacids for his stomach.

# Chapter 4.

Detective Hiro Tarsus sat behind his desk, which was located in the back corner of the homicide department. He was finishing his report on the shooting death of Peter Calhoun-Mitchell and the man that called himself Father Claudio. He was troubled, not by the statement form that he was filling out, or by the story that witness, Dr. Adam Calhoun, had told him about a priceless artifact that the mysterious Claudio was after. What troubled the forty-year-old homicide detective was something that he himself had witnessed at the home of Adam's aunt, Helen Morales.

Detective Tarsus recalled that after he took Adam's initial statement, he escorted the shaken-up doctor to his aunt's home to deliver the news about the deaths of her son, Jordy, and brother, Pete. When they arrived at

Helen's impeccably clean and well-maintained three-story colonial home, she was obviously totally blind. The detective recalled how she stared blankly directly in front of her as she opened the door. He also remembered how she walked carefully into the sitting room, seeming to count her steps to the couch. He recalled watching her very delicately set her cup of coffee onto the coffee table directly in front of her with both hands. Detective Tarsus noticed how her thumbs both scanned the surface of the coffee table finding the beveled edge marking the distance of the cup from the edge of the table.

The veteran detective also remembered the pain in Helen's face upon learning of the deaths of her son and brother. As a homicide detective, he had delivered tragic news to many people. It never got easier. Delivering the news always left him with a feeling of helplessness. His job was to investigate and solve murders that had already happened. Hiro often told himself that putting those criminals away was preventing future crimes, but that knowledge was usually little comfort when the pain of losing a loved one was shown to him mere feet away.

The detective remembered stepping into the hallway so that Adam and Helen could speak privately. He remembered the odor of an Italian dish wafting from the kitchen. Hiro thought the odor was from a lasagna being baked to perfection by Helen's son, Sean, who had been called from the kitchen by his mother. Paintings along the wall in Helen's hallway looked expensive and religious in nature. The table near the front door was an antique, as were most of the furnishings in the home.

He also remembered Adam's panicked cry for help, "Detective! Detective!" Hiro ran into the sitting room with his weapon drawn. He saw Helen still seated on the couch. Adam was standing in a defensive position, facing an older man dressed in priest's garb. There seemed to be no immediate danger to anyone in the room, so Hiro re-holstered his weapon. The priest turned out to be Father Vigano from the Vatican Guard. Hiro watched as Helen and Sean exited the room to leave the priest and her nephew in private. That was only a moment before Adam asked the detective if he would wait out in the hall so the two could talk in private. Hiro remembered going back out into the hall and returning his attention to the artwork and the smell of warm marinara and beef infusing together.

Then suddenly, Detective Tarsus' mind landed on what had been bothering him about that day. Helen's blindness. It had seemed to cure itself. She was totally blind when he and Adam arrived. Minutes later, Helen stood and told her son, Sean, "I'm fine, I'd like for you to take me to go see your brother." She was no longer blind when she and Sean walked out of the room.

"She was no longer blind." Detective Tarsus muttered to himself as he reached for his phone and looked at his notes for the cell phone number of Dr. Adam Calhoun. Hiro dialed Adam's number and listened as the phone rang three times before delivering Adam's short outgoing message.

"Dr. Calhoun, this is Detective Tarsus. Sorry to bother you, but I am finishing my reports and I have a couple of questions regarding the case. If you could call me back at your earliest convenience, I would greatly appreciate it." The detective continued with leaving his office number and the number to his cell phone before ending the call. He stared at his paperwork for several minutes, stroking his dark mustache and goatee with his left hand as he often did when he was deep in thought. His thoughts went to the body of the mysterious Father Claudio, the man with no ID, fingerprints, or any other traceable material on his corpse, then to Peter Mitchell, the deceased millionaire who drugged his own nephew in an effort to retrieve a necklace.

Next he considered Adam's cousin Jordy, the silver-spooned baby turned strung-out junky that got shot in an alley by the mysterious Claudio while trying to steal the necklace from Adam. Finally, he thought about the Grey brothers, Hiram and Horace, two thugs that kidnapped the doctor Rose Powell and ransomed her return in exchange for the necklace. They were both shot presumably by Claudio. All of these events seemed to revolve around the necklace that Adam was given by his great-grandfather shortly before his death. *This case is strange*, Hiro thought to himself. *There's something more to this necklace than Adam was letting on.* The detective couldn't shake the feeling that he was missing important information about this necklace, and it somehow tied in with Helen's sudden ability to see.

"Tarsus! I need to see you in my office, now." Hiro's train of thought was broken as he snapped his head toward the office at the head of the homicide department when he heard Captain Conrad shout his name and order.

Captain Hugh Conrad worked hard at appearing to be a stereotypical hard-nosed police captain. The balding, slightly overweight fifty-seven-year-old often rolled his sleeves to his elbows after draping his jacket over the back of his chair, neglecting his coat rack that stood in the corner of his office. He was normally seen with a dark-colored tie that matched his dark suspenders that held up his either khaki or brown flat-front pants. Captain Conrad completed his look with a pair of slightly scuffed black-leather, plain-toe oxford shoes, one of which he was tapping the toe of on his office floor as he watched Detective Tarsus quickly get up from his desk and make the twenty-foot journey into his office.

"Close the door behind you," Captain Conrad told Hiro as he walked into the room.

Hiro closed the door as per his captain's request. He noticed a man in a dark suit standing next to Captain Conrad's desk. The man was tall and broad shouldered. His dark brown hair was styled very precisely. The man's sideburns were squared off exactly at mid lobe on each ear. The hair on the sides of his head was shaved short and trimmed to a military standard one quarter inch above the ear lobe. His hair gradually lengthened as it neared the top of his head, but no longer than two inches in total length, just enough to create a part line and comb to the right. Hiro also noticed the man's suit, a black, Italian-styled, two-button jacket fit the man well, but it was bought off the rack, not tailored, as were the man's slacks and tie that were all made from the same material as the jacket. *This man is FBI*, Hiro thought to himself, *but not your usual run of the mill agent.*

"Detective Tarsus, this is Special Agent John Bulwark with Homeland Security." Captain Conrad said with obvious distain in his voice. "I need you to box up

35

everything you have on the Calhoun case and hand it over to him now."

"Sir, I am hardly finished with the reports, plus I have—" Hiro began to reply.

"It doesn't matter!" The captain snapped, his temper getting the best of him. "The case is now in the hands of Homeland Security. They're taking over as of right now, and they don't want to share any information with us. They have their reasons I suppose." The captain continued while giving a sideways glance at Special Agent Bulwark.

"Detective Tarsus," Bulwark said, "one of the victims in your case is a person of interest to the federal government. I wish I could read you in on the matter, but due to the delicate nature of the case, I am not allowed to. My department will handle all angles of the case, and I assure you that justice will be brought to those who deserve it. For now, I need you to hand over all of your evidence and reports and consider the case closed."

Detective Tarsus stood in silence for a moment. He stared directly into Special Agent Bulwark's light blue eyes, looking for weakness; there was none. He then turned his gaze to his police captain.

"Captain, you can't expect me to just quit this case," Detective Tarsus protested.

"I expect you to do what you're told. Turn over all materials and move on to another case," Captain Conrad sternly said.

"Yes sir," Hiro replied, "I'll get a box and start with what's in the evidence locker."

"Never mind with that," Bulwark interjected. "Everything in the evidence locker has already been gathered. What I need is what you have in your possession, Detective Tarsus. I need your reports and notes. All of them."

Hiro turned and walked out of the captain's office and headed straight to his desk. He felt pangs of distrust from his captain and Special Agent Bulwark. *Why would they clear out the evidence locker before they notified me they were taking over the case?* he wondered. *Don't they trust me, and if not, why?*

Hiro didn't notice the curious stares from the other detectives as he walked past them in deep thought. What he did notice was that Bulwark was keeping pace, right behind him. The agent from Homeland Security apparently wanted to make sure that Hiro turned in all of the reports and notes, and he was in a hurry for them.

Hiro quickly gathered up his report forms on the case and returned them to the yellow file folder that was lying open on the corner of his desk. He then put the folder in the large, brown, accordion-style folder carrier that contained all of the forms and files that Hiro had compiled on the case so far. He closed the top on the folder carrier and motioned to the special agent that the files were ready to be taken.

"I will also need all of your notes," Bulwark stressed.

"Everything that I have compiled is in this box," Hiro replied.

"Even your notes from the scene?" the special agent probed. "Most detectives take notes from the scene in little notebooks like the one in your jacket pocket," he added as he pointed to the jacket that was draped over the back of the chair at Hiro's desk.

"Oh, of course; I forgot about those," Hiro said as he took the small black notebook out of the jacket pocket. He then flipped passed the first couple of pages and tore out six pages of hand-written notes that he had taken as he took Adam's initial statement on the night of the murders. He re-opened the large, brown, accordion-style file folder carrier and carefully placed the six small pieces of paper in the front of the first file. He then closed the lid again and took a step back, away from his desk, signaling to the special agent that his task was complete.

Bulwark took the case in both hands and quickly walked out of the room without speaking another word.

"A thank you would have been nice." Captain Conrad said loudly out from the doorway of his office after the Homeland Security agent disappeared. He and Hiro locked eyes for a moment. The short shrug of Captain Conrad's shoulders reassured Hiro. It told him that the captain was on his side and that having the investigation pulled from him was not in the captain's control. The motion was a slight reassurance that Hiro felt comforted by.

Detective Tarsus seated himself at his desk and looked at his watch. It was a simple white-faced and black-numbered watch. It was four thirty in the afternoon. He opened the top left drawer of his desk and grabbed the envelope that was lying inside. It was addressed to his grandparents in Japan. Inside of the envelope was a check for nine hundred seventy-five dollars that Hiro made to his grandfather.

Every month, Hiro sent his grandparents twenty-five percent of his net income. He did this out of the great respect he had for his grandparents, and he also did it because he could. Hiro was earning a decent salary for a homicide detective, and he never lived outside of his means. In giving his grandparents a percentage of his income, he was ensuring them a greater quality of life in Japan, which gave peace to Hiro's soul. According to his watch, Hiro had thirty minutes to get the letter to the post office on St. Claire Street to be stamped and sent off before the post office closed. Hiro mailed the check and went home.

# Chapter 5.

The next morning, before going in to the precinct, Detective Tarsus made a stop at Helen Morales' house.

Hiro rang the doorbell and checked his watch. It was five minutes after nine on that Saturday morning. Sean Morales, Helen's son answered the door.

"May I help you?" Sean asked.

"Yes, I am Detective Hiro Tarsus," Hiro began as he showed Sean his badge, "and I need to ask your mother a few more questions concerning the deaths of your brother and uncle."

"I don't think mom wants to talk about it," Sean told the detective as he slowly began to close the door.

"Please," Hiro interjected, "I need to speak to her about her condition."

"Sean, let him in." Helen called out from within the

house just as the door was about to be closed in the detective's face.

Sean opened the door and grudgingly led the detective down the corridor to the same bright pink sitting room as before. Hiro sat himself on the long white couch and thanked Sean for showing him in. Sean quickly left the room without a word.

Moments later, Helen entered the sitting room. Hiro stood and noticed she was wearing a black, three-quarter-sleeved, faux wrap-around dress with a self-tied belt synched neatly to her left hip. Her shoulder-length hair was pulled tightly into a bun. Hiro also noticed that she was not wearing any jewelry. Her black, closed-toed flats completed her look of the mourning mother.

"Good morning, Mrs. Morales," Hiro said. "Thank you for agreeing to see me."

"I don't mean to be rude, Detective," Helen began as she sat at the opposite end of the couch, "but I've recently buried my grandfather, brother, and youngest son. I've become the executor of my grandfather's will. And a large portion of his estate now belongs to me. My brother Peter bequeathed his entire fortune to me as well. I find myself overcome with grief and responsible for a great many large decisions."

"News reporters are saying that mother is now the

richest woman in America," Sean interrupted cheerfully as he brought a silver tray with two tea cups, a teapot, and a small dish of shortbread cookies into the room. He set the tray onto the coffee table in front of Helen and then poured tea into the two cups. "Do you take milk or sugar in your tea, Detective?" Sean asked.

"No thank you," Hiro replied.

Sean handed Hiro his tea, smiled at the detective, and quickly left the room. Hiro thought the young man seemed awfully bright and cheerful for a man who had just lost his great-grandfather, uncle, and brother. He almost commented on the young man's odd behavior but then decided against it and turned his attention back to Helen.

"I am sorry for your losses, Mrs. Morales," Hiro said. Then he chose his words carefully. "The first time we met, I brought your nephew Adam here. Do you remember that, Mrs. Morales?"

"Of course I do," Helen replied. "What is your point Detective? Just ask the questions you came to ask."

"When you answered the door, you were blind. Then by the time you and your son left to go to the morgue, you had your sight back. How can you explain that?"

Helen shifted in her seat and took a sip of tea, then placed the cup back onto the coffee table. "I thought Adam told you that my brother Peter had been poisoning me to induce the blindness," she said.

"Yes he did, however if you could remind me as to why your brother was poisoning you?" Hiro asked.

"I can assure you, Detective, that I don't know," Helen replied. "My brother was a very rich eccentric man. He did a lot of things that I can't explain. What I do know is that he used chemicals to induce my blindness, and the chemicals that he used obviously wore off."

"It seems that they wore off rather quickly."

"I'm not seeing your point, Detective. Are you insinuating that I was faking my illness?"

"Of course I'm not, Mrs. Morales. I am just trying to understand what took place."

"What took place is my brother and son were killed by a crazed lunatic!" Helen snapped at him. "Your job is to investigate that, not what happened to me. The chemicals that caused my blindness wore off, simple as that. I'm no chemist, Detective, and neither are you. You need to find out why a man disguised as a priest came after my family."

"That is the second reason that I am here," Detective Tarsus replied timidly. "Your brother and son's case has been transferred to the Department of Homeland Security and is being investigated by a Special Agent Bulwark. I am no longer working on the case. I can give you the phone number of the—"

"Why is their case a federal matter?" Helen asked, cutting the detective off. "Who was the man that killed them?"

"I'm afraid that I was not able to identify the man that shot your son and brother before the case was taken from me. All I can tell you is that the man I was investigating had no fingerprints; there were no dental records that I could find that matched his teeth, and there were no photos that matched him in any database I used. He was a ghost, Mrs. Morales. And in my experience, that means that he was either a hit man or a spy."

"You mean like a Russian spy?" Helen asked.

"Well, the Cold War ended many years ago, Mrs. Morales, but if I were a betting man, I would say yes, just like a Russian spy."

Helen's demeanor changed suddenly. Her hands reached around her neck, looking for the hair that she usually grasped and pulled as a response to nervousness. She folded them tightly onto her lap. She knew that her brother Pete had poisoned her in an attempt to locate Grandpa Henry's necklace. She also had figured that the man disguised as Father Claudio was trying to steal the necklace as well. But upon hearing that there was a possibility that the man was a Russian spy changed everything. She knew that she had to keep the existence of the relic contained in the crucifix necklace that Adam had used to heal her blindness a secret, but there were other secrets that Helen was keeping as well. Secrets that included Helen's knowledge of the existence of a certain Russian spy many years ago.

"I'm sorry to have to cut your visit short, Detective," Helen said while she stood and ushered the detective to the door. "I have a lot to do, and if you are no longer handling my son and brother's case then I guess there is nothing else for us to discuss. Thank you for your time and efforts. Good bye."

Hiro stood on the porch of the large colonial home and stared at the closed door for a moment. Helen's behavior and sudden urge to see him out seemed strange to him. He turned and walked to his car. As he got in the black Crown Victoria, he reached for his seatbelt and buckled it. Then his cell phone rang. It was Adam, returning his call from the day before.

"Dr. Calhoun, thank you for returning my call," Hiro said as he put the phone to his ear.

"Yes, hello Detective," Adam replied, "sorry I missed your call yesterday. What can I help you with?"

"Well, actually when I called you, I had questions

concerning your Aunt Helen's eyesight on the night of your uncle's murder," Hiro said.

"What is your question, Detective?" Adam asked.

Hiro thought for a moment. The case was no longer his to investigate. Special Agent Bulwark made sure that the message was clear to Hiro that this was now a matter for Homeland Security. He thought on Helen's miraculous recovery and her sudden change in demeanor when she found out that the man posing as Father Claudio was not an ordinary thief. Hiro could easily wait for another case. Homicides weren't everyday occurrences in his small but growing city, but he was sure that there would eventually be another one. He could also assist another detective in solving their case. Most of the detectives in the homicide division weren't as territorial with their cases as television shows and the movies like to make them out to be. There were several things that Hiro could do instead of continuing to investigate the Calhoun family. Only Detective Hiro Tarsus' conscience would not let him. He knew that the questions that he had would continue to bother him if he didn't at least try to answer them.

"Can you meet me somewhere in person?" Hiro asked. "I have a few questions, and I think that a face-to-face meeting would be better. It doesn't have to be at the precinct; we can meet at a café or your home perhaps."

"I'm sorry, Detective, but I'm out of the country. I flew to Ireland and I can't say exactly when I will be back. If you could just ask me your question, I promise you that I will try to help as best as I can."

"Oh, I spoke to your Aunt Helen about her sudden recovery during our visit."

"Yes, and what did she say?"

"She told me that the chemicals used to induce her blindness must have worn off quickly."

"I'm afraid that I have nothing to add to her statement, Detective. If that is what my Aunt Helen says, then that's what happened."

"Yes of course, but later in our conversation when I revealed that the man posing as Father Claudio had no fingerprints and could not be found in any database and that the case had been taken over by Homeland Security, she became, well, frightened."

"What do you mean Homeland Security took over the case?"

"Exactly that, Doctor. It seems that what no one is willing to say is that the man who called himself Father Claudio is a man of special interest to our federal government. My guess is that he is either an assassin hired to kill members of your family, and if so, why? Or he was sent here from another government to retrieve something, and if so, what?"

Adam paused for a long moment. He did not want to reveal the relic to Detective Tarsus or anyone else. There had been enough death revolving around the object. Then Adam considered what the detective had said. If another country was trying to get their hands on the necklace, then that country would not give up with the death of one operative; they would send another. Adam recalled leaving the necklace tucked between the top mattress and box spring of Eli's bed. If someone else was looking for the necklace, then Eli was in grave danger.

"Detective, I can't answer your questions," Adam said. "Am I correct in thinking that you are no longer investigating my uncle and cousin's murders because the federal government has intervened?"

"You are correct, Dr. Calhoun," Hiro replied.

"Detective, are you a man of your word?"

"Yes, I believe so."

"Then I need you to give me your word on something."

"That depends on your request."

"I have a friend. His name is Eli Taylor. I usually visit him twice a week, and while I'm out of the country I'm going to miss my visits. I need you to go see him."

"I'm not sure that I understand your request, Doctor."

"He's my best friend and he's dying of cancer. I'm

afraid that he may only have days left, but I need someone to be there for him. I need you to promise me that you will go to his house and tell him that you are there in my place. He likes chess."

"You want me to visit your dying friend."

"I want you to keep an eye on him until I return."

Hiro agreed to visit Eli. Adam gave him the address and ended the call. Hiro then looked over at Helen's house. A curtain in the front of the house quickly swung back into its place. Someone from within the house was watching him. Hiro put the keys in the ignition, started the car and drove to the police precinct, where he would decide what his next move would be.

Twenty minutes later at the homicide department, Hiro draped his jacket over the back of his chair and sat down at his desk. He was unhappy with the way things had turned out over the last couple of days. Having a case taken from him was hurtful enough, but this case gnawed at him and that made it worse. Hiro kept going over details of the case with all of its victims fresh in his mind. He tried to block them out of his mind, but he couldn't. Hiro knew that he needed to find something that would calm his mind, but he couldn't think of anything. As the stress mounted within him, he reached for a file folder in his out basket and placed it over the clear spot on his desk where the Calhoun-Mitchell file had been. When he placed the file on his desk, a glint of light shining from underneath his out basket on his desk shone right in his eye, making him squint.

Hiro bent his head down, almost resting his cheek on the desk top and peered under the basket to see what the object was that was reflecting light back into his eyes. It was a cell phone. With two fingers, Hiro dragged the phone out from under the basket. He pondered over the phone for a moment and then remembered where the phone had come from.

During the investigation, witness Dr. Adam Calhoun had told the detective of a warehouse where Dr. Rose Powell had been taken and held for ransom. When Detective Tarsus went to the warehouse, he found the bodies of two men wearing ski masks. Horace Grey, the smaller of the two, was found lying on the floor, looking up. He had been shot in between the eyes with a nine millimeter. A large hunting knife was still gripped in his hand. Horace's brother, Hiram, was found several feet closer to the door than his brother. He too had been shot between the eyes with a nine-millimeter gun. A cell phone lay near his body. Detective Tarsus assumed the phone had come out of the large man's breast pocket and slid off the man's chest as he died. Detective Tarsus had taken the phone and intended to turn it in as evidence after he had it checked out by the forensics lab.

Hiro thought hard and could not remember what had happened that day that would have distracted him so much as to lose a piece of evidence. Nothing like this had ever happened to Hiro before. He was always meticulous with his notes and always followed procedure. He knew he should take the phone to Captain Conrad. He should turn it in to be given to Special Agent Bulwark. He would most likely be punished for misplacing evidence, but Hiro knew that it was the proper thing to do. Hiro also knew that no one other than he knew the phone existed. He could quickly check the phone out and quite possibly there could be information on it that may answer a question or two that he had concerning the case.

Hiro chose to keep the phone. He tucked it into his jacket pocket and left the building. When he got into his car, he pulled the phone out of his jacket pocket and pressed the power button in an attempt to activate the phone. It was dead. He looked at the charge port on the phone and confirmed that it was the same size and shape as the port on his own phone. He would take the phone home and charge its battery on his charger. Once the phone was powered up, Hiro would be able to check its contents.

# Chapter 6.

Eli Taylor was lying in his bed weaving in and out of consciousness. His blonde hair gently fluttered from the breeze provided from the ceiling fan above his bed. His condition hadn't worsened since his friend Dr. Adam Calhoun had visited him last, but it hadn't seemed to have gotten better either. Eli lay in wait to be taken into the arms of an angel and led to Heaven, where he would be reunited with his mother and loved ones.

Eli's hospice nurse, Terry Santos, was attending to the IV bag that she had just changed. As she adjusted the drip rate, Eli reached over with his right hand and grabbed her arm.

"Mr. Taylor, you scared me!" Nurse Terry cried out in surprise.

"I want to pray with someone," Eli whispered.

Nurse Terry felt the grip her charge had on her arm weaken. She noticed his fingers felt oddly cool. The usual charm she had grown accustom to was nowhere to be found in his voice or expression. For the first time since becoming his hospice nurse, Nurse Terry noticed that Mr. Taylor looked frightened.

"I'll call the hospital and tell them you want to see the chaplain again," Nurse Terry replied.

"Someone different this time," Eli quietly said. "Father Kellen is a nice man, but I want to hear another voice. Make it nondenominational." Eli cracked a small smile that appeared to take considerable effort as he tried to look confident and unafraid. His eyes, however, showed what he could not hide: his frailty and pain. "Someone I haven't met yet who could teach me a new prayer would be nice."

"You already know all of them," Nurse Terry replied, trying to keep the mood of the room light. She left the bedroom and went to Eli's home phone, which was an old cordless phone with a built in answering machine hanging on the wall just outside the kitchen. Eli had bought the phone when he moved into the house sixteen years earlier. She took up the phone and then went to her purse, which was hanging from a chair in the kitchen. She dug through her purse and pulled out a small green paisley address book. She thumbed through the book quickly and found the phone number to the chaplain's office at Hope Hospital. She pressed the on key and heard a dial tone. Then she dialed the number for the hospital and held the bulky grey and ivory antique to her ear as she dropped the green paisley book back into her purse. She counted three rings before the call was picked up.

"Thank you for calling Hope Hospital Chaplain Services. How may I assist you?" a woman's voice answered.

"Hi, I'm Terry Santos. I'm a hospice nurse. May I speak to Father Kellen?" Nurse Terry asked.

"I'm sorry, Father Kellen isn't in at the moment. May I take a message?"

"Yes. Eli Taylor is my patient. He's a friend of Dr. Calhoun's, and he's asking for someone to come to his home and pray with him. Father Kellen has been here before, but Mr. Taylor is asking for a non-denominational pastor this time. Nothing against Father Kellen, I think Mr. Taylor is looking to meet someone new."

"I will make sure that Father Kellen gets the message, and a pastor will be scheduled for a home visit at their earliest availability. Is this possibly a last-rights visit?"

The question made the usually stone-hard Nurse

Terry pause and slightly tear up. "It may be, actually, it should be. For some reason though, Mr. Taylor just seems to hang on. I'll say no. Not yet."

Nurse Terry ended the call by giving the receptionist Eli's address and telephone number. She pressed the on button on the cordless home phone and hung the phone back up on its cradle. She went back into the kitchen and sat on the chair where her purse was hung. She folded her arms on top of the table and rested her head. She stared at the wood grain of the oak table for a moment then closed her eyes. Exhaustion overtook the caregiver as she sat and slept at the table.

***

Pastor Faith spent the first several hours of his Saturday shift as a volunteer clergy for PR purposes at Hope Hospital, roaming the halls, meeting some of the patients, and introducing himself to the nurses and staff. He wanted to make sure that his position as a volunteer was secure for the duration of his wait for Adam Calhoun's return. He spent two hours on the pediatric oncology ward getting to know the staff there. He refrained from asking any questions concerning the whereabouts of Dr. Calhoun specifically. He did not want to rouse any suspicion as to his true purpose.

When he felt hungry, Pastor Faith went to the cafeteria to grab a bite to eat. He wasn't thrilled with the idea of eating hospital food, but he thought it couldn't be much worse than the diner food he'd been having lately. He followed the signs that lead into the cafeteria. Upon entering the cafeteria, he reached into his jacket pocket and took out a roll of antacids in anticipation of needing to take a few.

To his left, he saw a large refrigerated cabinet fully stocked with bottled waters and juices. Next to the juice cabinet was a case for prepared sandwiches and salads. Then the regular service line started, and Pastor Faith saw that the menu selection was far greater than he had anticipated. He took up a tray from the stack of trays at the beginning of the service line and got a small salad, a bottle of water, a small cup of split pea soup with ham, and a small dish of steamed baby carrots. He stood in front of the entre selections and gazed at the choices.

"What will you have, hon?" came a voice from the other side of the service counter that snapped Pastor Faith out of his daze.

"Oh, I beg your pardon," Pastor Faith said as he looked up and saw Lydia the cafeteria worker in her purple smock standing just behind the corned beef and cabbage. He beamed his famous smile at her as he said,

"It's just that everything here looks so good, and I just can't seem to make a decision."

"Well, take your time," Lydia replied. "We don't want you making any choices you'll regret later."

"What?" Pastor Faith asked.

"I'm referring to your ulcers," Lydia said as she gestured toward the antacids the pastor had placed on his tray. She did her best to hide the fact that she felt insulted at the idea that this man thought that her cooking would upset his stomach before he even tasted it.

"Oh, well I do appreciate your concern. I think I'll skip the corned beef and just have a serving of that lovely sliced turkey breast."

"That's a good choice," Lydia said as she served two slices of turkey breast onto a plate and handed it to Pastor Faith.

Pastor Faith took his tray and walked to the middle of the cafeteria seating area, looking for a seat. He saw Dr. Hammurabi and Father Kellen sitting together at a corner table. He quickly approached the table and asked if he could join the two men.

"Please, have a seat," Father Kellen said. "Dr. Hammurabi, this is Pastor Faith. The good pastor has agreed to volunteer some of his time here at the hospital."

"I wasn't aware that you were local to our

community," Dr. Hammurabi said to Pastor Faith. "I was under the impression that your TV show was shot in Chicago."

Pastor Faith swallowed hard and held his temper. Having his work referred to as a show always bothered him, but now was not the time to correct Dr. Hammurabi. He would have to play his cards right if he wanted to stay at the hospital long enough to be around for Dr. Calhoun's return.

"I do broadcast my sermons and healings from my church in Chicago," Pastor Faith replied. "However, when I heard of the Martinez Miracle, I felt a calling. I felt that God was telling me to come here. I can assure you, Dr. Hammurabi, that I'm not here to lay hands and heal those who don't believe. I'm here to listen, pray with, and witness with those who are in need."

"And the good pastor has agreed to allow us to use his name and a photograph of him praying with a patient for the hospital's website," Father Kellen said. "It will be great P.R. following the recent miracle."

Dr. Hammurabi's demeanor softened a bit. Father Kellen's use of the words "great P.R." were like music to his ears.

"Glad to have you aboard," Dr. Hammurabi said as he offered his hand to Pastor Faith to shake.

Just then, a nice-looking young man in his early twenties dressed in a navy blue suit, white shirt, and black tie approached the table. The young man was Michael Daniels, Father Kellen's assistant.

"Excuse me, I hate to interrupt, but a prayer service request has come in from Eli Taylor," Michael said.

"Well, I'm finished with my lunch anyway," Father Kellen began, recognizing the name.

"I'm sorry Father Kellen," Michael interrupted. "The request is for a non-denominational pastor. The request came in from Mr. Taylor's nurse and she said that he just wants to meet someone new, that's all. I'm sure it's nothing against you personally."

"I see," Father Kellen answered. "Well, we happen to have the perfect man for the job right here. Pastor Faith, you wouldn't mind holding a prayer service in the home of one of our hospice patients, would you?"

"Well, actually I was hoping to get to learn my way around the hospital more, and get those photos taken for public relations." Pastor Faith replied, trying to cleverly turn down the offer without having to actually say the word no.

"Oh, there will be plenty of time for that later," Father Kellen replied. "You'll like Mr. Taylor. He's a devout man of faith, and he happens to be a good friend of our own Dr. Calhoun who is out of town at the moment. If you stick around long enough, I'm sure you'll get a chance to meet him. He's one of our patient favorites. He's the pediatric oncologist who also witnessed the Martinez Miracle."

"Father Kellen, I would like nothing more than to go to the home of the friend of Dr. Calhoun," Pastor Faith said. He turned his attention to Michael Daniels and asked, "What's the name and address?"

# Chapter 7.

Adam and Rose stepped out of their top-floor suite, Suite 1022, and into the plush carpeted hallway of their hotel in Dublin. Adam placed the sign around the door handle informing the hotel cleaning staff that no room cleaning was required.

A woman wearing a cleaning staff uniform pushed a cart past Adam and Rose and stopped at the suite one door down and removed a master key card, unlocking the suite.

Rose led Adam by the hand down the hall towards the elevator lobby. The cleaning woman reached into her cart, removing a spray bottle of cleaner and a dirty rag. She turned her head to watch Adam and Rose disappear into an elevator and head off for a Sunday of sightseeing. As the doors closed to the elevator, the cleaning woman tossed her spray bottle back into her cart and proceeded to push the cart down to the suite belonging to Adam and Rose. She removed a pair of white gloves from her apron and placed them on. Then she flipped the service card over requesting cleaning services, swiped the key card unlocking the suite and entered the room.

The woman entered the bathroom, and in the mirror, her face came into full view. The cleaning woman had a small scar above her upper lip that appeared to be from a corrective surgery to repair a cleft lip. The woman methodically rummaged through the room, careful to place everything she touched back to its original position. She searched the drawers, the bedding, shoes, luggage, and even underneath the base of the lamps for the silver crucifix pendant. But nothing. The lady turned her attention to the room's safe located in the main closet. Another dead end. The door to the safe was wide open and empty, indicating neither Adam or Rose had even touched it during their stay. After completing a thorough search of the room, she locked the door and pushed the cart down the hallway. Once she reached the end of the hallway near the stairwell, she removed a cell phone from her pocket and sent a text message.

A fit, stylish man in his forties was on the receiving end of the text message. His hair was slicked back and bore an unusual, silver-streaked patch that went from his left temple, over his ear, and down to his manicured neckline. In the clandestine world of government operatives, this Russian assassin was known only as Vas. He was as smart as he was lethal. Fluent in Russian, English, Spanish, and Mandarin, he had accounted for a number of unsolved deaths around the globe over the past twenty years. Vas was seated on a plain wooden chair in a sparsely furnished, run-down flat when he opened the text message from the female agent. The message written in Russian read, *Room Service Requested.*

\*\*\*

Deep underground, beneath The Center of Special Operations in St. Petersburg, Russia, David Mosin sat in his prison cell, catching his breath. He had just completed his daily sit up, pull up, and push up routine, a routine that he had been adhering to throughout his thirty-four-year incarceration.

His steel blue eyes stared at the spot on the floor where the sweat that dripped from his nose began to pool. He dried the palms of his strong steady hands by running them through his long black and white beard then onto the grey pant legs of his prison jumpsuit. Pain shot through his damaged left hand as he did. He steadied his breath by taking in long deep breaths through his nose and exhaling through his beard-covered mouth.

With the index finger of his left hand, he reached up and scratched the itch on his face within the deep-set smile line that ran from the corner of his crooked nose to a dimple that hid beneath the thick salt and pepper beard. After scratching his face, he took a moment to examine the painful fingers on his left hand. His pinky and ring fingers curled in toward the palm and were twisted so that the ring finger actually crossed over the pinky. David spent minutes examining the damage done to his hand over the years during interrogations and one time during the attempted removal of his wedding ring, which he still wore.

David glanced up from his hand when he heard the lock at the end of the hallway snap open with a loud, echoing clank. He stood and faced the door when he heard the familiar clip and slide sounds made by the footfalls of the man coming down the hall as he limped his way to David's cell.

The observation panel in the thick solid steel door was slid open slowly by the frail hands of Pavel Volkov. David immediately took note of the optimistic joy in Pavel's face that couldn't be hidden behind the age spots and the large bags under the man's eyes.

Pavel ran his shaking, frail hand along the top of his head, ensuring what sparse white hair he had left was lying flat and covering a large age spot.

"I have good news," Pavel said with a large smile.

"I'm free to go?" David asked.

"No moy plennik," Pavel giggled. "Henry Calhoun is dead!" The jovial expression on Pavel's face turned to a menacing grin as he waited for David's reaction.

David sat on the edge of his cot. The emotional weight he felt within his chest at the news of Henry's demise took him by surprise.

"The relic is mine for the taking!" Pavel laughed as he slammed the observation window shut and limped his way back down the corridor that led to the outside world.

David sat in silence fighting back tears as he processed the news. Henry Calhoun was dead. This was news that David had been expecting to hear for a long time. He just wasn't truly ready for the emotional impact the news would bring. Because along with the news of Henry's death came the memories of David's involvement with the Calhoun family.

*The relic is mine for the taking!* David remembered Pavel cackling as he left. *At least he doesn't have it,* David thought to himself as he sat and waited for another day to pass.

Hours later back in Ohio, Hiro Tarsus woke up and rubbed the sleep from his eyes. He put on grey jogging pants, a tight fitting blue t-shirt that showed off his lean muscular v-shaped frame, and his running shoes. He set out on his morning jog, taking his usual path through his neighborhood to a nearby park. He jogged through the park, enjoying the cool morning air as it passed through his nostrils. After two laps around the park, which equated to approximately five and a half miles, Hiro jogged back to his small apartment.

Hiro undressed and stepped into his shower. As he adjusted the temperature of the water with the hot and cold knobs, getting his shower to the perfect temperature, Hiro's thoughts were on the case that was taken from him. While he lathered the soap and washed his body with a sea sponge, he recalled that while interviewing Adam, the doctor had said that his troubles started when his great-grandfather had given him an extremely old and possibly valuable necklace. Hiro showered quickly and got dressed. He wore a pair of light tan, flat-front chinos with a brown belt, a pink-striped slim-fit oxford shirt, and black leather lace-up shoes. Being single and hoping to someday bump into his future wife, Hiro preferred to always look his best, even on his days off.

While he ate his breakfast, which consisted of

steamed rice, miso soup, a small portion of grilled fish, a rolled omelet and dried seaweed, Hiro couldn't help but try to put the pieces of the puzzle together. Hiro recited the facts that he remembered of the case to himself while he ate.

"The late Henry Calhoun gave Dr. Adam Calhoun a necklace. Dr. Calhoun's apartment was broken into and he was physically attacked by two men looking for this necklace. Dr. Calhoun's cousin tried to steal the necklace and was killed by a man with no fingerprints or identifying markers who was disguised as a priest. Dr. Calhoun's uncle, Pete, poisoned his own sister to induce blindness then stole the necklace. Dr. Rose Powell was kidnapped by two men who were later shot dead by an unknown assailant. The mystery man dressed as a priest shot Pete and Dr. Powell to try to steal the necklace, killing Pete. Someone shot and killed the mystery man. Then Homeland Security took over the case."

After finishing his breakfast, washing, and putting away his dishes, Hiro took out a notebook and a pen and wrote down the following:

*Who is the man dressed as a priest, assassin or spy?*
*Who were the two thugs that mugged Adam?*
*Were the two men that kidnapped Dr. Powell the same*

*two men that mugged Adam?*

*Why is Homeland Security involved?*

*What is so special about that necklace?*

Hiro left the notebook open on the table in his kitchen and went into his bedroom to check on the phone that he brought home. It had been charging on his dresser overnight and was now fully charged. He pressed the power button to activate the phone and was pleased to see it turn on. The phone went through its activation sequence and then showed a photo of what Hiro thought was a rather tough-looking man, possibly the former owner's father. After closer examination of the photo on the phone, Hiro noticed the earrings and light makeup on the face of the person and determined that the photo was in fact most likely the former owner's mother. Hiro crinkled his nose at the sight of the woman and muttered to himself, "What an unfortunate woman. To have a son that ended up like this man. She must have been ashamed."

He slid his finger across the screen of the phone in an attempt to get past the screen saver photo. Four small boxes appeared in the middle of the screen with a keyboard below them and a message atop which said, "Enter Password."

Hiro looked at the phone for a moment, and typed the numbers 1,2,3,4 to the phone and hit the enter key. The squares went blank, and in red letters, the words "Incorrect: three attempts left" flashed on the screen. Hiro set the phone down and returned to the notebook in an effort to figure out the pass code to the phone before he locked himself out if it permanently. He worked on the possibilities for the password in the notebook. He started by writing down what he knew of the phone's owner.

*Two men. Illinois Drivers Licenses. Horace Grey. Hiram Grey. Brothers.*

After staring at the notebook for several minutes, Hiro remembered a promise that he had made to Dr. Calhoun. He promised to check in on his friend, Eli Taylor. Hiro closed the notebook and left his apartment, heading for the address Adam had given him over the phone.

Four blocks away from the apartment of Hiro Tarsus, the doorbell chimed throughout Eli Taylor's home. Nurse Terry walked through the house with a laundry basket in her hands. She set the basket full of freshly washed linens on the couch in the living room and answered the door.

"Hello?" Nurse Terry said as she pulled the front door open.

"Hello, I'm here to see a Mr. Eli Taylor," Pastor Faith said as he opened the storm door to let himself into the house, flashing Nurse Terry his bright white smile. "I've been asked to sit with him in prayer."

Nurse Terry showed Pastor Faith to Eli's bedroom, which was toward the back of the house.

Pastor faith greeted Eli with a huge smile and said, "I understand that you have asked to pray with someone."

Eli opened his eyes and looked at the man who came to his room. He took in the man's bright red hair that stood atop his head like a flame on a torch. The man's all-white suit and gleaming white smile made it appear that light was coming from him. Then Eli slowly began to speak.

"I have," Eli said in a soft, tired voice. "You look like an angel. Have I died?"

"No, no," Pastor Faith chuckled, "You have not died, and I am no angel. I am a man of God who has come here to pray with you while you fight to survive, young man. What would you like to pray for?"

"Remission would be nice," Eli said, his charm and warmth slowly returning. "But since I don't think that's going to happen, I'd like to pray for peace for everyone I know."

"You are a good man, Mr. Taylor," Pastor Faith said as he pulled up the wooden two-toned dining chair that Adam had previously set into the corner against the wall and sat at Eli's bedside holding his hand.

The two men began to pray, and Nurse Terry went back to the basket of linens and started folding. After the linens were folded, Nurse Terry went to the kitchen to begin preparing Eli's afternoon meal. Eli's appetite had decreased and his ability to chew was affected by his overall weakness, so Terry had become accustomed to making small dishes of vanilla pudding and slightly thin chocolate milk shakes for Eli's meals. If he was up to the task, he would enjoy the shake and pudding like a child. Lately, however his interest in food had faded.

A knock on the front door shook Terry out of her focus on the task of making pudding. She wiped her hands on the towel she hung from the refrigerator door handle and went to answer the door.

"A pastor is already here..." she started to say as she opened the door, but when she saw the handsome detective standing on the porch, Nurse Terry became speechless.

"Good afternoon," Hiro said. "I am Hiro Tarsus. Sorry to be a bother on a Sunday, but Dr. Adam Calhoun asked that I come and visit with Mr. Eli Taylor while he was out of town. May I come in?"

"Yes, please do," Terry said with her cheeks beginning to glow with embarrassment. "Mr. Taylor is in a prayer service with a pastor at the moment. If you don't mind waiting here in the living room until they're done, I can bring you some pudding. The prayer sessions don't usually take very long. You can sit on the couch. I made vanilla pudding. I'm rambling. Excuse me, but we don't usually get too many handsome visitors. Not that Dr. Calhoun isn't handsome; he's just not......you."

Hiro smiled. "Pudding would be nice," he said, giving Terry relief of her ramblings and a reason to leave the room and recover her thoughts.

Nurse Terry went into the kitchen to serve some pudding into a small bowl for the visitor. Hiro followed her into the kitchen and leaned against the doorway.

"That's a nice Cadillac convertible parked in front of the house. Is it yours?" Hiro asked the nurse as she turned around with the bowl and spoon in hand.

"Um, no," Terry answered shyly. "I take public transit. Save the planet and all."

"The Cadillac is mine," a voice coming from the living room announced.

Hiro turned around and saw Pastor Faith walking

from the hallway toward the front door.

"It's a very nice car," Hiro said.

"Thank you. It was a gift from my daddy," Pastor Faith replied.

Hiro extended his hand in greeting and shook the pastor's hand. "My name is Hiro Tarsus; it's nice to meet you."

"It's nice to meet you too," Pastor Faith said. "I would love to stay and chat, but I really must run. Hospital clergy business."

Hiro nodded and watched the man leave. Then he turned to Nurse Terry and asked that she show him to Eli's room. Terry led Hiro down the hall to Eli's room. Upon entering the room, Terry immediately noticed a change in Eli's condition. He was sitting up a little more upright on his pillows. He was smiling, and some of the brightness had returned to his eyes. He seemed to have more color to his skin as well.

"You're looking better," Nurse Terry said to Eli. "This is Hiro Tarsus. He's Dr. Calhoun's friend. I'll leave you two to talk, but not too long. Your pudding is waiting."

"I'll have it later," both Eli and Hiro said simultaneously. Hiro realized that Terry was talking to Eli and not him. He chuckled and sat in the chair left at Eli's bedside.

"So, you're a friend of Dr. Calhoun's," Eli said suspiciously. "How do you know the good doctor?"

"Forgive me," Hiro began. "Let me introduce myself. My name is Detective Hiro Tarsus. I am a homicide detective and I was tasked with investigating the murders of Dr. Calhoun's cousin, uncle, and his assailant. Dr. Calhoun has asked that I come and check on you while he is out of the country. He mentioned that you like chess."

"Ok," Eli said. "Just checking, but what is Dr. Calhoun's first name?"

"Adam," Hiro replied.

"Ok, where did he travel to?"

"He told me that he is currently in Ireland."

"Ok, how good at chess are you?"

"I am a worthy opponent."

"Two more questions. One, would you play a game of chess with me?"

"It would be my honor," Hiro said as he stood and retrieved the game board and the bamboo breakfast tray from atop Eli's dresser. He set the tray and game table on the bed. "And what is question number two?"

"It's a two-parter. A, are you single? I think Nurse Terry was looking at you like she might have a crush. And B, do you have a sister?"

After a fun-filled Sunday out sightseeing, Adam and Rose attended a wonderful choral service at the historic Saint Patrick's Cathedral and then capped the evening with supper in a local pub. Following dinner, Adam and Rose returned to their hotel and took a quick visit to the VIP guest services desk where Adam was greeted by the charming guest services manager, Daina.

"Evening Dr. Calhoun. How may I assist you?"

"Hi Daina. I was hoping you would be able to give me directions to either a clerk-register's office or a general register office? I'm trying to look up some information on my great-grandfather. Also, if you have any of their office hours for tomorrow."

"Absolutely. Let me see what I can find for you." Daina typed into her computer. After a few minutes, Daina located and printed some information for Adam. She stepped away from her desk, removed the printouts from the hotel printer, and then returned to give the papers to Adam.

"I would recommend arriving extra early. The queues for government agencies are typically out the door on Mondays," Daina said as she handed the printouts to Adam.

"I will do that. Thanks for the tip." Adam handed the woman twenty euros for her assistance.

"That's very generous. Thank you. Enjoy the rest of your evening." She smiled politely as Adam walked away towards Rose, who was seated in the nearby lobby.

# Chapter 8.

The next morning, surrounded by off-white walls and lit in fluorescent lighting, Adam and Rose sat in the hard, orange plastic chairs of the government office and waited patiently for their number to be called. Rose perused her guidebook on Ireland while Adam finished filling out the required paperwork needed to request vital information pertaining to his great-grandfather.

Seated beside Adam was a middle-aged woman in a pant suit who was tapping her right heel rapidly on the grey tile floor. She impatiently stared at her ticket whispering the number to herself. "Nine. Nine. Nine."

The lady's behavior only seemed to heighten the anxiety building inside of Adam. The clacking of her heel against the tile sounded like a woodpecker pecking away at his ear drum. Adam was thankful that at least he took

Daina's advice and arrived early because it seemed as if right after Adam and Rose took their ticket the room filled up with people.

A grouchy, prune-faced clerk in his late sixties was seated behind the one open window at the service counter. He pressed the loud speaker button and leaned in towards a thin microphone extended up from the counter. "Eight. Eight to the service counter."

"That's us," Adam said to Rose with nervous anticipation. He stood up and approached the sour clerk. Rose gathered her things and followed right behind him.

"Eight?" the clerk said in monotone, expecting Adam to hand him the #8 service ticket.

"Yes," Adam replied.

"Ticket?"

"Oh." Adam checked the paperwork he was holding to see if his ticket was there.

The clerk pointed his worn finger to a sign on the counter. In a raspy, irritated voice he said, "Signage clearly states to have your ticket ready."

"Sorry. I have it here," Adam said, searching his pockets.

"I'm nine if that bloke doesn't have his ticket." The impatient woman spouted from her chair as she gathered her dark blue purse.

"Without your ticket, you will need to take another number and fall back in at the end of the queue," the clerk instructed.

"Adam," Rose said as she leaned over and picked up the #8 ticket from the floor. "Here you go." She smiled, handing the ticket to the clerk.

"Morning." The clerk took the ticket, crumpled it up and tossed it into a waste basket on the floor. He then shifted his eyes from Rose back to Adam and waited silently.

"Hi, okay. Well, I am searching for some records associated to my great-grandfather. His name is Henry Calhoun."

"Did you fill out the required form?" the clerk asked pointedly.

Adam slid the completed document requesting vital records such as date of birth, marriage, and death information to the clerk for review.

The clerk picked up a pair of dark-rimmed reading glasses and fixed them to the bridge of his nose. He then methodically took the form from Adam and began to type the information listed on the document into his computer's database. The clerk's fingers were slender and knotted, bearing the signs of rheumatoid arthritis. They clicked away at the keyboard at a snail's pace. After a moment of entering data, the clerk stopped and glared at Adam. "Is this date of birth correct?"

"I believe so," Adam said meekly.

"The birth records in this office only date back to 1940," the clerk replied, further annoyed.

"I'm sorry. I wasn't aware," Adam said politely.

"For records prior to that time, you would need to check with the Office of the Registrar-General of Births, Deaths and Marriages. Good day."

Adam turned away feeling somewhat defeated. He began to slowly walk away from the counter when Rose noticed the clerk flinch in pain.

The clerk clutched his left hand. His fingers seemed to creak like a rusty hinge. The older man struggled to slowly open and closed his claw-like fingers. He hooked the curled fingers of his left hand on the edge of the counter and pushed his palm down to uncurl his fingers.

Rose traded places with Adam at the counter and leaned in slightly to the clerk. "Let me see," she said in a calm voice.

The clerk popped his head back slightly, giving her a suspicious look.

"I'm a doctor," Rose assured the man, turning her palms up and extending her hands towards his.

The clerk hesitated at first, but the compassionate

expression on Rose's face put the man at ease. He extended his left hand out to Rose.

"Here," Rose said as she took his hand. She then applied pressure with her thumbs to several strategic points on the elderly man's palm.

"Eegh," the clerk gasped slightly.

"Breathe out." Rose moved her thumbs in a circular pattern around the man's palm.

The clerk exhaled and his fingers seemed to relax. The pain decreased in his hand and a little bit of the swelling reduced. The man's flesh bloomed pink as blood began to circulate with greater ease.

"If you apply moderate pressure to these spots on your palm for fifteen minutes a day, it should help reduce some of the pain."

"Thank you."

"You're welcome." Rose turned to leave and then looked back over her shoulder. "Oh, one thing. You wouldn't happen to have an address for the Office of the Registrar?"

"I do. But it's quite a drive from here. They are located over in Roscommon. Might I suggest you place a request online? The cost for photocopies is about twenty euros per certificate."

"You wouldn't happen to have any idea how long that

might take?" Rose asked.

"Several weeks, I'd guess."

"I think we might just take the drive," Rose said.

"Suit yourself." The clerk then opened a drawer and rifled through several cards until he found the one for the General Registrar Office in Roscommon. "Here we are." He took out the card and handed it to Rose.

"Thanks again. And don't forget to apply pressure to those spots on your hand."

"Fifteen minutes a day."

Rose smiled and turned to join Adam, who stood admiring Rose.

"A bit of advice. They typically don't engage in family history research. But there is another option." The clerk said, stopping Rose. "You might want to check the National Library for Vital Records before you drive all the way to Roscommon. The National Library maintains copies of parish baptismal records, even dating prior to 1864. And best of all, the library is here in Dublin over on Kildare Street."

"That's wonderful. On Kildare Street?" Rose asked as she opened her guidebook to a map of the city. She placed the map on the service counter.

The clerk leaned over and pointed to a spot on the map. "Yes. You can walk there from here. We are right here. Just head down Bride Street. Then you can take this street across. The National Library is over here, across from Trinity College." He slid his finger to another part of the map. "I have a friend who works in the library's Genealogy Advisory Service. It's a free service. No appointment required. Otherwise you'll have to apply for a reader's ticket to access the main reading room. I will place a call for you, if you'd like, Doctor…?

"…Doctor Powell. But Rose is fine."

"And a lovely Rose you are."

Adam rolled his eyes in the background and shook his head, bemused.

"The chap's name is Nathaniel," the clerk said with a twinkle in his eye.

"You don't know how much this means to us." Rose gave him a warm smile and a gentle touch on the top of his hand. Her warm, soft fingertips sent a tingling sensation up the man's wrinkled arm. It was as if this was the first tender contact the clerk had had in years.

The clerk blushed. "You're quite welcome. Happy to serve."

Rose turned and walked off, taking Adam by the arm on her way to the exit. They walked out of the office suite and into the hallway as the clerk called over the loud speaker, "Nine. Serving number nine." The clerk looked directly at the impatient woman, who watched Adam and Rose leave the room. "Nine?" He said again directly to the woman.

"I seem to have misplaced my ticket," the woman said in return.

"Guest ten. Ten." The clerk continued about his business.

The woman removed a cell phone from her dark, blue purse and stood up. She began to dial as she calmly walked out of the office suite. The phone rang and was answered by Vas' deep, Russian voice, "Здравствуйте." As the woman began to move her deep ruby lips in reply, a small scar above her upper lip became clear.

Adam and Rose navigated their way through the corridors of the government building until they wound their way back to the front entrance. They walked out through the bulletproof glass doors and onto the street. The day was bright and clear.

Adam turned to Rose, still impressed with the way she had charmed the clerk. "You are incredible. You know, that."

"Yea, well, not all miracles come from your necklace," Rose said playfully.

"Apparently not. I always thought you had quite the bedside manner."

"Jealous?" Rose gave him an alluring glance.

"No... Maybe a little," Adam said with a winsome smile.

Rose placed her right palm on the side of his face and inched towards him for a kiss.

As the two kissed, they failed to notice Vas seated across the street on a metal bench. He wore dark, green-tinted sunglasses and was snapping photographs of the couple with his cell phone. Vas blended in with the office crowd shuffling along the busy sidewalk by wearing a simple striped, button-down cotton shirt, dark brown khaki pants, and a brown Irish Ivy herringbone driving cap to cover his now disheveled hair. He glanced down at the cell phone photograph he had just taken of Adam and Rose. Satisfied with the clarity of the photograph, he pressed the send button on his phone.

Within seconds, the text message found its way to the private cell phone of senior KGB officer Pavel Volkov. Pavel removed his phone from his coat pocket and opened it to see the photograph of Adam and Rose. A sinister smile came across his jagged face. Pavel's bony finger typed a reply message and clicked send before placing the phone back into his pocket.

Vas' phone vibrated. He glanced down and read the text message from his superior, Volkov. After a moment, the secret agent casually stood up from the bench and placed the cell phone into his pocket. He removed his cap, ran his fingers through his hair, straightening it, and watched Adam and Rose stroll down Bride Street. His silver patch of hair drifted out from under his hat as he fixed the cap back on his head. Vas picked up a magazine from off of the bench and began to casually walk after Adam and Rose.

Rose and Adam walked happily hand in hand, taking in the scenery as they continued down Bride Street towards Ship Street Little. Vas was careful to maintain a safe distance from the couple, blending into groups of people walking the streets so as not to alert the traitor Rose to his presence. Several yards ahead of Vas, two men walking, recognized each other and stopped abruptly in the middle of the sidewalk to greet one another. The sudden movement caused a minor traffic jam as other pedestrians tried to navigate around.

Vas found himself caught up in the mix. After realizing the inconvenience, the two men apologized to the pedestrians around them and slowly moved over to the side. Vas gave a subtle smile and nod to the men and slipped around them, scanning the street ahead for Adam and Rose. Vas had lost visual on the couple. He picked up his pace slightly nearing Ship Street Little. Just then, he caught a glimpse of Adam and Rose as they walked across to Ship Street Great. Vas jogged across Ship Street Little and then waited for the couple to momentarily slip out of sight before he rushed across onto Ship Street Great to continue following his targets.

Vas stared down Ship Street Great to discover Adam and Rose had stopped. Rose was referencing a map in her guidebook.

"We will want to turn left at Stephen Street Upper," Rose said to Adam as she pointed to the street ahead of them.

Vas took notice of Rose's hand gestures and used her body language to decipher their next move. He stepped up to a trash bin to throw away his magazine and allow the couple a few moments to put a little more distance between them and him as they turned up Stephen Street Upper. After he was satisfied with the distance, Vas proceeded after them. Vas neared the intersection of Stephen Street Upper and Ship Street Great when he saw Rose stop again unexpectedly in her tracks.

Rose peered down once more at the map in her guidebook. Adam was several steps ahead of her when he stopped and turned back to see if there was a problem.

"Did we make a wrong turn?" Adam asked.

Rose stood quietly, then she looked up from the

guidebook and turned around, looking back the way they came. She then glanced around at the street signs.

Vas was out in the open and found himself closing in on them quickly. He couldn't risk bringing attention to himself by slowing his pace or stopping, so the assassin continued to walk towards his targets as they stood on the corner. In the old days, Vas wouldn't have hesitated in seizing the opportunity and firing off a couple of slugs before disappearing into a shell-shocked crowd. But this wasn't the good old days. Now he was faced with the threat of highly sophisticated cameras on every traffic signal. Not to mention the private security cameras placed inside the storefronts and offices they walked past combined with all of the camera phones being carried by the tech-savvy by-standers on the street. Vas would have to wait for the right moment and provide a profile that would leave the police dumbfounded. He found himself within several feet of the couple. As he neared the street corner, Rose glanced over at him, but Vas casually walked past on her left side and continued to the crosswalk several feet away from them. There he waited patiently to cross the street.

"No. But I think the Whitefriar Street Church is really close by. Would you mind if we took a quick detour to look at it?" Rose asked Adam. "Henry used to go on and on about the church's stained-glass windows. We could cut across on Longford Street Little and down Whitefriar Place."

"Sure. I'm in no rush," Adam replied in a nonchalant manner.

"Fantastic." Rose grabbed his hand and led him across the road towards Longford Street Little.

Vas glanced over at the couple and proceeded to walk off in the opposite direction. He took his cell phone out of his pocket, dialed a number, and placed the phone to his ear. The woman with the lip scar answered on the other end and listened to Vas' instructions.

After about fifteen to twenty minutes of slow, casual walking, Adam and Rose found the entrance to the Whitefriar Street Church nestled away on the corner of the busy thoroughfare of Aungier Street. The charcoal-hued exterior of the Carmelite church was rather unassuming, plain, and somewhat dreary, but as they walked past the traffic signal and passed by the blue door to the Carmelite Priory, they approached a beautiful wrought-iron gate and the arched entrance to the church. The arched entryway was flanked by columns on both sides and two golden statues, one of Our Lady and the other of St. John. The stone columns had inscriptions such as "Carmelite Church, Whitefrairs, Foundation

1274."

Rose broke away from Adam to read one of the inscriptions while he admired the gate and glass doors to the building. She looked up from the inscription that read "Refuge of Sinners Pray for Us" and peered down the street in both directions. Rose noticed her breathing and heart rate had increased. She took a deep breath and tried to regulate her breathing.

The street was bustling, but no one stood out to her. *Am I just being overly cautious? Am I paranoid?* she thought. Rose knew the dangers that came with fleeing the organization. Hit squads had been issued in the past to eliminate defectors, and she had taken notice of the man with the green-tinted sunglasses, brown cap, and tuft of silvery hair after he had followed them for several blocks. *But if the man was an agent, he certainly would have overheard her asking Adam to take a detour over here to the Whitefriar Street Church*, she told herself as she scanned the area. *At the pace we walked, he would have had ample time to loop around and approach Whitefriar Street Church from the opposite direction. That's what I would have done*, Rose contemplated. The atmosphere made her uneasy. She felt like the mouse instead of the cat.

Rose began to second guess her plan to take this

journey with Adam. Her plan was to protect Adam from anyone who was after the necklace, but now she worried that her presence might have put him in greater danger from anyone who might be hunting her. Her heart raced again and her hands trembled from adrenaline.

Adam had opened the glass door and turned expecting to see Rose by his side. He saw her looking off in the distance. Adam slowly closed the glass door and walked back to Rose. He gently wrapped his arms around her waist. "You coming?"

Rose nodded, taking one last look down the street, but all she saw was a crowd of tourists that had formed at the intersection of Whitefriar Place and Aungier Street. She wrapped her arm around Adam's body and gave him a sideways hug before the two ventured through the entrance, arm in arm.

As the crowd of tourists descended away from the intersection of Whitefriar Place and Aungier Street toward the Whitefriar Street Church, a man separated from the crowd. In the man's back pant pocket was a folded brown cap and a pair of green-tinted sunglasses. Vas glared back over his shoulder towards Whitefriar Street Church and then disappeared from view. His plan was set.

Just inside the main entrance to the building, Adam

and Rose found themselves greeted by historical photographs along the hallway walls, a Shrine of St. Albert of Sicily, and over in the middle of the hallway the life-sized statues of the Calvary Shrine. They continued beyond a rare, 16th-century wooden sculpture depicting the Black Madonna of Ireland, "Our Lady of Dublin," and wandered silently into the Byzantine-designed church. They found themselves overwhelmed with the beauty of the church. Natural light streamed into the vast sanctuary, highlighting the tall ceilings, the majestic apricot-colored columns and arches trimmed in ivory white, the shrines, and the incredible stained-glass windows.

Adam and Rose stood before a set of splendid stained-glass windows known as the Rosary Windows, which depicted scenes from the life of Our Lady. The beautiful light shining through the windows illuminated their faces in a glorious rainbow of color. Adam wrapped his hand around Rose as she crossed her arms in front of her body, taking his left hand in her right. She held his hand tightly and closed her eyes.

"Are, you okay?" Adam asked sweetly.

Rose nodded. "Why do you ask?"

"I can feel your heartbeat."

"The perk of dating a doctor," Rose quipped. "We are

constantly checking each other's vitals."

"Sorry," Adam said blushing.

"I'm fine. I'm just...I'm happy. To be here with you."

Adam hugged her tightly.

"In your quest to discover your ancestry, this little tidbit might be of interest. Your grandpa said this church is where his heart was broken for the first time."

"I never heard that," Adam said, gazing at the Rosary Windows.

"Yep. By his first love, Deirdre," Rose affirmed. "I'm sure this is completely selfish of me, but I have to thank her for standing him up."

Adam gave her a curious glance.

"Because I wouldn't have you."

"That was kind of cheesy," Adam teased.

"Hey, come on. We are in the presence of St. Valentine."

Adam gave Rose a gentle kiss on her hand. "Speaking of St. Valentine. Shall we?"

"Have you ever thought what if? What if you made a different choice in life?" Rose asked as they walked towards the Shrine to St. Valentine. "You know, changed one small seemingly insignificant choice. But when you look back on that itty bitty choice, you realize that if it was changed that one change would have changed the course of your life forever?"

"I think about that with my mom. But it just gets depressing when I think too much about it," Adam responded giving Rose a doleful look. They both fell silent for a moment and then Adam murmured, "Life sure is full of those tiny moments."

As they reached the Shrine to St. Valentine, there was a petite, neatly dressed elderly woman standing there deep in prayer. The frail woman had one eye covered with the sort of gauze eye patch one would have after an eye injury or surgery. Her other eye was closed in meditation as she prayed out loud. The volume of her earthy voice was under her breath but loud enough for Rose and Adam to overhear the prayer. There was passion in her voice. She prayed for couples around the world that they would be granted the wisdom to recognize true love and commit themselves to one another. That through their union they would become closer to God and understanding his love, a sacred understanding that would serve as a cornerstone of their marriage and guide those couples through times of great hardship as well as times of great prosperity. She prayed that all lovers may be granted the understanding that love is more than lust.

Her voice pleaded, "May all lovers understand your teaching, that there is no greater love than the sacrifice of self for another. May they understand that this selfless commitment to each other is more valuable than...." The elderly woman hesitated and tilted her head slightly towards her left side in the direction of Adam and Rose. Sensing their presence, she cut her prayer short, used her right hand to bless herself and then placed the knuckle of her forefinger to her lip and kissed it. She opened her uncovered eye and gazed down upon the black casket containing the vessel stained in the blood of St. Valentine. Her crinkled face was etched in longing and sadness, but when Rose looked upon her, she sensed the warm glow of love and hope.

The elderly woman's words had struck a chord with the little girl inside of Rose that dreamt of a fairytale-like love, not a love that required rescuing but rather a love that you don't question ever faltering long after you've read the words "The End." A love that you know will keep those two souls together forever. Rose believed she had that unexplainable connection to Adam associated with love, but she was still slightly fearful that it might be a bond forged through trauma or one he didn't fully share. Sure, the way he looked lovingly upon her rang true, but neither one of them had verbally expressed the words "I love you." What Rose had no way of knowing was that Adam felt the same way. Moved by the woman's prayer,

Rose had a strong urge to connect with her even if it was only to share a comforting word.

"That was a beautiful prayer," Rose smiled gently.

"It was for you," the old woman replied.

"For me?" Rose asked, baffled.

"Both of you," the old woman disclosed. "Young people in love or searching for love. Your love is what he fought for—St. Valentine. He was beaten, stoned and ultimately beheaded all because he believed lovers had a sacred right to be united in marriage. He's my favorite saint."

Rose and Adam looked over at the woman and then back at the black casket with a new veneration for St. Valentine. The black casket was adorned with gold metal work and rested beneath the marble altar behind protective glass and iron. Behind and above the altar in a marble alcove stood a life-sized, carved statue of St. Valentine dressed in red vestments and holding a crocus. Rose gently sank her shoulder against Adam's chest as she placed her arm around him.

The elderly woman turned her opened eye peacefully towards the ceiling and whispered, "Rest in peace my dear Ollie." She then faced the couple. "Love on earth is short. Love up there," she pointed towards the heavens, "is eternal. You can do anything together united in God's love." She stepped towards Rose and touched her on the shoulder. A warm energy flowed through the paper-thin skin of the woman's hand and sent a tingling sensation throughout Rose's body. She smiled at Adam and Rose and began to carefully walk the short distance to the main entrance from the Shrine to St. Valentine.

Adam thought of the years he had worked so hard at staying away from love and reconsidered how he had viewed that time. It wasn't time wasted, but time well spent waiting. Perhaps the old woman's prayer had been answered. Adam was never much of a risk taker and rarely impulsive, but for once in his life all caution left him. He was certain that the way Rose had healed his fractured heart was true love. He wanted to drop to one knee and offer his heart to her. He slowly turned Rose towards him only to find a tense expression upon her face.

Adam had no way of knowing the conflict that was tearing Rose apart inside. She was a master at masking that conflict, but now she wanted so desperately to tell him the truth: the truth of her past, her mission to steal the necklace, but that she had fallen madly in love with him. She began to formulate the words on her lips but then the look in Adam's eyes stopped her.

Adam's voice spoke in an almost apologetic tone. "I love you."

Rose stood in silence. Adam gently touched her face.

The pressure of his fingertips seemed to trigger a stream of tears. Tears of joy and sorrow watered her face as if she was a character straight out of a Chekhov play grappling with the complexity of the moment. She felt Adam carefully funnel the tears off her statuesque cheek bones and away from her face.

"You don't have to say anything," Adam said, trying to reassure her. "And it is okay if you don't feel the same way. I have just made a habit of holding my emotions locked up for so long... And I don't want to do that anymore. I love you and I am so grateful that you are here with me."

Rose nodded and kissed the palm of his hand. She glanced into his eyes. "I love you too."

They held each other tightly. The moment was theirs but not theirs alone. At the front entrance to the main church, the elderly lady looked back on the couple. A smile creased her lips as she stepped outside into the hall area.

*** 

An hour later, Adam and Rose passed through the wooden double doors and onto the mosaic floor of the National Library's main building. The floor featured the emblem of an owl and the motto for wisdom, *sapientia.*

They continued past the colorful stained-glass windows depicting famous philosophers and literary minds and onwards to the Genealogy Advisory Service located on the first landing. The walls of the room were covered in wood paneling and reminded both Adam and Rose of Henry's own personal library back in Ohio. Several people were seated at computer terminals inside the Genealogy Service Room.

Adam noticed a storkish staff member who was wandering up and down the aisles offering assistance. "Excuse me, sir," Adam said quietly. The staff member peered over at Adam, who continued, "I'm wondering if you could help me locate Nathaniel. He is—"

"Expecting you, yes," the staff member said politely. "I'm Nathaniel. And you must be Dr. Powell?" the man said, turning his attention to Rose.

"Yes. Nice to meet you, Nathaniel," Rose replied.

"Let's find your great-grandfather, shall we?" Nathaniel said optimistically to Adam. "Follow me, please."

Nathaniel led Adam and Rose out of the Genealogy Service Room, past the main staircase and into a reading room. The reading room was filled with twenty or so microfilm readers and several microfilm reader printers.

Nathaniel guided them to an unused microfilm

reader. "If you can write down all the information you have on your great-grandfather, then we can get started," Nathaniel said as he turned on the reader.

"Here you go." Adam handed Nathaniel the vitals form he had filled out earlier at the clerk's office.

"Cheers. This will do nicely. I will run a search in the Catholic Parish Registers and also one for the War Department. You did say he fought during World War I?"

"Yes. He did," Adam replied.

"Splendid. I'll be back in a few minutes."

After several minutes, Nathaniel returned with several microfilm cartridges. He placed one each in a reader for Adam, Rose, and himself and the three began searching the contents.

After half an hour or so of searching, Nathaniel located a hit. "Here we are. I seem to have located his attestation papers."

"Attestation papers?" Adam asked curiously.

"Those are Henry's enlistment papers," Rose said, intrigued by what the papers might reveal.

"This is a fantastic starting point. I'll print them out for you," Nathaniel said, sending the document to the printer. He then walked over to the printer and waited for the printout.

"This is pretty exciting," Rose said as she clutched

Adam's hand. He sat silently. "Aren't you excited?"

"Yeah. Yeah. I just never thought we would actually turn something up," Adam said, astonished.

"See. Have a little faith, right?

Adam nodded and kissed her hand.

"Here you go." Nathaniel placed the printouts on the desk top in front of Adam.

Adam turned his attention to the printouts and began to scan the document with his finger. Rose looked on, reading over his shoulder. Adam slid his finger to the section listing the names of Henry's parents and then he scribbled the names Matthew and Catherine Calhoun down on a scratch piece of paper. Adam flipped over the first page to reveal Henry's signature. He touched the signature gently with the fingertip of his right index finger.

"Look at the date," Rose said, excited. "It's dated in September of 1914. Isn't that the year of the poem you were given from Pete?'

"Wait." Adam reached into his jacket pocket for the poem. "I don't think that's the year."

"It has to be. That was Henry's eulogy and Pete said Henry wanted you to have it."

Nathaniel glanced over from his microfilm reader at Rose and Adam, intrigued by their excitement.

Adam removed the eulogy from his pocket. "No. It' not. The poem is *September 1913*."

"William Butler Yeats," Nathaniel smiled. "Intriguing poem. Yeats is very clear in some ways and others, well, certain stanzas certainly could be open to interpretation based on the eye of the reader. For instance, the yellow-haired woman in the poem some note is Yeats way of suggesting that men go to war to impress a lass. He's mocking the men of the day for lacking ideals. But according to other scholars, the use of the color yellow also might suggest the woman is distorted in some way or that there is something fake about her. There are a number of scholars who claimed Yeats was simply taking a shot at an old flame who married someone else after Yeats travelled to America. The color yellow was often associated with prostitutes or immorality in literary work dating back to the Middle Ages, when prostitutes were forced to wear yellow to separate them from the general populace.

"But one thing is certain, *September 1913* is a political poem more than anything. Yeats used the poem to express his disgust with the current society that he felt was consumed by greed and their own self-interests over the fate of the country—that Ireland's heroes had died in vain and the traditions that made the country great died along with them. The poem unloads his literary wrath, chastising society. He even points a critical finger at religion. Or how men of the time were using the face of religion in their lives, viewing them as no longer men of action but men who would rather spend their time consumed by a love of money and in prayer."

"Wow. This poem certainly has a lot to try to digest," Rose said.

"I'd be happy to print out several critical essays that analyze the poem for you from a couple different viewpoints."

"That would fantastic," Rose replied.

Nathaniel jotted down a few notes on a pad of scratch paper as to not forget the promised items. Then he stepped over to a nearby computer terminal and began typing.

"This is interesting. Check it out," Adam said, pointing to the handwritten portion of the attestation papers where Henry spelled out his name.

Rose leaned over to view the document closer.

"He spelled his first name wrong? Henri with an 'i' not a 'y.'"

"Do you think it's a clue to something else?" Rose asked.

"I'm not sure."

"Is his name misspelled under the oath to be taken by recruit at attestation section?" Nathaniel queried, overhearing their conversation.

"It sure is," Adam replied.

"That's the section where soldiers declared their allegiance to the King of England and his heirs. We have found a number of Irishmen spelled and signed their names incorrectly under that section. It's symbolic more than anything. A way to thumb their noses at the British crown.

"You see your great-grandfather was part of what was considered the first all-Irish division in the British army. Even though the 10th Division did have Englishmen fighting in its ranks, the majority of the soldiers were Irish and their hearts were loyal to Ireland.

"This might help." Nathaniel clicked print on the computer screen, causing a nearby printer to spit out the document. "I was able to locate Henry's service record, giving you more information about the battles he fought in, including the one that took his life," Nathaniel said as he removed the printout from the printer and walked back over to Adam.

"That can't be his service record. He didn't die during World War I," Adam replied.

"Henry Calhoun. Parents Matthew and Catherine

Calhoun?" Nathaniel referenced the printout.

"That's right, but he just died this year," Adam confirmed.

"Perhaps he had gone missing in action during the war and was presumed dead. This record is from 1915. It lists Henry Calhoun as serving with the 7th Battalion, 10th Division and dying a war hero during the Battle of Gallipoli."

Nathaniel handed the printout to Adam for review. The doctor slowly took the paper and began to scan it.

"I'll see what I can gather regarding your great-grandfather's parents," Nathaniel added before heading back to the other computer terminal.

Adam peered up from the document. "Would you be able to check one more name? Alroy Byrne."

"Certainly," Nathaniel said, as he seated himself down at the nearby computer.

"Thank you, Nathaniel."

"My pleasure, Dr. Calhoun." Nathaniel smiled, turned to his monitor, and began typing.

Rose nestled up to Adam as he began to quietly read the document out loud.

"On the 9th of August, 1915, Corporal Henri Calhoun's selfless act of bravery saved the lives of...

Bombs erupted on the hills inland on the Gallipoli Peninsula. A twenty-something year old Henry Calhoun stared up at the smoke rising from the mouth of the Turkish howitzer that was blasting shells at the foothills behind him. He was so close he was able to read the Arabic inscription painted on the armor plating of the large gun. Translated, the inscription read, "God is with us." Henry glared at the inscription and thought. *Has God forsaken me and my mates?*

Bodies of his fallen brothers lay strewn across the ground. Some of the men were nothing more than a limb, a grim remembrance of the men they once were: brothers, fathers, sons, Irishmen, and soldiers of the 7th Battalion. But to Henry, they were simply his pals and they had been overrun by the might of the Turkish forces, who held every advantage in this battle. In the distance, Henry saw Lieutenant Murray give the signal for retreat.

"Calhoun!" bellowed out in the night air.

Henry turned to hear the low voice of his mate, Private McDonough. "Get the hell out of there, mate," the private hollered at him and fired a shot, striking a Turkish soldier who was charging down the hill towards Henry.

The smoking howitzer fired another shell, striking the ground near five men of the 7th. The men screamed in agony as shrapnel punctured their bodies.

"Calhoun! Now!" McDonough yelled before turning and retreating with the rest of the able-bodied men.

A third shell crashed several yards from the wounded soldiers. The heat from the shrapnel ignited the dry brush into a wall of flames. Fear of burning alive filled the eyes of the wounded men as they struggled to kick and claw their bodies away from the firestorm.

Henry's blood pumped with terror-fueled adrenaline. He could not allow his fallen brothers to suffer a fate of being burned alive or horrifically bayonetted by the Turks as they lay wiggling wounded on the ground like bait for sharks. He raced up towards the Turkish gun crew as they rushed to reload the heavy field howitzer.

The brush fire inched its way, lunging its fiery tongue toward Henry's mates. Bullets struck the ground around him, kicking up shards of rock and dirt, but he would not be denied his target. McDonough watched helplessly as Henry moved within range of the gun crew. With a grenade in one hand and his rifle in the other, Henry seized his moment, hurling the deadly hand bomb at the howitzer. He hit the deck and watched as one of the Turkish gun crew spotted the grenade and reached for it. But the man's attempt to capture the grenade and fling back at Henry was short lived. The grenade erupted into a meat-grinding tornado. Henry charged with his bayonet and seized control of the howitzer.

McDonough, aided by Lieutenant Murray, rushed to save the five fallen soldiers, pulling them one at a time out of the path of fire. As they dragged the third man to safety, Murray turned back to help the remaining two soldiers and found himself staring in disbelief at what he would describe as the most selfless act of heroism he had ever witnessed. An exhausted Henry had the body of one soldier over his platform-like shoulder and the other man under his left arm. Henry's muscles twisted and crackled under the strain, but he continued forward. Murray raced to Henry's side, and the men were taken back to the field ambulance tent behind their front line.

Lieutenant Murray would write in his commendation of Henry, "If they say war brings out the worst in mankind, Henry Calhoun is proof that it also brings out the best."

Days had passed with both sides locked in a chess match. Allied bodies, including many of Henry's mates, had begun to fill up the makeshift cemetery behind the front lines. Henry sat with his head resting against the dirt wall of the trench dugout he shared with his cocky and high-spirited friend, Private Robert McDonough. McDonough chewed on a stinky, beef-soaked biscuit and reminisced about his love back home in an attempt to take their minds off the gruesome cloak of war. Night had begun to set in. The clouds of artillery smoke bellowed in the air and faded into the dark backdrop of God's starry night. The bursts of cannon fire seemed to give way to the loud sounds of locusts whistling and frogs croaking in the few puddles of brackish water leftover from the dried-out water wells near the trenches.

A cat-sized rat gnawed on a dried out biscuit several meters from the men. Its cloudy eyeballs beamed like devil moons on the dirt deck. McDonough grabbed a stone and heaved it at the rat, striking its hind quarters, but the plump beast barely budged. McDonough simply shook his head in disbelief. *War,* he thought, *even the damn rats aren't afraid of us.*

McDonough reached into his breast pocket and removed a picture of his fiancée Johanna and handed it to Henry with pride. "She's doing clerical work in a hospital."

"The Lord modeled a fair piece of clay, mate." Henry said. "Maybe I ought to hang onto this?" he kidded as he pretended to place the picture in his own pocket.

"Hey, hand it over. And don't be getting any ideas. I plan on making it out of this war with my bollocks intact."

The men laughed at one another until Henry

suddenly grasped his swollen guts and gasped in pain. After taking a deep breath, Henry forced an exhale through clenched teeth in an attempt to muscle through the agony of his intestines locking up and shuttering. If a bullet or rocket shell didn't send the men to the beyond, then illness due to the combination of brutal heat, incessant flies, and lack of clean water was doing the job. The hulking Irishman was no exception. Before the war, Henry felt indestructible, especially on the rugby pitch, but now the effects of war had quickly humbled him. His bowels were bathed in blood as dysentery ravaged his body.

McDonough knew without medical help Henry would succumb like many others from their unit. But despite McDonough's best efforts to convince his pal to seek medical attention, the rugged Henry refused to leave his mates behind to fight without him. It was this brotherhood and loyalty to his pals, not pride, that kept Henry in the fight, and McDonough admired Henry's will, for it seemed to have no bounds.

"McDonough. Calhoun," a firm voice rang out near their dugout. The voice belonged to Lieutenant Murray, the last of their officers. The once baby-faced lieutenant now had the signs of a man who had aged ten years in a week. The fighting had turned him into quite the leader, and the men were honored to serve alongside him. He peered his war-wrinkled face into the dugout. "We're on the move. The chaps from the 31st are under heavy fire on the ridge near Kidney Hill, and command refuses to order a withdrawal."

"7th to the rescue," McDonough said as he hurried to eat his last biscuit.

"Calhoun, you should sit this one out," the lieutenant said as he watched Henry grimace and struggle to his feet.

"You need someone to be your guardian angel, sir." Henry cracked a half smile.

"Bring up the rear then," Murray said simply.

Henry nodded, reached for his rifle, and followed McDonough and Murray down the trench to gather the other men.

Murray led a force that included McDonough, Shannon, and Henry and about a dozen or so other men who had been patched together from various units. They snaked through their trench, past the Allied encampment of Jephson's Post until they reached the front line and prepared to be spit out at the base of Kidney Hill. The shifting sand of the dunes trembled beneath Henry's feet from the constant pounding of artillery. The air was ripe with a symphony of wind instruments of war. The full might of the grim reaper's baton was on display. Soldiers on both sides of the line cried out as bullets and shrapnel made mincemeat of the men.

The Turkish soldiers had positioned themselves on the southern slopes as they fought the Allies for control of the northern boundary of Suvla Bay, a ridge known as the Kiretch Tepe Sirt. From that position, the Turks lobbed grenades and fired rockets over the crest of the ridge and onto the men of the 6th, trapping them under a canopy of modern brimstone. Henry watched the rocket fire eat away at the steep, shrub-covered slopes. The only way to slow the Turkish attack and provide support to the 6th was to cross an open plain that lay at the feet of Kidney Hill. Unfortunately for Henry and his mates, this open plain provided clear visibility for the Turkish artillery, leaving the pals dangerously exposed.

Murray swallowed hard and was the first to go over the top and into the no man's land. In a wave of green, the remaining men joined suit as they charged towards the hill. Grenades and shelling swept the plain and hillside, striking four of the men before they reached the slopes of the hill. The heat of the shrapnel and explosions set the thick shrub of the open plain on fire behind the men.

Murray reached the base of the slope first and raged up it. The rock was loose, and he suddenly lost his footing on the steep slope, hitting the deck hard. He winced, blood running from a cut near his eye. He dug in his heels and pushed forward. A Turkish grenade bounced on the ground near his feet. He quickly scooped it up and lobbed it back towards the summit, where it exploded.

Henry spotted the dark outline of enemy snipers against the orange bursts of grenades. He aimed his rifle and squeezed the trigger. Unable to confirm his hit, Henry continued his pursuit up the sharp slope. The fire raged behind him and ate away the darkness. With a wall of fire to their backs and the only live bodies in front of them belonging to the enemy, Henry and his pals knew there would be no retreat in this battle. So the men pressed forward into the gnashing teeth of the Turkish line.

Murray, followed by Shannon and several men, elected to change course and rush the hill up a steep path that was clear of burning brush. Soon that route became drenched in blood. Henry watched in horror as Murray took a bullet through his heel before a machine gun rendered him unrecognizable. Henry fired several shots in the direction of the machine gun fire and then sprinted for a crater in the hillside. He dove into the hole just as the machine gun sprayed a volley of gunfire towards his last position. This gave Shannon and another soldier on the steep path a momentary reprieve to break for cover. Shannon and the other soldier sprinted for the seaward slope known as the Pimple.

Henry carefully scanned the hillside for other men from his unit. The remainder of the men were following Shannon towards the Pimple. Henry was alone and trapped in the crater. The only positive news was the apparent change in direction of the Turkish forces, who gave chase and focused their attack back on the northern slopes. Henry's heart rate slowly settled, and his ears adapted to the noise. Through the gunfire, he heard a weak voice call out to him: "Henry. Henry."

Henry slid his face against the ground and peered out from the crater to find McDonough lying wounded, several feet from the crater.

"Are you badly hit?" Henry whispered.

"More or less," McDonough replied.

"Splendid," Henry said wryly. He then rapidly grabbed his friend by the upper body and pulled him into the shelter of the crater.

McDonough's left leg was clinging to the rest of his body by his shredded thigh muscle and exposed tendons. His thigh bone was completely splintered, severing the femoral artery. McDonough had jammed his fingers into his upper thigh and was pinching the artery with all his might to stave off the bleeding.

Henry quickly detached his rifle sling from the rest of the weapon, hoping to use it as a field tourniquet. He pulled the sling high up on McDonough's leg, near his groin, and struggled to tighten it deeply between McDonough's groin and hip. Henry removed his bayonet from his weapon and slipped it through the sling, using it as a lever to tighten the tourniquet.

"At least I still have my bollocks, pal." McDonough grinned before choking for breath.

"Jephson's Post isn't far off. Hang on, Robert. I'm getting you out of this."

Henry cautiously slid his face up out of the crater, cheek hugging tightly to the rocky ground. He glanced south in search of a clear path, but the brush behind them was still in flames. He tilted his head north. At that moment, a bullet struck the rocky ground in front of him, sending a spark flying into his forehead. Henry wiped the cinder and stared to the north, beyond the bodies of both rotting and newly fallen soldiers. In the flashes of exploding grenades, he was able to make out the remainder of his regiment. They had managed to push through to the northern slopes, but Henry would never make it that far with McDonough. Henry's only option was to race McDonough over to a dangerously steep slope southeast of them, navigate their way down, and then follow a maze of gullies back to the field hospital at Jephson's Post.

Henry watched and waited for a moment as the Turkish forces turned their full attention back to the troops north of them. His chance had come. Henry slid back into the crater and turned to McDonough. McDonough was breathing in hefty, staccato bursts as his hands trembled to unbutton his breast pocket.

"Time to go, Robert," Henry said.

McDonough shook his head and pointed repeatedly to his breast pocket, as if his finger were a woodpecker's beak. Henry leaned into the man and helped him unbutton his pocket. McDonough pulled at the open pocket with his right index finger.

"I'll get it, mate," Henry said as he delicately removed the photograph and placed it in between McDonough's trembling fingers.

McDonough gazed through his bloodshot eyes lovingly upon Johanna's picture. The rhythm of his breath slowed, and the heavy, staccato panting turned into a series of slow, drawn out sighs.

"We have to go, mate. Now's our chance," Henry urged.

"The loves of our lives are the only significant things

in this world, Henry." McDonough reached out his left hand and gently patted Henry on the cheek.

Henry watched as McDonough's hand drifted from off his cheek down to the rocky soil and his body sank, heavy with death. Rage welled up inside of Henry as he gently shut his dear friend's eyelids. He clasped his rifle, mustered his courage, and climbed out of the hole to follow after his regiment. In that moment, a sniper's bullet seared through his chest, followed by another round, and another. Henry stumbled forward for several steps until a fourth round split his midsection, singeing a path through his swollen guts and effectively stopping Henry in his tracks. He collapsed. The air fell silent as his mind registered the severity of his situation. The pain was surprisingly absent as endorphins flooded his nervous system. Henry's eyes rolled to the back of his head, and his senses fell silent.

Time stood still and Henry lay awaiting his fate. The flash of light and heat on his face from the bombs bursting in battle faded. The fighting had ceased. As the minutes drifted away, Henry heard the gentle sound of rocks crunching under foot.

"There's too many. We can't get them all, sir," an Allied medical orderly said while he and a medical officer set a stretcher down on the ground.

"Take the ones that can be saved and tag them. Leave the rest for the Almighty," the medical officer instructed.

The field ambulance unit only had a short window to salvage who they could, and they briskly went about the business of sorting the living from the dead or soon to be dead. The men who had a shot at life received the only priority. This was the cold reality of war.

Henry lay still in the no man's land, unable to speak, the life seeping out of the wounds in his body as he stared up into the starlit abyss. The medical orderly hiked his way in the vicinity of Henry. The orderly was so close Henry felt the ground vibrate with the man's steps. Would the orderly take pity on Henry and at least carry him off for a proper burial? Or would he simply leave him here for the sun to scorch him and the flies to feast on him? Henry watched, his vision going in and out of focus, as the orderly glanced at his wounds.

The orderly rolled Henry over onto his right side and inspected his exit wounds. As Henry's head fell to the side, he saw the rows of the charred remains of his fallen brothers. The orderly turned Henry back onto his back, made the sign of the cross with his thumb on Henry's forehead, and walked away.

The night fell silent. The field was desolate, and the temperature had dropped. Henry prayed silently to himself and hoped that God was free for a few seconds to listen. *My time has come, Lord. Please be merciful in your judgment and forgive my trespasses.* Henry closed his eyes. He felt as though his body were floating inches above the ground. Weightlessness and the cool caress of the nighttime breeze overtook his body as his mind pictured a wash of blue. As Henry drifted out of consciousness, he felt as though his body had begun to rotate and spin on an axis, still floating inches above the ground, all awhile being blanketed by a fog of blue mist. The light touch of the blue mist was comforting and cool. The light blue cloud slowly wafted all around his floating spinning body until he was fully covered in the blanket of comfort.

Hours later, in the dead of night, a cold wisp of air sent a shock through Henry's system, snapping him back into consciousness. He shivered violently. His khaki uniform was stiff with blood. He began to think about his mother and his father: their well-being without him, the promise he had made to return his mother's locket, and the disappointment he would cause his father when they learned of his death. Henry's resolve began to fortify. He refused to rot on this ashen hillside of hell.

Henry stared up at the night sky, confident with his chances for survival. He slowly moved his fingers, making sure they would follow his commands. He repeated the task with his elbows, knees, ankles, and toes. He seemed to be in remarkably good working order for someone who had been shot several times. There was weakness in his muscles however. Though his movements were slight, Henry noticed the considerable effort that was put into completing each task. As he continued to stare up into the star-filled blanket of darkness, he slowly rolled his head to the right. His head felt heavy, but his muscles continued obeying his command. He then turned his head to his left. That's when he saw it.

Henry felt his pulse quicken. His spirits were suddenly lifted. The ridge was within his sight. The top of the hillside that separated him from a downhill descent to the trenches where his Allied mates were surely held up for the night was merely yards away. Henry raised his right arm and crossed it over his body. He grabbed a handful of grass and tugged at it, pulling himself onto his side. Pain shot through his body as he lay on his side staring at the crest of the hill that would surely lead him to safety and life-saving assistance. He regained his strength and repeated the task until he rolled himself onto his belly. Henry rested on his belly for a moment, flicking grains of sand away from his left eye with his eyelashes as he blinked. His breathing became labored.

He felt wetness as his blood began to pool underneath his body. Henry swallowed hard and began to make the painful laborious journey toward the ridge.

With his arms stretched out before him and all of the strength he could muster, Henry dug his fingers into the ground and pulled himself a few inches forward. He reached out and repeated the motion, gaining only inches with each pull. He clawed at the brush around him. The holly needled his hands as he pulled his body toward the steep path that swerved up the hill. He set his focus on the edge of hill. If he could reach the incline, he would tumble down the hill, closer to the front line. Hopefully someone would see him and alert a medic to his presence. The no man's land was no more than ten meters in some places. Henry was running on pure will. He slithered his body inch by grueling inch. He was close now; the slope was only a couple feet away. He pushed off the ground; his chest pounded with pain as he lifted his torso off the ground and lunged at an angle, tucking his chin with his head pointed downward. His shoulder hit the steep area, and gravity did the rest. Henry tumbled end over end until he landed hard on his back at the bottom of the hill. His body twisted and cracked its way, crashing into burnt brushwood below.

Only feet from the trench, Henry thought to himself,

*Surely, one of my mates had to have heard my fall.*

"Ambulance," he cried out faintly. Henry was surprised at how faint his voice sounded compared to the amount of effort he was putting into being heard. It felt to him that he was screaming at the top of his lungs, yet he could barely even hear himself.

The battle had claimed over seventy percent of the forces who charged the hill. The remaining soldiers had abandoned the trench to help carry the wounded to makeshift field hospitals. No one was there to hear his cries. As Henry's heartbeat faded, a black clothed figure appeared in the darkness. *Is it a Turk? Did he somehow hear my faint cry for help? Has he come to put me out of my misery with a quick thrust of his bayonet?* Henry left himself to God's hands saying softly, "Your will be done." His eye lids closed leaving him in darkness to die. Henry's consciousness left him and this time all was silent, dark and still...

"Excuse me, excuse me? Adam? Rose?" Nathaniel's voice broke Adam and Rose away from reading Henry's service record. He was standing, holding a file folder containing a number of printouts. "I was able to find an old photograph." The rangy man said quite pleased with himself as he handed a printout of the portrait to Adam.

"That is your great-great grandfather Matthew Calhoun. He was a constable in Dublin and died April 26TH during the Easter Rising in 1916. Pretty cool, eh? I mean not his death—of course his death wasn't cool—but the photograph, wouldn't you say?" Nathaniel stammered whilst grinning ear to ear.

"This is very cool. Thank you for all of this," Adam replied.

"Oh, and you appear to have at least one relative still living not far from here. There's property owned in the family name. Bridget Gildea. The daughter of your great-grandfather's aunt on his mother's side. I'm not allowed to give out her address but she has a telephone number listed as public record. You may like to give her a ring."

"Absolutely, I would. And anything on Alroy Byrne?

"I was able to locate a few names between 1890 and 1930. They have all since passed away as one might imagine. All of them lived to adulthood except one, so they might have relatives living in Ireland." Nathaniel handed Adam the file folder of printouts.

"And what about the one that didn't live to adulthood?" Rose asked curiously.

"A child that died in an asylum, sad to say, in 1896. I've included everything I was able to find. There's even a photograph of the workhouse in there," Nathaniel boasted.

"May I see it?" Rose asked Adam.

"Sure." Adam handed her the file folder.

Rose opened the folder and thumbed through the printouts until she came to the photograph of the workhouse. There was something ominous about it and she didn't know why but her gut was telling her to take a closer look.

"Again, thank you so much, Nathaniel. I'd like to make a contribution to the library if there is any way you could give me the information of who I may contact?"

"With pleasure. Please follow me," Nathaniel said, motioning for them to head out of the reading room.

"I will catch up with you both," Rose said as the men continued out of the room. She stared at the black and white photograph of the workhouse. There was a misery to the buildings but also a strange familiarity that she couldn't quite put her finger on. Henry had a conversation with her once about a series of schools, clinics and orphanages that his foundation had funded, and in that conversation the term Magdalene Laundries was used on more than one occasion. *I wish I had listened closer*, Rose told herself as her mind toiled to find a connection. Frustrated, she placed the printout back into the file folder and went to join the men.

Back at Adam and Roses' hotel, a pair of white-gloved hands unlocked the door to their hotel suite. The hands belonged to the woman with the lip scar. She slowly pushed a cleaning cart inside the suite and then into the bathroom to carry out Vas' directive. She systematically removed a kit from the bottom of the cart, removed several items from it, and began tampering with the sink faucet. After several moments, the woman's work was done. She placed the kit back into the bottom of the cart, wiped down the area, and sent a text message to Vas that read "Reservation Placed." She placed the cell phone into the pocket of her apron and awaited her next order.

# Chapter 9.

After quite a long day of research and walking, Adam and Rose made their way back to the hotel to rest for the night. Their next stop would be the farmhouse belonging to his newfound cousin, Bridget Gildea. Nathaniel had been nice enough to lend Adam use of his personal office telephone for the call after supplying the doctor with the contact information for the head of donor relations with whom Adam intended to leave a sizeable donation for the Genealogy Advisory Service. Before taking the elevator up to the floor of their suite, Adam stopped off at guest services where Daina assisted in acquiring him a rental car.

"Will you require an early check out?" Daina asked Adam after handing him the paperwork for the rental car.

"No. Please hold the room for us for the full ten-day

reservation. Just in case," Adam answered with a smile.

"As always, if you are in need of anything else, don't hesitate to call down."

"Thank you." Adam gathered his papers, said good night to Daina, and met Rose near the hotel elevators.

Several minutes later, they were both tucked away inside their hotel suite retiring for the night. Adam walked into the bathroom and removed his toothbrush and toothpaste from his toiletry bag. He reached for the brass water handle. The water sputtered out of the faucet as he turned it on, causing a stream of water to seep out of the base of the handle and puddle all over the granite surface. "Seriously?" Adam said, annoyed. He switched the water off and reached for the phone attached to the wall in the bathroom. He punched in the number for guest services.

Daina answered after one brief ring. "Guest services, Daina speaking," she said politely.

"Hi Daina. This is Adam in Suite 1022."

"Yes, Doctor Calhoun. How may I help?"

"The bathroom faucet just started leaking from out of nowhere. Would you mind sending someone up?"

"Oh, I do apologize for that. I will send facilities up immediately. So sorry for any inconvenience. Would you like me to provide you with a temporary suite?"

"It's all right. Thanks." Adam hung up the phone and walked back into the living room of the hotel suite. Rose was changing in one of the suite's two bedrooms. Adam turned on the television and sat down in a large lounge chair.

The phone rang in the hotel maintenance office. The head facility workman on duty, a stout man in his fifties, answered the phone. "Hello?"

Daina relayed the work order for Adam's room to the man.

"Suite 1022. Leaky faucet in the loo. Got it." The workman wrote down the work order and then hung up the phone.

"I'll take that one, mate." A low voice boomed behind the workman. The workman turned, startled to find another man dressed in a facility work outfit. A workman's cap hid the man's silver-streaked hair.

"You startled me, mate," the workman said before clearing his throat. "I don't believe we have ever met. Do you work the swing shift?"

"I'm a new hire, mate. Just trying to make a good first impression."

"Alright. Well pace yourself. We don't get tips down here. Cheers." The older workman said, handing the man with the silver-streaked hair the work order. "You will need that tool kit over there," he said referring to a large grey toolbox.

"I have my own."

"Right. Of course you do." The older workman smiled at the man's enthusiasm and patted him on the back.

Vas grinned back and then left the utility room and headed for the freight elevator. He pushed the up button and waited for the lift doors to open. The door to the elevator slid open with ease, and standing inside was the woman with the lip scar, standing behind a cleaning cart.

Vas stepped nonchalantly into the freight elevator. He uttered to himself. "Everything in life has an antithesis."

As the doors closed, the woman replied back, "What once was lost will be found again. We are of the same flesh."

Vas knelt down and removed a dark grey toolbox resting on the base of her cart. The freight elevator clicked its way up to the tenth floor. The woman removed a key card from her apron and handed it to the man as the elevator reached its destination. The door slid open, and the man stepped out.

Rose sat down in a lounge chair opposite from Adam when a knock was heard on the door to the suite.

"Were you expecting someone?" Rose asked Adam, as

he stood from his seat to answer the door.

"I called guest services. The faucet was leaking. They were sending a repairman up.

"A luxury suite shouldn't have a leaky faucet." Rose stood up from her chair and leaned her head out into the small hall leading to the door.

"It's okay." Adam opened the door.

"Evening sir," Vas said, posing as a workman. "Leaky faucet?"

"Right here." Adam held the door open and motioned to the bathroom located in the foyer.

Rose watched suspiciously from the living room area as the workman entered the foyer.

The workman nodded at Adam and tipped his hat to Rose. "Evening madam."

Rose flicked her fingers up in a quick wave. Adam turned his back to the man and walked towards Rose. Vas adjusted his cap and turned to enter the bathroom. The light in the foyer shined down on the man, highlighting a streak of silver hair that popped out from under his cap and across his ear. Rose quickly noticed the streak of hair and focused her attention on his facial features, but the man had slipped into the bathroom.

"This might be quite loud," the man said as he closed the bathroom door. "I will keep the door closed until I'm done."

"Adam, we should go out and grab some coffee while he works," Rose whispered to Adam as he walked past her.

"I'm beat. I don't think I can do another minute of walking."

Inside the bathroom, Vas set his toolbox down next to the sink. He then flicked the water on and off. After doing so, he opened the toolbox to reveal a MP-443 Grach; a standard military-issue sidearm issued to all branches of the Russian military and law enforcement. He removed his cell phone from his pocket and typed the following text message: *Target Acquired. Requesting Authorization.* He rustled tools around in the toolbox as he waited for his superior's final authorization to carry out the hit on Rose and Adam.

Pavel Volkov walked into the small kitchen of his modest home. He got a clear plastic glass from the dish strainer next to the sink, filled it with water from the tap, and set the glass on the small, green, Formica-topped kitchen table. Then from his pocket, he produced a packet of two Alka Seltzer tablets he had gotten from the medicine cabinet in his bathroom. As he tore open the packet, the cell phone that was sitting on the table next to the water glass vibrated. Pavel paused for a moment and growled at the phone as it buzzed and lightly hopped across the light green table top. He shook the tablets out of their packet as he scooped up the dancing phone with his other hand. One of the tablets fell into the water glass, the other landed on the table next to it. Barely noticing the rogue tablet, Pavel looked at the phone and saw that he had received a text. The text was from Vas, seeking Pavel's authorization to eliminate both former agent Rose Powell and her American counterpart Adam Calhoun.

With his shaking hand, Pavel lifted the glass and took a long gulp of his fizzing water. The not yet fully dissolved tablet from the water glass floated into his mouth. He chewed the sour mass and swallowed it. A belch bubbled up from his gut and burst out his mouth. He wiped his lips and raised his phone. He began typing the authorization code with his thumb when a small red light coming from a box sitting on a desk in the corner of the kitchen caught his eye. The flashing red light was an indicator that a silent alarm had been tripped.

Before Pavel had time to react, the door to his apartment burst open and he found himself surrounded by Russian security forces. The Federal Security Service of the Russian Federation had been observing the commander for some time, gathering evidence against him. This text was the final piece of evidence they needed to stop him for good.

Grigory Popov, a tall, tough-looking senior security officer marched into the apartment. He calmly crossed through the security forces that had guns drawn on Pavel. "Pavel Volkov, you have been found guilty of treason by means of carrying out unauthorized operations," Grigory said as he confiscated Pavel's cell phone. He erased the partial confirmation code that Pavel had typed and replaced it with a code signaling the agent awaiting authorization to stand down and abort the mission. The op was over. Adam and Rose were not to be touched. Grigory then dropped the phone into the left breast pocket of Pavel's suit and patted it twice with his hand as he ordered two security officers to escort Pavel to the armored vehicle that would transport him to the prison where he would live out the rest of his days.

The security officers slammed Pavel face down on the green kitchen table, where Pavel took notice of the lone Alka Seltzer tablet. He thought fast about how he could work his way out of this situation and slid his mouth over the tablet as the officers handcuffed him. The two security officers yanked Pavel off the table and escorted him out of his apartment while the remaining men seized anything they could find of interest.

"Confiscate everything," Grigory said to his men as

they tore Pavel's apartment apart. "We must ensure every rogue long-term, deep-cover operation is shut down. Locate all files regarding any agents still in the field. Every sleeper agent must be identified and returned home. We must abort all ghost operations."

Outside the apartment building, Pavel felt the pressure from the foam that was mounting in his mouth from the dissolving Alka Seltzer tablet. He feigned choking and foaming at the mouth as he collapsed on the sidewalk between his escorts. The security officers turned to each other, unsure of what to do to help the convulsing older man. One of the security officers ran to the armored vehicle and got on the radio to call for an ambulance while the other unlocked the handcuffs that had been keeping Pavel's hands behind his back. The security officer then rolled Pavel over and tilted his head forward in an effort to keep him from choking to death. He quickly took out his wallet in order to place it inside Pavel's mouth to prevent him from possibly biting his own tongue.

Pavel quickly twisted his neck and fiercely bit down on the man's hand while un-holstering the agent's gun and shooting him point blank in the head, killing him instantly. Pavel stood and spit foam from his mouth onto the officer's lifeless body as the dead man's partner jumped out of the armored truck to see what was happening. Pavel shot and killed that officer before he could react to what he was seeing. Then he walked past the armored truck and escaped, disappearing into an alley.

Back in Adam's hotel suite, water was heard gushing out of the bathroom faucet. After several minutes, Adam approached the bathroom door. Rose watched him and grabbed a nearby metal pen to use as an improvised weapon.

"How are things going in there?" Adam asked. There was no reply. Concerned, Adam reached to open the bathroom door.

"Adam, no!" Rose rushed towards Adam as he pushed the bathroom door open.

The bathroom was empty.

"Hey, are you okay?" Adam asked taking Rose in his arms.

Rose nodded, breathing a sigh of relief. "I'm sorry." She held onto him tightly.

"The stuff that happened back home has me still pretty shook up too," Adam said to comfort her. "But we can't live in fear, right?"

"No. We can't," she said, looking up at Adam.

Adam kissed her forehead and gave her another

comforting hug. "At least the faucet's fixed," Adam said, making light of the situation and bringing a smile to Rose's face.

# Chapter 10.

In his small cell beneath The Center of Special Operations in St. Petersburg, David Mosin sat cross legged on the cold concrete floor, meditating. He had meditated after he prayed twice a day every day with the same dedication he gave to his exercise routine. This evening's hour-long after-prayer meditation was almost over. David had reached the third meditative stage. His mind was tranquil and at peace with the universe. His mind had become void of all thought. David was on his way to the beginning of a higher meditation.

David's meditation was cut short by the sound of the lock at the end of the hallway snapping open with the ever-familiar loud, echoing clank. He listened as the footsteps of a man he didn't recognize approached his cell door. David remained seated on the floor of his cell, waiting for the steel observation panel to slide open. Instead, David was surprised when a key was inserted into the cell door, unlocking it.

The cell door swung open, revealing Grigory Popov. The senior security officer filled the void where the three-inch thick steel door had been. "You are David Mosin, prisoner of Pavel Volkov," Grigory began. "Is that correct?"

"Yes, I am David Mosin," David replied as he stood to face the man in the doorway. "Who are you? Am I being moved to another facility again? Or have you come to get rid of me?"

"I am Grigory Popov, senior officer with The Federal Security Service of the Russian Federation. Pavel Volkov is no longer affiliated with the Russian Government, Agent Mosin. He is a criminal guilty of committing many crimes."

"Are you saying that I'm being released?" David asked. He scanned the man's face, looking for indicators of a deception while keeping an eye on the tall Russian's hands. David did not want to get shot in this cell, and if the Russian wanted to terminate him, David planned on not going down without a fight. The man's hands, however, stayed at his side and his face gave no hint of deception. "What's going on?" David asked, confused.

"I am prepared to offer you amnesty," Grigory said.

"What do you mean by 'prepared to offer'?" David asked, wanting Grigory to get to the real reason for the strange visit.

"The Cold War is over, Agent Mosin. In fact, it's been over for a very long time. The relations between Russia and the United States are very different than they were when you were imprisoned. The world outside is not the one you last saw thirty-four years ago."

"Everything changes," David replied. "I myself have even managed to age a little. What is the condition for my amnesty?"

"Pavel Volkov has evaded capture," Grigory said with a bit of shame. "Locate and eliminate this embarrassment and you will receive amnesty. Refuse to cooperate and you will never set your eyes on the sky again. This obsolete concrete prison will become your tomb."

"It doesn't sound like you're giving me much of a choice," David said as he stepped toward the doorway of his cell.

Grigory reached into his right front pant pocket and pulled out a small piece of paper. On the slip of paper was an address in Ireland. He handed the slip to David.

"We believe this is the location where former agent Volkov is heading. We believe he is going to attempt to assassinate a man and a woman. Remove Pavel Volkov from the face of the earth, and you will have earned your freedom. Now, please shower; you smell like old mold. There is a change of clothing waiting for you in the shower room, and I will arrange transportation for you while you clean up."

David showered and dressed. While he waited for his escort to take him to his transportation, he wondered how much the world had changed. He wondered who the targets were that Pavel Volkov was set to assassinate. Henry Calhoun was dead; therefore, Pavel would be after whoever was getting between him and the relic. David wondered if Peter and Helen, Henry's surviving grandchildren, were the man and woman in question. He wondered if he would see them, and if he did, what he might say to them; after all, he had been missing for thirty-four years.

# Chapter 11.

After several hours of driving, Adam and Rose found themselves lost in the Irish countryside.

"At least the country is beautiful to look at," Rose said optimistically.

"Daina wasn't kidding when she said the signage wasn't the best out here in the country," Adam said.

"Understatement of the year," Rose replied lightheartedly.

"Any luck with the GPS?"

"Still no signal. Maybe we should head back towards that village we saw about a half hour ago? You know, stop and ask the locals for directions."

Adam smiled and nodded his head in defeat. "Okay. You win." He slowly turned the car around and headed back in the opposite direction.

Finally, after one stop at an eating house, a second stop at a bed and breakfast, and a third stop at a roadside flower and fruit vendor, all to ask for directions, Adam and Rose managed to locate the unpaved road that led to his relative's rural farmhouse. The landscape along the road was painted with a combination of thick trees and green fields. The car bumped its way down the narrow, curvy road that was covered in pot holes before reaching the turn into the long gravel driveway of the farmhouse. The property boundary was marked by an old stone wall that varied in height and appeared to be holding back the encroachment of a forest of alder, ash, and oak trees.

The sound of gravel crunching under the rolling tires and the scenic landscape reminded Adam fondly of his grandpa Henry's own estate back in Ohio. As the car slowly navigated its way down the driveway and over a small hill, the farmhouse became visible: first the dark thatched roof, then the sturdy tan and grey stone walls of the multi-story farmhouse. Adam drove the rental car down the hill and circled the vehicle into the vast open gravel area in front of the farmhouse and parked.

Henry's first cousin, Bridget Gildea, stepped out of the front door and slowly walked towards Adam and Rose, who were exiting the vehicle. Bridget wore an off-white Aran cardigan over her simple, wool dress. The light color of her clothes seemed to make the elderly woman's hazel eyes sparkle as the sunlight bathed her weathered face.

"Bridget Gildea?" Adam said in a pleasant manner as he walked up to the woman.

"Yes, but I haven't gone by that name since I was knee high. It's just Biddy, dear," she replied. Her voice was modulated and reminded Adam of his great-grandmother Florence, minus the brogue. "You must be Adam."

Adam nodded and extended his hand.

"Not on your life. These old bird wings were meant for hugging," Biddy said with a bright wrinkled smile. Her warmth was contagious and immediately made Adam feel like family. She gave Adam a gentle hug. Then she turned to Rose. "And is this beautiful lass your wife?"

Adam found himself tongue tied, but Rose quickly came to his rescue. "His girlfriend. Rose," she replied as she hugged Biddy. "It's so nice to meet you."

Biddy held onto Rose tenderly by the forearms and looked into her eyes. Rose felt calm and unsure of herself all at once. She felt as if Biddy's gaze might have the ability to sum up Rose's character with a single glance.

"Ah, well, good thing I have one bedroom for each of you." Biddy smiled.

"We don't want to impose," Adam chimed in.

"Nonsense. I insist you stay for at least the night. There's so much of our family's history here. It would be a shame if you rushed the visit. I hope you didn't have too much trouble finding the place? I was getting worried when you didn't show a couple hours ago."

"Uh, no, not too much trouble. Well, maybe a little," Adam said.

"We had a lot of trouble," Rose chimed in, looking Biddy in the eyes.

"My Hugh was the same way when it came to asking for directions," Biddy said with a wink. Then the two women instantly broke into laughter. "Navigating your way around this land is a might bit difficult. But that's one of the reasons old folks like me never became townies. The peace and quiet of seclusion," Biddy said, patting Rose gently on the hand. Biddy turned and guided Rose towards the house. "I'm sorry, I'm getting to be as slow as late dinner nowadays." Her steps were paced and calculated, yet she seemed quite spry and hardy for a woman in her early nineties.

"I can't tell you how much I appreciate you allowing us to come out here," Adam said as he followed close behind the women.

"Allowing you?" Biddy glanced over at Adam. "Family visits are rare these days. Henry was very dear to me. He was more of an uncle than a cousin. You are most welcome. Now you two look famished. Let Biddy fatten you up a bit. Come inside."

They sat at a small table in the kitchen and enjoyed a steaming hot cup of black tea with sugar and milk. "I do hope you two will consider staying a day or two? This home is as much yours as mine," Biddy said as she placed two bowls of stew on the table, one in front of Adam and another in front of Rose. "Biddy's pot luck. In the old days there was always water simmering over the fire and whatever the fellas brought back from the fields just went into the pot. You never knew what kind of meat you'd get. It was all luck of the pot. Pot luck."

Rose glanced down at the stew with a suspicious eye.

"Don't worry love, it's just mutton, hearty potatoes and carrots with some seasonings. Family recipe," Biddy said as she fixed herself a bowl.

After they finished their lunch, Adam politely cleared the table and went to work on washing the dishes.

"Don't bother with that, Adam. You're my guest. Relax and enjoy another cup of tea," Biddy instructed.

"I don't mind doing a few dishes."

"Would you like to see a portrait of your great-great grandmother Catherine?" Biddy countered.

Adam quickly rinsed off the dishes and turned to take

Biddy up on her offer.

She escorted them out of the kitchen and up the wooden staircase to the second floor. At the top of the stairs were four doors leading to bedrooms. Two to the right and two to the left and a fifth door leading into a water closet at the end of the hall. The staircase narrowed as it circled around and up to a third-level attic space.

Biddy walked up to the second door on the right and used an old metal key to unlock the door. The lock cringed as the internal mechanism rotated, rubbing the old metal as the bolt slid open. Biddy opened the door and motioned for Adam and Rose to enter first.

The room was a time capsule of the early twentieth century. The early afternoon sun shone through the window, giving it a golden brown haze. On the wall opposite the window and to the left of the door was a painted portrait approximately 18 to 20 inches across and 24 inches in height. The portrait was of a beautiful woman in her mid-twenties with crystal blue eyes, ivory skin, and curl upon curl of yellow hair.

Adam gazed at the portrait. Her eyes seemed to call to him, and a piece of the riddle slowly became clear. He stared at her angelic, yellow hair when the epiphany struck. "It's her," he said softly.

"Your great-great grandmother Catherine," Biddy

said with pride.

"Yes. But I mean, she's the woman with yellow hair," Adam replied, turning to Rose. "There's a line in the poem regarding a yellow-haired woman."

"My mother Anna always said Catherine was a sight to behold. The poor soul was taken much too soon. In this very room. The décor is a tad morbid I know. But I promised your great-grandfather many years ago that I would leave it untouched."

"You knew him?"

"Of course. I knew Henry quite well." Biddy motioned to the portrait of Catherine. "Would you like to visit her?"

"Catherine?"

"Yes, boy. The family has a private cemetery on the grounds. Scores of Calhouns are buried here including Uncle Matthew, your great-great grandfather."

\*\*\*

The family cemetery was on a gentle sloping hill that looked out over the property. The grass was well manicured and dotted with wildflowers and headstones. Fresh crisp air that smelled of lavender and a touch of rain blew across the land.

Biddy directed Adam and Rose to the simple yet elegant headstones that marked the resting place of

Matthew and Catherine. Matthew Calhoun's headstone had a quote that read:

## THE JOURNEY MAKETH THE MAN

This seemed prophetic to Adam, as his great-grandfather had sent him on this journey of self-discovery. He noticed his great-great grandparents had died within a short time span of each other.

"April 26th and June 6th in 1916," Adam noted.

Biddy stepped closer to Adam. "My mother said Catherine died of a broken heart, but truth was she was quite ill with consumption for almost a year. Henry was by her side when she passed away. There was nothing anyone of them could have done.

"Times were harsh back then. My grandmother died during childbirth. The pregnancy was not exactly what my grandparents expected at their age and my grandfather was not exactly physically equipped to raise a daughter on his own. So my aunt Catherine asked him for my mother to come live with her and Uncle Matthew. They raised her until she was a teenager and she moved back here to look after her father.

"He lived here until he died, only a few years before sweet Catherine. My mother cared for him and then for

Aunt Catherine until she passed. Less than two months after the riots claimed my uncle Matthew. I must imagine it was a very difficult time for Henry. He looked after my mother like a sister. My mother married late in life for those times—and I was born."

A strong breeze blew across the lush green grass of the cemetery. Biddy rubbed her arms to stave off the chill.

"We can walk you back to the house if you'd like," Adam said gently.

"Oh no. A little cool air is good for the lungs. My bones just aren't as thick as they once were."

Rose removed her light windbreaker and placed the jacket over Biddy's shoulders. "Here."

The rugged woman patted Rose's hand in thanks. "Take all the time you need. I don't get many visitors out here anymore. I suspect one day I will just put myself out to pasture like a maimed sheep dog," she jested.

# Chapter 12.

Back in Ohio, Hiro Tarsus rolled over in his bed, sliding his hand and arm under his pillow to elevate his head as he opened his eyes to greet the new day. He stretched, got up, dressed for his morning jog, and set out for his daily run around the park.

As he jogged, Hiro thought of his upcoming visit to his new friend, Eli Taylor, later. Today's visit would be Hiro's third, and Hiro had noticed that not only was Eli's skill in chess improving, but his humor and overall health seemed to be improving as well. Hiro also thought about Eli's caregiver, Nurse Terry. It was pretty obvious to Hiro that Nurse Terry had a crush on him, but he was also beginning to have feelings for her as well. Her smile, the warmth in her eyes, and the cute child-like scrubs she chose to wear all filled Hiro's mind as he ran his last lap around the park and headed for home.

Hiro showered and got dressed in the black suit, white shirt, and black tie that he normally wore to work. He sat down at the kitchen table, and while he ate his traditional Japanese breakfast, he looked over the notes he had made concerning the cell phone and its possible four digit pass code.

He scanned the series of possible choices that he had written down and placed a checkmark next to the ones that stood out to him as logical choices. The first code that he checked was MOM1. Hiro thought that since the photo of Hiram Grey's mother was used as the cover photo for the phone that his mother may be used as his password. Hiro had looked up the Grey brothers' mother in Chicago. She had passed away several years ago, and her name was Alice, therefore Hiro knew that Hiram couldn't have used her name as the password. The second choice that Hiro checked was the number sequence 1111. Hiro checked that particular sequence because he remembered the date of birth on Hiram Grey's driver's license when he checked it the day he discovered the bodies of he and his brother. Hiram's date of birth was listed as November 11th. The third option checked was simply Hiram's last name GREY. Hiro would double check the list and try to access the phone after work.

He finished his breakfast and drove to the precinct, where he checked his in-box and found it to be empty. There had been no homicides assigned to him that day. Hiro checked in with Captain Conrad, who allowed Hiro to take the day to run errands or whatever it was that Hiro wanted to do that day just as long as he stayed close to his radio.

Hiro drove to Eli's house. As he parked, Hiro saw Pastor Faith's long white Cadillac convertible parked in front of the house. He rang the bell, and within seconds, Nurse Terry answered the door. She greeted Hiro with a warm smile and invited him into the house.

"Mr. Taylor is in another prayer session," Terry said. "I've just finished making my lunch. Do you like meatloaf?"

"I do," Hiro replied. "How long has the pastor been here?"

"He got here about five minutes before you did." Terry answered. "They usually pray for about a half an hour or so. Are you in a hurry?"

"No, I was just curious. The meatloaf smells great."

Terry brought two plates of meatloaf, green beans, and mashed potatoes to the table. As they ate, Hiro regretted not bringing flowers. He was trying to build up the courage to ask her if she would go on a date with him, but it seemed odd for him to do so without flowers, so he kept the conversation focused on Eli.

"How is Eli doing today?" Hiro asked.

"He's actually getting better," Terry answered. "I don't know if it's your chess games, the pastor, or a combination of the two, but something is really affecting his health. He's feeling better, his vitals are improving, and he's asked for a Salisbury steak frozen meal for dinner."

"Those things are pretty gross," Hiro chuckled.

"I know, but he seems to like them. The important part of that request though is he's up to eating solids. That's a vast improvement from just the other day."

"That's good to hear," Hiro said. "If his condition continues to improve like this, soon he'll be beating me at chess."

Eli closed his eyes and prayed silently as Pastor Faith placed his hands on his forehead. Eli felt warmth in the pastor's hands. He suddenly felt as though he was no longer in his bed, but floating on a cloud. The smell of freshly cut grass infiltrated his nostrils, and the scent made Eli think of playing in his yard as a young boy. He had a red fire truck with an extendable ladder that he would push through the grass, imagining the grass was a forest and the fire truck was sent to the forest to put out fires. As a young boy, Eli would imagine himself to be the fireman who put the fires out and saved the kittens that had climbed the trees to escape the flames. Eli often played the hero when he was young. Then he would run into the backyard and try to climb the apple tree that grew there. Occasionally, he would treat himself to one of the apples from one of the lower branches.

Eli remembered lying in the grass underneath the apple tree staring at the sky. He focused on how blue the sky was and how the sun peeked at him from between the leafy branches of the apple tree. The warmth of the sun caressed his face. Then Eli felt the warmth engulf his whole face and body. The warmth generated all through him and even moved to the back of his head. The back of Eli's head went from feeling sun-kissed warm to feeling as though a hot needle had been jabbed into the back of his head.

Eli opened his eyes and let out a loud yelp, causing Pastor Faith to stop his prayer and jump back away from Eli's bed.

"Are you alright?" Pastor Faith asked.

"I don't know," Eli replied. "I think I might have just died there for a second."

"Well, you certainly aren't dead now," Pastor Faith said, recovering from his scare. "In fact, I'd say that the good lord is allowing you to heal through the powers that I bring to you in prayer."

Just then, the door flew open. Hiro entered the room followed by Nurse Terry.

"Is everything alright?" Hiro asked.

"I'm fine," Eli answered. "I just dosed off for a second and had a dream. I guess I yelled myself awake."

"How do you feel?" Nurse Terry asked as she came around Eli's bed to check on him.

"I'm a little warm, but I feel fine," Eli said. "In fact, I have been feeling a lot better lately."

"You have been getting better lately," Pastor Faith said. "God is allowing me to heal you, son. He wants you to continue his good work. How many more visits it will take until you are fully recovered? He only knows. But I think I will call it a day and allow you to rest and—"

"Thank you, Pastor," Nurse Terry interrupted. "I'll walk you to the door. Eli, Hiro is here to see you. If you're up to it he'd like another game of chess."

Terry escorted Pastor Faith out of the room and to the front door of the house. Once the pastor was on the front porch, Terry took a deep breath and said, "I appreciate what you are doing here, and I know that you believe that

Mr. Taylor's condition is improving. Please refrain from telling him that he is being healed, though. Mr. Taylor's condition is terminal. He may appear to be improving, but to be honest with you, his days have been numbered for some time. My job is to keep him comfortable, and although it may seem harmless to fill him with false hope, I don't agree with it."

Pastor Faith smiled his signature smile and said, "But my child, he is healing. You cannot ignore the evidence before you. That man in there is in much better condition today than he was before I came to visit him. You may not believe, but he does." Then, he turned and went to his car. He sat inside the long, all-white Cadillac, put the key in the ignition, and paused. He held his hands palm up and looked at them. The palms of his hands were red and warm with energy. This was a warmth he had never felt in his hands before. Pastor Faith had laid hands on and healed hundreds of believers before, but none of the healing sessions that he had done in the past left him feeling warm and energized.

Pastor Faith smiled as he started the car and drove away. The idea of healing Eli Taylor sounded good to him. It would definitely instigate a personal meeting with Dr. Adam Calhoun. Then Pastor Faith's mind began to whirl, devising a plan on how to trick Dr. Calhoun into revealing the location of the crucifix pendant during that meeting.

Nurse Terry watched the Cadillac drive away. Once the car had turned the corner at the end of the block, she went back into the house. She went to the kitchen and cleared her and Hiro's dishes from the table, put them onto the counter next to the sink, and began washing them.

Inside Eli's bedroom, Hiro and Eli were continuing a game of chess they had started on Hiro's last visit. Eli quickly moved one of his pawns on the table.

"You're sacrificing a piece," Hiro said.

"I'm protecting my king," Eli replied.

"Be sure not to carelessly lose pieces. Each piece, even pawns, are valuable to your game. You cannot win a game of chess without pieces to checkmate," Hiro answered back with a smile.

"Speaking of checkmate, have you asked Nurse Terry out yet?" Eli asked.

"What makes you think I'm interested in dating your nurse?" Hiro asked, avoiding a direct answer to Eli's question.

"I'm not blind. I can see the way you two look at each other. Plus, she's cheerful after you've visited. Almost too cheerful. She clearly likes you, and I think you might like her too if you took the time to get to know her. That, and your babies would be adorable."

"Hold on there, cowboy," Hiro said as his face turned red with embarrassment. "Dating and babies are two completely different subjects. Let's not make me a father just yet. I haven't' even figured out where she would want to go on a first date yet."

"So you have thought about asking her out."

"Yes, I have. Not that it's any of your business."

"Hey, if my friend and my nurse are going to hook up, I think I have a right to know."

"Thank you for calling me your friend."

"When you're in a condition like mine, you have to make friends fast or you might not make any at all."

"Well, you seem to be looking healthier, and we're talking about a date, not hooking up, and no you don't. Besides, checkmate."

"Wait, what?"

"Checkmate. It is time I left anyway. There is something I have to do at home." Hiro stood and removed the tray with the game from Eli's lap and placed it back onto the dresser. He then took the chair that he had been sitting on and put it against the wall near the door. "Besides, I hear its Salisbury steak night here, and I wouldn't want to encroach on that."

Hiro went into the kitchen where Terry was sitting at

the table, reading a book. He said goodbye. She stood and offered him a goodbye hug. Hiro took Terry in his arms and held her tightly. He felt the urge to turn his head and offer her a kiss, but he fought off that urge, fearing that a sudden show of boldness may take her off guard and cause her to shy away. She felt good in his arms. He noticed that she lightly rested her head on his shoulder. He held the hug at what he hoped was for the appropriate amount of time. He said goodbye again, let himself out of the house, and drove home.

# Chapter 13.

Hiro arrived back home, walked through the front door, and took off his jacket and tie. The entire car drive back home from Eli's house all Hiro could think about was Nurse Terry and Hiram Grey's locked cell phone. He unbuttoned the top button of his white oxford shirt and rolled up the sleeves to his elbows as he walked into his kitchen.

He sat at the kitchen table with the fully charged cell phone and notebook in front of him. He examined the choices for possible passwords that he had check marked before. He eliminated MOM1 from his first choice, thinking that a thief and a thug like Hiram Grey was too narcissistic to have a password that didn't deal with himself.

Hiro took up the phone and pressed the power button.

The screen lit up with the photo of the late Alice Grey staring at him along with the four boxes and a keyboard. He typed the letters, GREY, to the phone and pressed the enter key. The squares went blank, and in red letters, the words, "Incorrect: two attempts left" flashed on the screen.

Hiro held the phone in his left hand and scanned the notebook. The next choice checked in the notebook was the series of numbers associated with Hiram's birthday. Hiro typed in the numbers, 1111, and pressed enter. Once again, the squares went blank, and in red letters the words "Incorrect: one attempt left" flashed on the phone's screen. Hiro went back to the notebook and scanned all of the options he had written down, and none of them seemed correct. He thought about the man who the phone had belonged to. "He was a thug," Hiro said to himself. "His birthday was November 11th, and he was a kidnapper, a bully, and an opportunist." Hiro looked at the phone and noticed how it rested in his left hand. Or rather, he noticed how his left hand rested around the phone. More specifically, how his thumb hovered above the screen directly above the number five on the keyboard. "He is also lazy." Hiro said out loud as he typed in the number sequence 5555 and pressed enter on the phone.

This time, the phone lit up and the photo of Alice Grey was replaced with a screen containing three icons. The icons on the screen were for the phone function, a calendar, and a solitaire game. Hiro pressed the phone icon and the screen changed, revealing a dial pad. Above the dial pad for the phone were the four words; Keypad, Recent, Favorites, and Contacts. Hiro pressed Recent and a call history revealed itself to him. Hiro turned to a fresh page on the notebook and began writing down all of the recent calls on the list. The nine most recent calls to and from Hiram Grey's phone were with a Mr. P. Mitchell; then Hiro noticed that the next series of calls were all with a P.F. There were also three calls from his brother, Horace, and one from an S.S.

Hiro looked at the call history on the phone and wondered if the Mr. P. Mitchell on the list was the same Peter Calhoun Mitchell. Hiro pulled his own cell phone out of his pants pocket and dialed the number associated with the name Mr. P. Mitchell on Hiram Grey's phone. Hiro listened as the signal connected and the phone rang several times. Just after the fourth ring, Peter Mitchell's voice delivered his outgoing message for his voicemail, "You've reached Peter Calhoun Mitchell. Leave a message." Hiro ended the call, grabbed his jacket, and drove to Helen Morales' house.

Sean Morales answered the door and greeted Hiro Tarsus with a disapproving scowl. "Hello Detective, I'm sorry, but mother's just about to have her afternoon tea. You'll have to come back another day. Perhaps you could call ahead next time."

"I apologize for the intrusion," Hiro said, "but I must speak with your mother. I have questions concerning your uncle's involvement in the kidnapping of Dr. Rose Powell and the men—"

"Like I said," Sean interrupted. "You'll have to come back some other day."

"Don't you want to know what happened to your brother?" Hiro asked.

"My brother was a drug addict and a leech," Sean said through clenched jaws. Hiro could see Sean seething with anger as he continued. "While I've taken care of mother my whole life, my brother spent his time getting high and wasting mother's money on drugs and whores. I know what happened to my brother, Detective. He got what he had coming. Now if you don't mind, please leave."

"Sean, let him in!" Helen's voice broke the stare down the two men were engaged in on either side of the threshold.

Sean spun around and saw his mother standing right behind him. "Mother, I'm sorry, but the detective isn't even allowed to be working on the case anymore," Sean stammered.

"Sean, that's exactly why I want you to let him in. Detective Tarsus is not giving up on finding the truth, and I admire that. Also, I know what your brother was. Despite all of his flaws, he was my son. We should have done more to help him."

"Yes mother," Sean replied, hanging his head like a scolded child.

"Detective Tarsus," Helen said as Sean sulked into the kitchen. "Come in and join me for tea."

"Thank you," Hiro said as he followed Helen into the sitting room.

Hiro sat on the long white couch next to Helen. He pulled Hiram Grey's cell phone out of his jacket pocket and showed Helen her brother's name and phone number on the call history.

"Your brother, I believe, hired the men who kidnapped Dr. Rose Powell," Hiro explained. "I found this phone next to one of the two murdered men in the warehouse: the warehouse where Dr. Powell was held captive, the same warehouse your brother happened to own. Two of the earlier calls on this list align with the day your nephew Adam was attacked in his own home."

"What are your thoughts?" Helen asked Hiro. "What

do you think my brother's involvement was?"

"When I interviewed Adam on that night, he told me about the necklace that his great-grandfather had given him. He said that it was a valuable antique and that he suspected several people may have been after it."

"Antique," Helen smiled. "I guess it was an antique. My grandfather's necklace is valuable, Detective, and my brother went to great lengths to get it."

Helen considered telling the detective the whole story of the necklace: How it had the tip of one of the nails from Christ's cross in it. How it had the healing powers of Christ within it. Helen reconsidered and decided to not tell the detective the whole story. She didn't know his true intentions after all. So she told him what she felt was enough information for him to put the pieces together without revealing the necklace's true power.

"Originally, Grandpa Henry had left the necklace to me. I was to make sure it got put in a safe place. After he died, the necklace went missing. I suppose he gave it to Adam. I can't imagine Adam taking it without his permission. As you know, Detective, my brother poisoned me to induce my blindness. I suppose he thought I would reveal the necklace's whereabouts if I were in need of help. I suppose it's within reason to assume that Pete also hired the two men to ransack Adam's apartment looking for the necklace. I don't think he meant for them to harm Adam. I think Adam must have surprised them. When that didn't work, I guess Pete had the men kidnap Dr. Powell in a desperate last attempt to force Adam into giving him the necklace."

"I believe you're right," Hiro said. "Only without my notes or any other evidence at my disposal, it will be difficult to learn more about these men. This phone is the only piece of evidence I have left."

"Have you tried finding out who the other people are on the call history on that phone, Detective?" Helen asked. "I noticed there are other callers other than just my brother on that phone."

"That will be my next move," Hiro replied. "If you wouldn't mind assisting me with a pen and paper, we can call these numbers and find out who answers."

Helen got a pen and a writing pad from the antique writing desk in the far corner of the sitting room. Hiro wrote down the initials P.F. and the number associated with that name on the first sheet of paper. He then took out his own phone and started to dial the number. Helen, however, had pressed the number on the dead man's phone and the call went through. Hiro activated the speaker function and set the phone on the coffee table so that he and Helen could hear the answerer together. The phone rang three times.

"Hello, who is this?" a voice answered.

Helen and Hiro exchanged glances, and then Helen spoke. "Hello, may I ask who is speaking?"

The phone went silent as the connection was disconnected.

"I think we may be onto something, Detective." Helen said to Hiro as she turned the top sheet of the writing pad over and wrote the name Horace and the phone number associated with that name on Hiram's call history.

"I believe that name and number belongs to the other man in the warehouse," Hiro told Helen. "Horace and Hiram Grey were brothers who worked together as small-time thieves."

Helen wrote Horace Grey below the phone number, skipped two lines, and wrote Hiram Grey below it. She then jotted the initials P.F. in the upper right hand corner of the page and wrote the corresponding phone number beneath them.

"Who's next then?" Helen asked.

"The letters S. S." Hiro answered.

Helen skipped two lines below Hiram Grey's name on the sheet and wrote S. S. and the corresponding telephone number next to it.

Hiro dialed the number and set the phone to speaker

as he had done before. The phone only rang once before it was answered by a woman's voice.

"Good afternoon and thank you for calling Salvador International. How may I direct your call?"

"I'm sorry, I may have dialed the wrong number," Helen said. "Whose office have I called?"

"This is the global headquarters for Salvador International."

"Oh, I've dialed the wrong number, sorry to bother you," Helen said and then ended the call.

Hiro took a deep breath and looked at the list of names and telephone numbers that Helen had written on the pad of paper. "We have four names, including your brother Peter," Hiro said. "We have three area codes as well." Hiro picked up his cell phone and accessed Google. He typed in the numbers 773 in the search bar and hit enter. The search took him to a Wikipedia page for the area code 773, an area code for the city of Chicago established in 1996.

Helen wrote the word "Chicago" beneath the numbers for P.F. and Hiram, because those numbers both started with the area code 773.

Hiro then cleared that search and typed in the area code number associated with S.S., 312. The search took them to another Wikipedia page. This area code served the downtown area of Chicago.

"It seems the Grey brothers had dealings in Chicago," Hiro said. "That's not much to go on at the moment. I'll have to sleep on it and consider my next move."

"That's a good idea, Detective," Helen agreed. She then took the notepad and pen and headed back toward the writing desk.

"Excuse me," Hiro blurted, as Helen began walking away. "If you don't mind, I would like to have that sheet of paper with the information on it. It will be useful in helping me gather my thoughts."

"Oh, but of course." Helen tore the sheet off from the pad and handed it to Hiro.

"Thank you," Hiro said as he took the sheet, folded it into a small square, and put it into his jacket pocket. He then walked to the door to leave, and as he turned back to say goodbye, he noticed that Helen had taken a sharpened pencil from the writing desk and was holding it in her hand. "Goodbye, Mrs. Morales," Hiro said. "If I find anything, I will be sure to inform you."

"Thank you, Detective," Helen replied with a smile. "I look forward to that call."

Hiro let himself out and stood on the porch for a moment. He turned his head and looked back at the house. Specifically, he looked back at the window of the sitting room he had just left. The sheer curtains were drawn on the sitting room so he couldn't see in great detail what Helen was doing seated on the couch slightly hunched over the coffee table, but he assumed that Helen was using an old trick, rubbing the graphite from the sharpened pencil across the page on the writer's tablet to highlight the indentions pressed into the paper from the page that had been torn out above it. Helen was going to look into the names and numbers herself. Hiro then walked to his car and sat in the driver's seat and watched the house. Only seven minutes went by before Helen and Sean emerged from the house. Sean brought the car from out of the garage. Helen got into the passenger seat and the two drove off. Hiro followed.

Hiro followed Helen and Sean all the way to the former home of Helen's grandfather Henry Calhoun. Hiro parked on the outer road roughly fifty yards from the entrance of the private tree-lined drive that led to the immense estate. Hiro sat in his car and wondered what it was about the names and phone numbers that were on Hiram Grey's cell phone that would lead Helen to the estate of her late grandfather.

Helen told Sean to wait in the car once they reached the large estate house. She unlocked the front door, entered the house, and locked the door behind her. She then went into Henry's library and opened every drawer in his desk, looking for something specific. She did not find what she was looking for in his desk or on any of the shelves or reading tables in the library. She then went into the den and looked there, with no luck. She proceeded to the second floor and checked the bedrooms as she made her way down the long corridor that cut through the center of the immense structure. She ventured to a small office on the west end on the second floor. The door was locked. Helen went through the series of keys on the key ring that she had inherited along with Henry's home. After several failed attempts, she finally found the correct key and opened the office door.

The room was musty and full of cobwebs. It was apparent that no one had been in the room for years. The layer of dust on the dark walnut furnishings gave everything a dry and chalky look. Helen opened the desk drawers and searched for her prize. It was not in the desk. She then hurried to the bookshelves that ran along the north wall of the room. As she came around the desk on its left side, a loose floorboard squeaked beneath her foot as she stepped on it. Helen froze in her tracks and looked down. She pressed her foot down onto the board, making it squeak again. She then got down onto her hands and knees and pried the loose board up with her fingers.

Beneath the board, Helen found what she was looking for.

An ancient scroll, possibly thousands of years old, preserved in a wooden cylinder lay beneath the floorboard of Henry's private office. Helen lifted the cylinder and carried it out of the office and down to Henry's den on the first floor. She turned on the lights and then the computer and cleared a place on the desk. She opened the cylinder and took out the scroll, which was wrapped in a leather case embellished with circular gold studs. Then she pressed the gold studs, causing the leather case to pop open. Next she accessed Google from the computer and typed in "Horace Grey."

Just then, she heard the horn from Sean's car honk several times. Helen became flustered and placed the scroll back inside the leather case before going outside to see what Sean was bothering her about.

"Sean, I told you to wait outside quietly!" Helen shouted as she exited the house. She looked out at the car and saw Detective Tarsus standing next to Sean beside the car.

"Sorry to bother you, Mrs. Morales," Hiro said, "I couldn't help but suspect that you had information that you were withholding. I would appreciate it if you were more honest with me in assisting me in finding out the truth behind your son's and brother's deaths."

Helen stared at the detective for a moment. Her initial emotional reaction to seeing him was anger. She couldn't believe he would have followed her to Henry's mansion. Then her temper cooled as she realized that the detective was only doing what he was made to do. He was trying to help. He was seeking the truth.

"Come inside Detective," Helen said as she held the door open. "Sean, go into the kitchen and make us some coffee. It could be a long night."

Hiro walked passed Helen and entered the house. "Please, call me Hiro," he said. "It may help in your learning to trust me."

"Alright, Hiro," Helen said as she led him to the den. "I've got something to show you. When I was a little girl, my parents would sometimes bring us kids here to play and visit our grandparents. Pete always liked to play outside, while Mary always wanted to spend time with our grandmother in the kitchen. I was never more than arms reach away from Grandpa Henry. He called me Helen Doll, because he said I looked like a doll that had been left on the floor by his feet. I have several wonderful memories of Grandpa Henry working away in his office, looking for new discoveries. I remembered him telling me about how he found this."

Helen showed Hiro the opened leather casing. With

the care and precision of a museum curator, she removed the scroll from its casing and opened it, laying it out on the desk for Hiro to see. She placed weights on each corner to keep the fragile document from rolling itself closed. The document Helen had opened was an ancient numerology codex.

"This scroll, I believe, will be particularly useful. My grandfather found it in Turkey in an underground city. He brought it to the U.S. and spent a great deal of his time studying and deciphering this and other scrolls he found. I believe that once Grandpa Henry passed away, the evil that caused my brother and son to act in the ways that they did was directly set upon them by the antichrist. I need to find who it is and stop them before evil descends upon our entire planet."

Hiro looked at Helen with curious eyes. He examined the ancient scroll that she had unrolled onto the desk. He took out the folded piece of paper that he had placed in his jacket pocket earlier and laid it next to the scroll.

"Please, tell me everything you know about this scroll," Hiro said.

"I'll do you one better than that, Detective, I mean Hiro. I'll tell you the real story about my grandpa, Henry Calhoun, and how he discovered the site of his most precious archeological finds in Turkey. My grandfather would tell me it was just the luck of the Irish, but I believe it was fate.

"He was fighting in the trenches of Gallipoli, Turkey. He was shot multiple times and left for dead. When he awoke he found himself deep underground lying on his back looking up at a ceiling with the scene from Christ's crucifixion painted on it.

"*Where am I?* He wondered.

"A round faced Armenian man named Davit had been caring for him under the orders of a priest by the name of Father Keshishian. The priest had found Grandpa Henry lying on the battlefield, nearly dead, and brought him to their cave city. Grandpa Henry had rested on a table and slowly recovered.

"'I have to get back to my unit,' my grandfather kept saying," Helen revealed with a smile.

"But they made him stay on that table until he fully recovered. It took a while, but eventually he was able to sit up. Soon, he was able to stand.

"'Please, you should stay on the altar,' Davit pleaded with Grandpa Henry the first time he stood up.

"'I'm well enough to stand,' my grandfather said. 'I'm well enough to get back to my mates.' He staggered and fell back onto the table.

"It wasn't long after that, with some care and

determination, he was walking.

"'You have fallen in and out of consciousness upon the altar of our small chapel, and you need to finish healing before you go,' the priest told my grandfather one day. I don't think Grandpa Henry realized at the time that he had been laid upon an altar to heal.

"'I must get back to my unit,' he kept saying over and over again as he tried to retrain himself to walk.

"The priest agreed to help Grandpa Henry return to his unit, but only if he stayed with them long enough to fully recover.

"Grandpa Henry and Father Keshishian took many walks through a maze of candlelit caverns. They were short walks at first, but they grew in length as the healing continued.

"On their walks, the priest educated Grandpa Henry about many things. Mostly their talks dealt with faith and religion, but not all. He told about his village and how the Ottoman Army drafted men ranging in age from fifteen to sixty. He revealed something far worse than a fight for land which is what people are told war was always about.

"The Turkish government began disarming the men and placed them in labor camps, where they were murdered. Many were arrested in Constantinople. Among them were teachers, doctors, officials, and even clergy. This spread throughout the country. Thousands were taken and did not survive.

"Father Keshishian had been forming a resistance. Most of the men were in hiding. They had refused to become Turkish conscripts; others had deserted the military to escape the labor camps. Turkish forces were continuing to raid their cities. Many did not make it out alive. Some were sold into slavery; others raped and killed by Kurdish bandits as they fled. There are even stories of women and children being locked inside of churches and the churches being set on fire."

Helen paused for a moment, wiped a tear from her eye, re-gathered her thoughts, and continued.

"Grandpa Henry continued his recovery. Like I said, his walks with Father Keshishian grew in length and frequency over the days.

"One day, Grandpa Henry said, 'I was shot several times, and I have healed to where there's barely a scar. How?'

"'You've been lying on Christ's cross. This ancient underground city has been here for a very long time, Henry. The treasures protected here are not only the people within its walls,' Father Keshishian revealed to him.

"You see Hiro," Helen said, staring deep into the man's eyes. "The cross that Christ our savior was crucified upon was part of that altar. Grandpa Henry was healed completely by just lying on it. His faith in God is what allowed that to happen, and the priest knew that."

"Were there no doctors?" Hiro asked.

"Not one," Helen replied. "Only the priest and his refugees were in that cave city."

"That sounds incredible," Hiro said, truly impressed.

"The priest grew to trust Henry through their talks and his show of faith by the speed in which he healed. One day, on their walk, Father Keshishian set his lantern on the ground and rolled a fairly large boulder to one side, revealing a room with shelves and urns within it. Some of the scrolls in that room were saved from the libraries of Alexandria while others came from various other sources. Some possibly were touched by or even written by Jesus Christ himself. Father Keshishian revealed that his order had been protecting the scrolls and their whereabouts for centuries. This scroll, the one I've laid out onto this desk before you, is one of those scrolls. Father Keshishian told Grandpa Henry that this very scroll contained a codex that held the key to a cipher that can foretell the name of the antichrist."

Hiro examined the ancient scroll. The brown-stained

material appeared to be as delicate as ash. The bottom edge of the scroll was blackened and jagged. To Hiro it appeared that possibly it had been burned at some point in time. The writing was organized in narrow columns and equally spaced on the scroll, but he couldn't make heads or tails of the markings. The scroll was written in a language Hiro had never seen before.

"You've got to be kidding me," he scoffed in disbelief. "The antichrist? I'm supposed to believe this scroll will reveal the antichrist?"

"Have an open mind, Detective," Helen growled at Hiro, her irritation with the man's disbelief clearly visible.

"I apologize," Hiro said maintaining his usual calm demeanor. "I do not mean to be disrespectful. Only, it has been my experience that evil is committed by people, not supernatural entities."

"The antichrist is a person!" Helen snapped. She sat down at the desk and pulled her shoulder-length hair into a ponytail as she took a deep breath. As she slowly released her breath, she relaxed her hands, folded her arms, and locked eyes with the detective. "As a homicide detective, I assume that you have seen some truly gruesome crime scenes. I'm also assuming that you have met and spoken with the men and women who have perpetrated these crimes."

"I have."

"Some of the people you've met must have seemed to be driven by something unexplainable. Sometimes a person does something unbelievably evil for no foreseeable reason. And at the same time, someone else will do an unbelievably kind act for no reason. Am I correct?"

"Yes, you are."

"And do you believe in balance?"

"Yes, I do."

"Well, Detective, there is one person on this planet who has as much evil within them as the kindest person in the world has kindness—one person who will endeavor to tip the scales and disrupt the balance in the favor of evil. And when that happens, Satan's reign on earth will begin. When I say the antichrist, Detective, I'm not speaking of a character from a story. I'm speaking of a living breathing human being, and I intend to stop them."

"This is a lot to process. But you are correct. I have witnessed some things that can only be described as pure evil. And I have witnessed pure good as well."

"Yes you have," Helen said. "You have even witnessed a miraculous healing."

"Go on," Hiro said. His full attention now focused on

Helen.

"When you asked me about my blindness, I lied. My blindness was caused by my brother. That is true. He was trying to get me to reveal the location of an artifact."

"I don't understand."

"The artifact that my brother was looking for is the one that was used to heal me. You were correct, Detective, I was blind but now I see."

"This artifact you speak of. It came with this scroll as well?"

"Let me continue with my grandfather's story."

"I apologize for the interruption. Please continue."

"My grandfather said that he spent many days exploring the underground city: its architecture and construction, but mostly he studied the scrolls. He returned to the room with the scrolls often.

"One day he was examining this scroll when he felt the room shake. The cave city was being bombed. Explosions from above caused such violent shaking, and then Grandpa Henry heard gunshots. He grabbed the scroll and made it back to the small chapel with the altar he had been lying on that was made from Christ's cross.

"As the bombing continued, somehow his belt got caught on a piece of metal that was protruding from one of the crossed planks in the altar. My grandfather pried the nail loose from the altar to free himself. He fled the underground city with the nail and the codex.

"That nail, Detective, is one of the nails that pierced Christ's flesh during his crucifixion. It has the power to heal the faithful and deserved. Somehow, the tip of that nail broke and my grandfather put the tip inside a locket. Later, he incorporated that locket into the construction of a crucifix necklace. The tip of the nail that resides in that necklace is what healed me. It is what Pete was after. More will be after it if I don't stop the antichrist."

"You said that your grandfather fled with the nail and the codex," Hiro said, trying to fully understand Helen's story. "What about the other scrolls and artifacts? What about the altar itself?"

"My grandfather returned years later after the war with a search party from the Vatican, only to find the True Cross was missing. But the chamber containing the remaining scrolls remained untouched. Many of the items are on display in museums around the globe. But he did keep several artifacts for himself, like the codex and a clay jar protecting a dozen scrolls that some believed to have been written by Jesus Christ himself." Helen motioned to a weathered clay jar resting on display in the back corner of the den next to an end table.

Tarsus approached the clay jar and peered inside. "It's empty."

"Of course it's empty. What did you expect?"

"What happened to the scrolls?"

"They were stolen in the late 1960s."

"Any idea who stole them?"

"My grandpa Henry always saw the best in people. I think he believed that the scrolls would find their way into the hands of who needed them most somehow. I don't know who stole them, Detective, but I believe my grandfather had his suspicions."

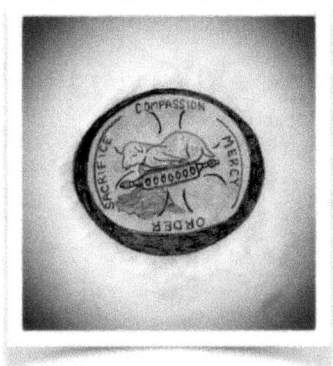

# Chapter 14.

Steven Salvador wore white gloves as he stood in front of a podium holding a rectangular case inside a climate-controlled preservation room. The case, a polished wooden book holder with a museum-quality glass lid, contained a historic scroll. The lid was hinged open, allowing Steven to examine the scroll.

As he deciphered the scroll, he turned to a large manuscript where he was writing down a translation of the scroll. Steven lifted a calligraphy pen and went to work. The man's lettering was a beautifully crafted calligraphy reminiscent of the handy work found within hand-painted medieval bibles.

A satisfied expression came across Steven's face as he pressed ink to parchment. He was near completion on a project that had taken him the better part of a decade. He felt that same rush of adrenaline a long-distance runner might feel as he sprinted the last fifty yards towards the finish line. After finishing his translation, he closed the glass lid, sealing the scroll inside, and turned his attention to his manuscript. The cover of the heavy book was embossed with a seal. The seal was the emblem of the slaughtered lamb resting on a scroll with seven seals of rubies, an exact replica of the one on Steven's golden ring. The book bore the title *The Revelations of Jesus Christ*.

Steven placed the manuscript inside a velvet-lined container and then left the climate controlled room through a special air-tight door that led into his high-rise office. He closed the door behind him and punched an access code into a key pad, locking the door to the chamber. Steven massaged his temples, stretched his back, and then grabbed his overcoat from off of a coat tree and left his office.

# Chapter 15.

Adam and Rose cozied up on a couch in Biddy's living room across from a stone-mantled fireplace that crackled and popped. Biddy placed three shot glasses on the coffee table in front of them and opened a corked bottle of whiskey.

"I usually only have half a night cap," Biddy smirked as she poured a full shot glass of whiskey for the three of them. "However, it's not every day long lost family members walk through your door." She lifted her glass. "Cheers."

They clicked glasses and sipped the whiskey, enjoying the warm glow of the wood-burning fireplace.

"Henry was more of an uncle than a cousin to me, you might say. When he moved to America during the Second World War, he asked my family to come live there permanently. He was afraid we might be bombed by the Nazis. But my parents couldn't bear the thought of leaving their home. Our blood is in the soil of Ireland, my father used to say." Biddy finished her drink. "I believe it is time for me to retire for the evening. I don't believe I have stayed up this late in half a century. I made the beds up in the two upstairs bedrooms across from one another at the end of the hall."

"Thank you for your hospitality, Biddy," Adam said.

"No need to thank me every two minutes, my boy. You both have made me a happy old woman."

"I wish I had gotten to know you sooner," Adam said.

Biddy's lips curled in an appreciative smile. Then she glanced back at Adam. "Hmmm. You sure do look a lot like him."

Rose took a long hard look at Adam. "I guess you and Henry share the same eyes."

"Not Henry, love." Biddy said in a sweet tone to Rose. "My memory isn't what it once was but there's no doubt you are your father's son." Biddy nodded and made her way towards the staircase, leaving Rose and Adam alone.

Rose snuggled up on Adam's chest and stared into the fire. She listened to his heartbeat. "Now whose heartbeat is racing?"

Adam tilted his head down, glancing at her. They

locked eyes in a loving exchange. "Must be the whiskey." Adam cracked a sly smile as Rose playfully punched him in the chest. "Ouch. Nice, left hook."

"And here I was trying to be all loving," Rose snickered back at him. She took the last sip of her whiskey and stood up. "Well, I will leave you to your thoughts, Doctor." She kissed him softly and walked off to bed.

Adam rose to his feet and slid his socked feet across the wooden floor towards a large window that overlooked the rolling hills of the property.

He imagined his great-grandfather playing in those same hills as a child. He wondered how much the property had changed over the years. He questioned why Henry never made mention of this family home? Perhaps the memories here eventually proved too difficult for Henry to bear. Henry always had a reason for everything he did. Perhaps he meant for Adam to discover this home for himself, and by doing so, give it a value unique to his own experience—to fall in love with it because of his own personal experience and not because of Henry's recollection of it. *Another lesson to be learned*, Adam conceded. Adam suddenly became aware of the wonderful sense of peace that had overcome him. It was a peace he could not quite explain, nor did he want to.

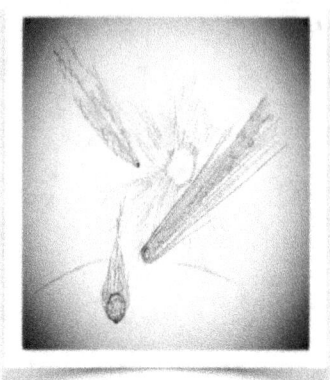

# Chapter 16.

Steven Salvador found himself standing alone on the edge of a pebble-strewn cliff. He was sharply dressed in a custom three-piece, dark grey suit and black bespoke shoes. The dark blue Pacific Ocean was spread out in front of him as far as his eyes could see. The pebbles began to rattle around his feet and inch towards the edge of the cliff. He felt the nauseating effect of losing his equilibrium take hold of his body. The pebbles trembled with greater intensity and rolled off the edge, tumbling down the cliff face like speeding marbles crashing into the waves below.

A streak of hot light burst above Steven, temporarily blinding him. He covered his eyes with the palms of his hands out of shock and fell to his knees. He could feel the heat from another streak of light pass over his back.

Using his forearm as a shield, he glanced up into the sky.

Fireballs rained from the sky like tears of fire. The boulders of coal burned from the inside out and seemed to melt the sky apart, separating the blue lining from the air around it in jagged rows of burnt orange. Steven had nowhere to run. He stepped towards the edge of the cliff and considered jumping.

At the bottom of the cliff, a circular opening was visible between the crashing waves. The opening tunneled underwater and into the earth. He heard screaming coming from below. A crashing wave brought bodies of people to the surface, each clawing their way for earth and air. A man dove under the wave and disappeared into the tunnel.

The fireballs streamed through the sky in slow motion, all sound disappeared, and then darkness covered the coast. Salvador suddenly found himself transported under the water, deeper and deeper until he found himself alone inside a concrete room. That was the moment he awoke from his dream.

His heart tried to pound its way out of his chest while he sat up in his twin-sized bed. His master bedroom was simply furnished with only the essentials: a closet with his wardrobe, a mahogany dresser, and the twin-sized bed that rested on a low-profile metal frame. Steven rolled out of bed and over onto his knees. He rested his hands on the mattress in a prayer position, took several deep breaths to relax his mind, and closed his eyes. After several minutes, he took to his feet, dressed himself, and left his bedroom.

Steven wandered the chilly streets of the downtown area of Chicago. He carried a stainless steel, insulated beverage bottle with a screw-on lid in one hand. He ventured past an alleyway filled with dumpsters. After a moment, he returned to the alleyway and took several steps towards one of the dumpsters near the entrance.

Hidden and pressed against the side of the dumpster was what appeared to be a woman of the street. But upon closer inspection, the pallid face of a teenage girl became visible hidden behind bruises, frozen tears, and cheap make-up. The girl shivered violently.

Steven approached her. The girl kicked at him instinctually as he lowered himself down to her, taking off his heavy overcoat. He placed the overcoat like a blanket across her body. He knelt beside her and unscrewed the beverage bottle, revealing hot soup. He held the soup to her mouth and helped her take a drink. The soup was a jolt to her system and caused her to gasp.

Steven removed his cell phone from his pocket and dialed his driver.

"Please don't call the police," she whimpered.

"Ssssh." Steven helped the girl take another sip of soup.

The teenage girl was admitted to a bed in the emergency room of Mercy Hospital. Steven reviewed the paperwork he had filled out for her, listing her as a Jane Doe with the hospital staff.

"I don't know if she has any family. But bill me for any treatment she might need. I've listed all of my information," Steven told the emergency room attendant as he handed the man the completed paperwork.

"Yes." The attendant picked out Steven's name from the paperwork. "Mister Salvador."

Steven checked the young man's name tag. "Riley. Would you please give her this card before she leaves, and use of a phone?" Steven handed Riley a business card that read *Ministries of the Merciful Lamb*.

"You a minister or something?"

"Just someone looking to help."

"You know she's probably just going to end up back on the streets. It's like a revolving door in here."

Steven glanced at him, then diverted his eyes, considering a response. "The meek shall inherit the earth, Riley," he said simply, then turned and left the hospital.

# Chapter 17.

Joy filled Adam's heart as he dipped his hands into the basin of the kitchen sink in the old farmhouse. His sleeves were rolled up past his elbows as he soaped up the breakfast dishes with a dish rag. Doing chores brought him back to childhood at the home of his great-grandparents. "Chores were an integral part of raising a healthy young man," his great-grandmother Florence would say. And Adam would laugh when he found his Papa Henry right beside him at the sink responding, "Which is why your Nana Florence has me cleaning all the time." He knew only of love in that house, and they did all they could to protect Adam. Biddy reminded him so much of his Nana Florence.

"You are spoiling me, Adam. I'm not going to let you leave." Biddy laughed as she took a cleaned dish from the rack, dried it, and placed it up in the cupboard. "Just like my Alroy. God bless him."

The name struck Adam like a bolt of lightning. He stared down into the soapy basin. His face reflected in the water as the soap separated.

"Alroy?"

"My son. You remind me so much of him."

"I would love to meet him if he's near?"

"You visited my dear Alroy yesterday. Up in the family cemetery."

"Oh, I am sorry. I didn't mean to...."

"Don't worry a hair on your head. It has been well over thirty years since he passed He was a good lad. He flew rescue helicopters." Biddy continued putting away the rest of the dishes. "When he was a small boy he had the cutest, chubby little cheeks you'd ever see. Everyone used to pinch them, but not Henry. He adored Henry. Henry used to tell people, 'Stop pinching that boy's cheeks, you're going to give him cancer.'" Biddy chuckled, mimicking Henry. "He was his godfather. In fact, my husband and I had hoped to name Alroy after Henry, but Henry humbly asked us to name him Alroy."

"Did he ever say why?"

"No. Just said he was always fond of the name." Biddy closed the cupboard.

"This might seem like an odd question, but your son didn't happen to be named Alroy Byrne?"

"No, lad. Alroy Henry Gildea," she said with pride. "Why do you ask?"

"It was a name my Papa gave me before he passed. Your son is the closet reference I have besides some old records from almost a hundred years ago."

"I wish you the luck of the Irish." Biddy winked at him and placed the tea kettle on the stove.

"Biddy, last night you said I looked like my father?"

"You're right. I did."

"You met him?"

"I wouldn't have said you looked like him if I hadn't."

"When?"

"I only took a plane once in my life and that was to your parents' wedding. Henry insisted. Your father even danced with me." Biddy looked out of the kitchen window in front of them. "Lovely view outside."

Adam glanced out of the window and saw Rose. "Yes, it is." To Adam, she was the picture of serene beauty, as she stood taking pictures of the countryside with her digital camera. Little did Adam know that Rose was actually quite paranoid inside and was using her camera to scout the hillsides.

Biddy took notice of Adam as he gazed lovingly out at

Rose.

"There's nothing quite as romantic as a stroll in the Irish countryside." Biddy nudged Adam. "Go."

The lush green grass and tiny wildflowers that speckled the landscape swayed to and fro in the breeze, brushing against Rose and Adams' pant legs as they hiked to the top of a hill. Behind them, the stone farmhouse had seemed to have shrunk to the size of a country dollhouse in the distance. In the lowlands ahead of them, three donkeys grazed near a series of tiny ponds. A thick tree line ran along a stone wall that bordered the property.

During their walk, Adam relayed the information he had discovered about Biddy's son Alroy. They both agreed that they were on the right track, but solid answers continued to evade them. Biddy's son was named Alroy Henry, not Alroy Byrne. So all they could decipher was that perhaps Alroy Byrne was someone from Henry's youth—possibly a friend, a soldier, a child. They did have a lead of a child by the name of Alroy Byrne who had died in a local convent not far from Biddy's farmhouse back in 1896. That would be the next destination on their journey. But Adam couldn't help feeling like the farmhouse had more answers. They just needed to ask the right questions. Adam and Rose sat down on a hillside to contemplate the meaning of the poem *September 1913* and its significance to Henry.

"Why would Henry choose a poem that criticized religion as his eulogy?" Rose asked.

"I know it has to make sense, but it doesn't. Faith was everything to him," Adam replied. "He wouldn't have taken that lightly."

"Did he feel wronged in some way?"

"The statement Yeats is making about people being consumed with wealth and prayer...maybe my Papa felt this referred to false prayer—or committing atrocities in the name of religion?"

"Let's focus on what we know," Rose said as she opened the guidebook with all of her notes and removed a pen.

"Well, the portrait of my great-great-grandmother Catherine. Her blonde hair. Let's assume she is the reference to the yellow-haired woman."

Rose jotted the reference down in the book, then asked, "Did he go to war for his mother? Is his view of her distorted?"

"If so, why?"

"Nathaniel said the poem was political, referencing heroes who died in vain. Maybe Henry felt like his own father had died in vain during the Easter Rising."

"Yeah, yeah." Adam grew excited and stood up. He began to pace back and forth. "Okay, what else?"

The two doctors continued to bounce ideas off of one another out in the open pasture. Hidden amongst the thicket of trees, a pair of wool-gloved hands held binoculars. The lenses were fixed upon Adam and Rose.

# Chapter 18.

"Check!" Eli exclaimed happily as he sat up in his bed. "I've got check! What do you think about that?" he asked with a large grin.

"Anastasia's mate. That is very good positioning, Eli." Hiro said as he quickly lifted the tray from Eli's lap, keeping him from knocking the game board to the ground in his excitement.

"Is everything okay in here?" Nurse Terry asked as she came into the room. She had a glass and a dish towel in her hands.

"Everything is great." Eli replied, "I was just schooling my friend here in chess."

"Oh, you let him win one?" Terry asked Hiro jokingly.

"No, Eli won fair and square," Hiro said.

"Hiro was just telling me about this really romantic

restaurant he was thinking of taking you to. You like Argentinean food, right?" Eli said to Terry with a mischievous smile.

"If Hiro was going to take me to a restaurant, he would tell me about it, not you," Terry fired back, while giving Hiro a wink. "Speaking of restaurants, I need to know what you want for lunch today."

"I want to try one of those chicken fried steak meals today."

"You know, I can cook," Terry said to Eli while hoping Hiro would take notice. "I can make you food from scratch. You don't have to keep eating those frozen dinners."

"I like them," Eli said in his defense.

Just then, Hiro's cell phone vibrated in his pants pocket. He took out the phone and checked the screen. The call was from Helen Morales.

"Excuse me," Hiro said to both Eli and Terry as he left the room to take the call. Once he was in the hallway, Hiro answered the phone. "Hello?"

"Hiro, this is Helen Morales. Are you available to come to my Grandpa Henry's estate? There's something I need to tell you."

"Yes Mrs. Morales," Hiro replied. "I can be on my way soon. Is it something that you can tell me on the phone?"

"Probably, but I would rather do this in person."

"I understand," Hiro said as he ended the call.

"Is everything ok?" Terry asked as she came from Eli's room.

Just as Hiro was about to excuse himself, the doorbell rang.

"That must be the pastor. His visits have become almost as frequent around here as yours," Terry said as she stepped past Hiro in the hallway to answer the door. "Not as popular, though," she said. She turned back and gave Hiro a wink.

Hiro went back into Eli's room and told his friend goodbye. He left his chair at the edge of Eli's bed, assuming that the pastor would be sitting there soon.

"Healing hands have arrived," Pastor Faith announced as he came into Eli's room.

"Good morning, Pastor," Eli said from his bed.

"Are you going to stay and pray with us this time?" Pastor Faith asked Hiro. "You are more than welcome."

"No," Hiro said. "I have some business to attend to. Eli, it was good seeing you, and thank you for the good game."

Hiro left Eli's and got into his car. Before he drove off, he took another long look at the pastor's car. The long white Cadillac convertible was in immaculate condition and Hiro couldn't help but admire the car. Hiro looked back to Eli's house. Terry stood in the doorway and waved goodbye. Hiro shut off the car and got out. He ran up the steps and stood a few feet in front of Terry.

"Would you like to have dinner with me this Friday?" Hiro asked. The lump in his throat tightened.

"Argentinean?" Terry asked with a giggle.

"Unless you like something better," Hiro said.

"I would love to go to dinner with you," Terry answered with a smile. "You can pick me up at six thirty."

"Six thirty it is," Hiro said, relieved and overjoyed.

Hiro walked back to his car and drove to the Calhoun mansion humming a tune and tapping the steering wheel with his fingertips along the way.

Pastor Faith sat next to Eli's bed and laid his hands on Eli's head. Both men closed their eyes and began to pray. Eli prayed silently while Pastor Faith repeated the words that he had used in prayer over the sick and put in the book he had written a year earlier. "Lord, heal your servant. Lord, heal your servant. Lord, give me the power to heal your servant."

As before, Eli felt warmth in Pastor Faith's hands. As the warmth in Eli's head passed from atop his head where the pastor's hands lay to the back of his head, Eli drifted off to sleep once again.

Eli dreamt he was a young boy standing atop a grassy hill. In his right hand he held a hammer. His left hand held a pencil. There were papers at his feet. Eli looked closely at the papers and saw that they were drawings of buildings—architectural blueprints to be precise. The buildings young Eli had drawn looked to be hospitals.

Eli felt the warmth on the back of his head grow and turn into a burning sensation. He felt a distinct burning directly over the spot where his skull and spine met. The searing pain in the back of his head brought young Eli to his knees. He took the pencil and clenched it tightly in his fist and jabbed the sharpened tip deep into his skull where the pain originated. He screamed out in pain as he drove the pencil into his head deeper and deeper until he felt the heat from his malady enter the wood of the pencil. He withdrew the pencil, slowly pulling it from the wound with great care not to create too wide of a tunnel.

There was a popping sound when the pencil exited the wound. Eli felt the pressure within his skull drop and he heard a hissing sound as a black tar oozed out of the hole he just created in the back of his head. The thick black goo stained his golden blonde hair as it traveled along the back of his head and dripped to the ground creating a glob of foul-smelling disease atop his drawings. Once all of the black poison had escaped his head and lay piled on the papers, Eli took up the hammer that was in his other hand and began smashing the pile of black goo. Every strike of the hammer sent more of the black goo into a vaporized frenzy as young Eli destroyed the sickness and turned it into white smoke that drifted away in the breeze.

Eli opened his eyes and saw Nurse Terry standing over him with one hand pinching his nose shut and the other holding his chin in place. She had been breathing into him, performing CPR. Eli's eyes widened as he took in a deep breath on his own.

"I didn't realize we'd gotten this close," Eli said to a visibly shaken Terry, trying to relieve the tension of the moment.

"Praise the Lord, you are alive," Pastor Faith chimed in from across the room.

"Sorry about the spit. I'm a little rusty," Terry joked back, letting Eli know that all was well. She gave Eli a wink.

"I believe you were just saved," Pastor Faith said as he approached Eli's bed. "The heat in your head became intense then you stopped breathing. Your nurse came in and breathed the breath of life back into you so you can continue God's good works. How do you feel?"

"You know what, I feel like getting out of this bed," Eli answered.

"I don't think that's such a good idea," Terry interjected. "You need to rest."

"Nonsense, I feel great. Like really great," Eli said. "In fact, I want to move the furniture."

"You are not moving any furniture," Terry interrupted.

"Your view out the window won't be as good if you were to move the bed," Pastor Faith added.

"I don't want to see the yard from a bed," Eli said. "If I want to look out the window, I want to walk over to it and look out. It will be good motivation to continue to get better."

"I'm going to call your doctor," Terry said as she stepped out of Eli's room and headed for the house phone.

"You don't mind helping me move some things around, do you?" Eli asked Pastor Faith.

"I'm not much for manual labor," Pastor Faith said. "But I suppose I could help with some small things."

Pastor Faith pulled the wooden kitchen chair that he had been sitting in away from Eli's bed and placed it back in its original spot against the wall. When he turned back, he saw Eli standing next to his bed.

"Shouldn't you wait for your nurse?" Pastor Faith

asked nervously.

"No need," Eli explained. "I feel like I'm a teenager again. In fact, I don't feel like I was ever sick."

Eli took a couple of steps and looked at himself in the mirror atop his dresser. He saw how frail and emaciated he had gotten. He raised his hand and took a long look down his thin stick-like arm.

"Wow, I look bad," Eli said.

"You are bad, get back into bed!" Terry scolded as she walked over to Eli to put him into his bed.

"No!" Eli demanded. "I'm telling you I want to move things around. I've been staring at that stupid fan for too long! I know you're doing your job, and I actually like you, but I'm the one who feels fine, so I'm saying grab a chair and start moving!"

Terry had never seen such fire in Eli before. He had seemed to be feeling better lately and his mood and energy levels had increased. His vital signs had also indicated that his health had been improving. He had been so close to death for so long, she was finding it hard to believe that he had the energy to stand, let alone walk around.

"Alright," Terry said, "where do you want your things moved to?"

Eli smiled and pointed toward the back wall of the

room. "I want the bed over there. I want to have to get up and walk to the window to look out."

"Okay," Terry said, "but first, I need to move your fluids and cart out of the way. You're still attached you know." Terry grabbed the chair that was for guests and brought it to where Eli was standing.

Eli sat in the chair and watched as Terry and Pastor Faith removed the drawers and maneuvered the wide mirrored dresser and a tall six-drawer chest to his specifications. Then their attention was focused on the bed. Terry wanted to remove the mattresses from the bed and move the frame into place first, while Pastor Faith thought the job would be completed more easily if they just pushed the large sleigh-framed bed into place all at once.

"You don't understand. This is an adjustable bed. There's machinery underneath it that weighs a ton," Terry told Pastor Faith, making her point as to why the bed needed to be disassembled first.

"Why don't we call Hiro to come over and help?" Eli suggested.

"Yes, get your strong friend to do the heavy lifting," Pastor Faith added.

"He got called away for work," Terry said. "Besides it will only take the two of us if we do this right."

"I guess it would be awkward to call your boyfriend and say, 'Hey, come move a bed with me,'" Eli joked.

Terry grabbed the top mattress at the head of the bed and lifted. As the mattress twisted and began to slide off the bed, Terry heard a slight clink as something metallic hit the wooden floor. She twisted her neck and looked at the floor between the mattress and the bed frame and saw the silver crucifix pendant and chain lying on the floor. Terry leaned the mattress against the frame of the bed and bent down to retrieve the necklace. She held it up to show it to Pastor Faith.

"Pastor," Terry asked. "Is this your crucifix?"

Pastor Faith looked at the necklace in Nurse Terry's hand and denied having ever seen it before.

"Adam," Eli said out loud.

"What?" Terry asked.

"It's Adam's," Eli said, realizing that Adam had tucked the necklace between his mattresses on his last visit. Eli also realized that Terry was holding the object responsible for the deaths of Adam's uncle Pete and cousin Jordy.

"Give it here!" Eli blurted out, not able to hide his nervousness concerning the object. "It belongs to Adam. He must have left it here. Call him and tell him you found it and that he needs to come and take it back."

Pastor Faith observed the emotional outburst and slowly realized that the crucifix in the nurse's hand was probably the pendant he was looking for. His heart raced and sweat began to bead on his forehead as he chose his words carefully.

"I can take it to the hospital and give it to his nurse to hold for him until he returns from his trip," Pastor Faith told Eli in as calm of a voice as he could muster.

Terry, ignoring the pastor's request, gave the necklace to Eli who put it in the front pant pocket of the pajama pants he was wearing.

"You call your friend," Terry said. "I'm your nurse, not your secretary." She then trained her attention to Pastor Faith. "Now you, help me move this bed."

"I'm afraid that I have another appointment that slipped my mind earlier," Pastor Faith said as he backed his way out of the room cautiously. "I'm sorry to have to leave the job undone, but there is another soul who needs my attention." Faith then turned and walked quickly out of the house and drove back to his motel room.

Faith needed to plan his next move carefully. The call earlier in the week from the cell phone of the dead hired hand Hiram Gray had shaken Pastor Faith slightly—not enough for him to give up his plan to wait for Dr. Calhoun to return from his trip, but enough for him to be on his guard. *The woman's voice on the other end could have been a detective investigating the case after all*, he thought. But now that he'd possibly located the cross pendant on his own, he could easily take it from the frail and sickly Eli Taylor and quickly return back to Chicago and none would be the wiser.

*Now that everyone knows I'm here though*, Faith thought to himself, *I will have to be careful. My plan must be flawless.*

Faith sat at the small desk in his motel room, composed himself and dialed. A woman answered the call.

"Good afternoon and thank you for calling Salvador International. How may I direct your call?"

"This is Pastor Faith. I need to speak to Mr. Salvador please."

"One moment please."

The phone clicked and music began to play as Pastor Faith waited. He did not have to wait very long.

"Well?" Steven Salvador's voice was calm and quiet.

"I found it." Pastor Faith said, barely able to contain his joy. His snickering almost became full on laughter.

"Then bring it to me," Steven said, his voice becoming a little louder and less patient sounding.

"I don't have it yet," Pastor Faith said.

"Why are you calling then?" Steven asked.

"I will get it tomorrow. I just need some assistance." Pastor Faith continued. "I need some hired hands to...."

"No!" Steven shouted. "Your associates and their clumsy methods do not work, Faith. You will get the necklace on your own and you will bring it to me. For the Lord God giveth them light."

"And they shall reign forever and ever," Pastor Faith replied. "I will get the necklace sir, and I will place it around your neck by tomorrow night."

"Good," Steven said and hung up the phone.

Pastor Faith had no idea how he was to obtain the necklace on his own. He wanted to hire a couple of thugs like the Grey brothers and stage a home invasion robbery. He sat at the small desk and stared blankly ahead, trying to devise a plan. Moments passed, and then a small hint of a smile crossed his lips as he slowly turned his head and looked at the restaurant flyer on the dresser. He had his plan.

He drove to the diner and ordered a whole rhubarb pie to go. He paid for the pie in cash then drove to a convenience store where he bought a package of paper plates, plastic cutlery, and plastic wrap which he also paid for in cash. He delivered the goods to his motel room then took the plastic bag the convenience store clerk had given him for his purchases and drove west out of town along a small blacktop rural roadway. He parked his car on the shoulder of the road and walked into the woods. Twenty yards off the roadway, the ground beneath his feet became saturated with water.

Pastor Faith didn't have to search the marshy area very long to find what he was looking for. He saw several small trees with vines trailing up their sides. The leaves on the vines were oval with pointed tips. Small violet flowers shaped like five-sided stars decorated the vines and brought attention to the point of Faith's search: bright red oval berries hung from their stems.

He wondered how many of the poisonous berries he would need to subdue the pesky little nurse and Eli. Pastor Faith knew that this particular plant wasn't as poisonous as it's more famous cousin, belladonna, but this variety, more commonly known as bittersweet nightshade, was rumored to be poisonous enough to kill livestock.

"If it can kill a cow," Pastor Faith said as he began picking the berries with his gloved hands, "it should be enough to incapacitate two people easily enough."

He picked more than enough berries for the job. In fact, Pastor Faith lost count at eighty. He took the bag of red poison to the motel room, where he crushed the berries, still in the bag, in the bathroom sink with the heel of one of his white patent-leather shoes. Then he quartered the rhubarb pie and placed each slice on a paper plate. One slice, he placed on a paper plate that he marked with a small tear on the edge. Then he wrapped it with plastic wrap right away. He removed the top crust from two of the other slices and laced them with generous amounts of the poison berry juice. He replaced the crust and wrapped the slices to make them match the safe slice in appearance.

Pastor Faith smiled at his cleverness. "Tomorrow," he mumbled to himself, grinning from ear to ear, "I will have the relic." He then helped himself to the untainted remaining slice of rhubarb pie.

The same time Pastor Faith bought the whole rhubarb pie, Hiro Tarsus had parked his car behind Helen's in the driveway of the Calhoun mansion. He stepped out and smelled the air. The crisp air that surrounded the huge estate seemed cleaner and energized Hiro with a renewed sense of purpose as he went through the front door of the massive home. Hiro noticed the change in air quality as he entered the foyer. There was a stale mustiness that suggested inactivity. The building didn't feel like a home to Hiro. Since the death of its former inhabitant, the house felt more like a museum.

Sean Morales met Hiro at the bottom of the staircase. Sean was carrying a tea set on a silver tray and led Hiro to the den where Helen was waiting. Hiro noticed there was none of the usual anger and defensiveness in Sean's demeanor. In fact, it seemed to Hiro that Sean was almost pleased to see him.

"Thank you for coming Hiro," Helen said as Sean placed the tea set on the desk. "Sean, would you be a dear and take the car down to the bank? Tell them that I want to open a new expense account and place thirty thousand dollars from my personal savings into it. I have a new business venture I want to look into."

"Yes mother," Sean replied with a smile as he left the room and closed the door behind him.

"Please sit and have some tea, Hiro," Helen said. "We have some business to discuss."

Hiro sat in the early twentieth-century office chair that Helen had gestured to. The spindle supports underneath the shaped top rail and carved arm rests creaked under the weight of the man as he sat back in the seat.

"The chair will hold," Helen said noticing the detective's nervous facial expression as he sat. "It's an old chair, but it was built to last. People used to know a thing or two about quality back when this office furniture was built. People took pride in their work and made things that were designed to outlive their owners so that they could be passed down. Not like now. Now things are designed to fail after a predetermined period of time and built by people who only desire an easy paycheck. I miss the old days."

The seat was much more comfortable than Hiro had expected. He sat for a moment waiting for Helen to continue her speech about the way things were, but he noticed that she was simply staring out into space. Helen appeared to be frozen in thought. *Perhaps she's caught in a daydream or a memory*, Hiro thought to himself. After a moment, Hiro cleared his throat and poured two cups of tea. It wasn't until after he had placed a cup of steaming tea in front of Helen and sat back into the groaning chair that Helen snapped back into the present.

"Remember the phone call we placed the other day?" Helen asked suddenly. "I did some poking around and I found that Salvador International is a huge company whose main operations deal with drilling tunnels and such."

"So, the man that kidnapped Dr. Powell was calling a mining company?" Hiro replied, not hiding the confusion in his voice.

"It's not just a mining company, but that's not my

point," Helen said. "Salvador International was founded by a man named Thomas Salvador."

"And who is Thomas Salvador?" Hiro asked.

"That's what I wanted to know," Helen replied, agreeing to Hiro's line of questioning. "So I looked him up on the internet. And you can imagine my surprise when I saw the photo of Thomas Salvador and realized that I had seen him before." Helen turned the computer monitor around on the desk so that Hiro could see the photo of the man she was referring to.

"Where?"

"Right here, in this very room. It had to have been almost fifty years ago, but I remember him. I heard yelling from down the hall, so I came to see what had upset my Grandpa Henry. I peeked through the open door and I saw my grandfather and this man, Thomas Salvador, in a heated argument."

"What were they arguing about?"

"I don't know, but I had never seen my grandfather so angry before."

"So, this hired thug that kidnapped Dr. Powell was in contact with a man that knew your grandfather fifty years ago?"

"It appears so."

"But why?"

"For the crucifix necklace, of course. That's why I have to protect it. I have to make sure that it never falls into the hands of evil men. Which brings me to the other reason why I called you, Mr. Tarsus. I am moving here to my grandfather's estate," Helen said. "Sean will remain living in my home and he will take on the role of administrative assistant in the venture that I am offering you."

"I'm afraid I don't understand."

"I want you to work with me, Mr. Tarsus," Helen continued. "I'm in search of the antichrist. I believe he or she is living in our time and that the evil that will be brought to our world cannot be stopped without our combined efforts. Sean is currently opening an expense account for you to use. I'm placing thirty thousand dollars into it as an incentive. Additional funds will be added to help you transition from police detective to private detective. I will pay you a salary of ten thousand dollars a month plus expenses until we find the antichrist or I run out of money, whichever one comes first."

"I appreciate your offer, but—" Hiro began to decline, but Helen cut him off.

"Hiro, I know that you send money to your family in Japan every month."

"How do you know about that?"

"Sean isn't just a good cook and housekeeper." Helen took a deep breath and continued. "You are a righteous man Hiro Tarsus. You refused to let go of this case even when your superiors demanded you do so. You know deep inside that you are destined for bigger things. Aren't you tired of investigating death after it happens? Wouldn't you rather be preventing evil before it overcomes its victims? I know that together we can locate and stop the antichrist. We can save more lives than you can imagine. Let me finance you. You and your family will be very well taken care of for the rest of your lives."

"This is a lot to process," Hiro said. Then with a softened tone he added, "I am not so certain that I can leave the police force."

"What if you keep your job and work with me on your time off?"

"Homicide detectives don't really have time off."

"Please, help me, Hiro. This is a golden parachute for you and quite possibly one that saves the world."

"Let me sleep on it," Hiro said as he stood and let himself out of the room.

Hiro drove home with his mind spinning from the emotional rollercoaster that had been the day. He had finally asked Terry out on a date, and she had said yes. He had been offered a job which could possibly be more rewarding than investigating and capturing murderers and he may be financially well off. He would not sleep well this night. Hiro had much to consider.

# Chapter 19.

The octogenarian Thomas Salvador rested in his bed with oxygen tubes and other machines attached to his body. His bedroom suite was warm and luxurious even though Thomas was confined ninety percent of the time to his bed. Only several strands of hair remained upon his head, and his fragile skin was colored a pale cream with a tinge of blue.

His son, Steven Salvador, stepped slowly into his father's room. The elder Salvador's eyes sparkled at the sight of his son but then turned crestfallen.

"You're tired, son," Thomas pointed out.

"I haven't slept much," Steven admitted.

"The dreams?"

Steven nodded and then sat down on the edge of the bed. He relayed his most recent dream to his father. After he had finished, his father placed his hand delicately upon Steven's and said, "They are signs from God, son. Informing us of the paths we were meant to take in life."

To the younger Salvador, the dream meant death, the end of humanity. Steven could not help but feel that in some way a secret tunneling project he was under negotiations with, with the United States Navy, might be playing a part in the dream—his subconscious getting the best of him. Or perhaps Pastor Faith was right and humanity needed a swift push towards salvation. Would the healing relic really be able to provide such a push in our modern age? If nothing else, the relic would provide the much needed healing for his father.

"I've completed the translation of the scrolls," Steven whispered. Thomas' eyes smiled at the news. "And we know where the relic is, Father. Pastor Faith lost his way but is making amends. We will recover it for you."

"Not for me, son. For you. Always for you. You are the light. I am an old man who has done some terrible things in my time in the name of—" Thomas coughed violently expelling a pinkish phlegm.

"If part of the nail that crucified Christ is inside that necklace and can heal you, we will obtain it."

"I have had the fortune of being blessed by its grace." Thomas' weak hands trembled as he shook off his bed sheet and touched his chest. "Henry Calhoun was my friend, my mentor. Did I ever tell you how we met, really met?"

Steven shook his head.

"We meet in 1959 on the ice-packed plains of Greenland. Our government contracted us to work on a secret military base. The official purpose released to the public was that the facility, known as Camp Century, was being constructed to conduct scientific research on the icecap—part of man's attempt to master nature and learn how to survive in the artic wilderness. It's amazing what the public will believe. But the real reason was to have a quick-strike nuclear facility that was close in proximity to the Soviet Union. The Soviets had bases in Cuba, the U.S. had Project Iceworm, among others."

"Why would Calhoun be involved with a military contract?" Steven asked.

"He was the foremost expert on ancient civilizations. The government hired him to consult from, let just say, an aesthetic purpose. The base was to be constructed deep under the polar icecap. Henry provided the inspiration for the design, even suggesting the addition of a chapel and a movie theater. I was recruited by the army straight out of college and served as one of the engineers. I worked primarily on the tunneling system constructed to deploy missiles from under Greenland's ice sheet. There was another man, a geologist named Max Hinder, if that was even his true name—a traitor.

"I caught him secretly taking documents of the nuclear reactor with the intention of reporting this information back to the KGB, we suspect. The base was powered by this reactor.

"The majority of the buildings for the base were prefabricated offsite and then buried in the massive trenches and tunnels we dug into the snow and ice. A portable nuclear reactor powered the entire facility. This was cutting-edge technology for the time.

"During mess one evening, we had a cave in. It was a tunnel near the mess hall. The tunnel separated the mess hall from the water supply building and connected them to the maintenance building that housed the reactor. Henry was the first one to his feet and the last one out of the facility. He led the evacuation. Grown men, trained men, panicked at the terror of being buried alive. But not Henry Calhoun. He rose to his feet and, with his booming voice, calmed each and every man, leading them in an evacuation. I have never witnessed anyone that calm and in control in the face of danger. He was the last man out and the first man to go back in to inspect the damage. I felt compelled to join in, and so I did. We walked back down the ramp leading into the tunnel we nicknamed Main Street. We were not expecting what we found."

Secret U.S Army Base, Greenland, 1960s

Henry Calhoun, still sturdy and strong as ever in his sixties, rubbed his father's field knife for luck. The dull blade was sheathed and attached to his utility belt under a dark, heavy winter coat. He began the slow and cautious march down the ramp and into the tunnel and heart of the camp.

A fresh-faced, twenty-one-year old Thomas Salvador flipped his fur-lined hood over his head and followed after Henry into the ice-packed coffin.

"The reactor is still functioning," Thomas said, pointing out the string of glowing lights.

"Listen for any rumbling. Even the slightest sound might alert us to another collapse," Henry cautioned. He noticed Thomas was trembling and his pupils were large with fear. "Just another casual stroll down Main Street, eh Tommy boy?" Henry smiled, giving Thomas a hearty pat on the back.

Thomas nodded, swallowing down the lump building in his throat.

"I won't let you die, kid. Now let's handle business,

shall we?"

They followed the runway of lights that ran the length of the tunnel attached to thick cables draped down the snow-packed sides of Main Street. This gave the walkway a continuous and eerie yellow and grey glow that disappeared into a pit of black. The vapor of their breath condensed into fog-like clouds as the men wandered towards the darkness. The entrances to the various buildings branched off either side of Main Street. The men reached the first building used for fuel storage. Henry peered inside the entrance to the building. All appeared normal. They continued down the path. The steel-constructed roofs of the buildings groaned and creaked under the snow pack.

"You check the buildings to the right. I'll take the left," Henry said as he opened the entrance to the stand-by power building.

Thomas continued towards the entrance to the R & D offices. Snow crunched loudly under his boots, contributing to a growing sense of paranoia. He had difficulty telling the difference between the echoes from his footsteps and the creaks of the shifting snow above. He closed in on the door to the offices and suddenly heard the sounds of something moving inside the room. *There is no reason for anyone to be inside the base. All the men were ordered to evacuate*, Thomas thought to himself. The air was cold, but sweat curled the hairs on the back of his neck. He had a bad gut feeling. "Now's not the time to be timid," he whispered to himself. Thomas drew his government-issued sidearm from its holster and slowly pushed opened the door to find Max Hinder removing documents and blueprints from an unlocked safe.

"Hinder?" Thomas said, shocked to see him.

"Thomas, thank goodness. Help me," the man spoke at a rapid pace. "I felt the collapse and raced in here fearing we may lose all of our research."

"Hinder. Those files are above our clearance."

"Thomas. Lower the gun. That's not necessary."

Thomas noticed a heavy kit bag several feet from Max. The kit bag was open and contained a number of explosive devices. Thomas shouted back towards the tunnel known as Main Street. "Henry! Henry hurry!"

Max rushed to his feet and charged at Thomas. Thomas aimed his revolver back at Max, who froze in his tracks.

"Get on the ground," ordered Thomas as he cocked the hammer on the revolver.

Henry raced to the entrance to find Thomas with his revolver fixed on Max.

"He's a traitor," Thomas said angrily.

"Max, get up slowly," Henry said. "Keep your hands out in front of you."

Max crunched down, grimacing. The sound of his tooth cracking resonated in the room.

"No!" Henry rushed to the man as foam streamed from the corner of his mouth. Henry turned the man to his side and then Henry removed a necklace from around his neck, bearing a silver crucifix. Henry firmly placed the pendant on the man's cheek and began to pray to himself.

What Thomas witnessed next would change him forever. The foam that was eating away the inside of the man's mouth turned to a clear liquid. The convulsions ceased. His eyes, which had rolled back inside their sockets, suddenly began to adjust to their normal position. The grim reaper was bested before Thomas' eyes. Max coughed and took in a deep breath. He looked up at Henry, unsure of what he had experienced.

"You've taken my honor," the man said, defeated.

Thomas leaned over to help the man to his feet. Henry and Thomas would escort him to the base commander to deal with as a traitor. Max Hinder knew his mission and capture would be viewed worse than death.

"Aagh." Thomas gasped as he gripped Hinder's upper arm. A lightning bolt of pain streaked through his breast.

He looked down in horror to see a knife protruding out of his chest. Max had slipped Henry's field knife from its sheath and struck Thomas. Thomas fell to his side, gripping the handle of the knife. Henry threw Max forcefully to the ground and raced to grab Thomas' revolver.

Max scrambled to his feet. "How many miracles do you have, Henry?" he said, slowly backing his way towards the entrance.

Henry glanced over at Thomas' wound. It was a fatal strike unless Henry acted fast. Max continued to back out towards the entrance.

Henry knelt down beside Thomas, whose face had fallen pale.

Max raced out of the room. He charged his way up Main Street and out the ramp, where several men waited for Henry and Thomas.

"Help! Hurry. Hurry. They are trapped. Another collapse near the officer's latrine!" Max shouted at the soldiers above with panic in his voice.

The men raced heroically into the tunnel as Max disappeared in the direction of several field vehicles.

Anger shone in Thomas' aging eyes as he finished telling his son the tale. "No one knows what happened to

Max Hinder, but I doubt anyone could have survived for long out in the artic wilderness. A few years later the camp was shut down. But Henry's choice gave me a future, and the future contracts I received due to Project Iceworm laid the foundation for the company we have today."

"You should rest, Dad. Soon, everything will be well."

"When a man nears the end, life becomes about legacy, the world. Steven, souls depend on the revelations. Men, throughout their lives, have the opportunity to experience enlightenment of a spiritual nature. Without Henry Calhoun, I wouldn't have been alive to bear witness to that. Years passed and the friendship between Henry and I flourished. He brought me into his world—knowledge I don't think I was prepared for or fully understood until your birth. I asked him to join our order and be part of the vision for salvation—Henry was less than receptive."

"I don't understand. He was a man of faith and a man who strove for knowledge."

"You are the light, son. This is your purpose. You were born to lead them into the light. You are unique, chosen. The Cold War taught me one very important lesson. Mankind will always search for ways to destroy itself in the name of peace and security. They need salvation. They need a presence, a face to follow. And miracles to witness. And then the shepherd shall have his sheep."

"And what if I am not this person? We will have the necklace for you, Father. This talk is not necessary. I'll be able to help you then."

"Our country is at war, Steven, religiously divided more than ever before. Terrorism will strike and eyes will turn to you for order, for unity. You are destined to be the light after the purge. Complete the city and a new world will be reborn from the protection of that capital. Fear is mankind's greatest motivation. Fear is the maker of sheep amongst men and you shall be their shepherd."

# Chapter 20.

Hiro had started his day the way he normally did. He woke from a restless night of tossing and turning. He put on his grey jogging pants and a tight-fitting white t-shirt that showed off his lean muscular v-shaped frame and went for his regular five-and-a-half-mile morning jog. He couldn't help but think about his conversation with Helen Morales the night before. After his jog, he showered and got dressed. He dressed himself in a classic black suit with a white shirt and black tie and ate his usual traditional breakfast.

Hiro went to the police station and hung his jacket on the back of his chair before he seated himself at his desk. The energy in the room felt different to him. It was as if he was seeing the homicide department through a different pair of eyes. Hiro realized the difference in the room was him. He was no longer looking around the room as a man who needed his job. He was looking around the room with a different perspective. He now had the perspective of a man who had the option to leave. He considered Helen's offer while checking his box for work. As he suspected, there had been no homicides reported. Hiro went to his files and reviewed them. He organized his desk and started his time card for the day. He was beginning a nine-day shift rotation.

Instead of having lunch at his favorite sandwich shop near the station, Hiro drove to the Calhoun mansion to see Helen. He was going to politely turn her offer down. He was a police officer in a quiet town, and even though he usually yearned for more excitement, he had a satisfying life. He had just recently met and fallen for a beautiful Filipino nurse who he was certain he had already fallen in love with. He made enough money to send his family the assistance they needed. Helen Morales' quest for the antichrist would have to be conducted without him.


Pastor Faith woke up in his motel room feeling energized about the day ahead. He showered, dressed, packed his clothes, and loaded everything into the trunk of his car. He placed the sack of pie slices in the trunk next to his luggage and checked out of the motel.

After having breakfast at the diner where he had bought the rhubarb pie the night before, he drove to a nearby gas station and filled the tank of his long white 1962 Cadillac in preparation for his drive to Chicago later in the day. He then drove to Hope Hospital. He went to Father Kellen's office to construct an airtight alibi for his actions that would come.

"I'm afraid I will have to cut my volunteer work here at the hospital a little short," Pastor Faith told Father Kellen. "There is an emergency that I must attend to. One of my ushers' mothers has passed away, and I must attend to him and his family in their time of need." The lie, Pastor Faith hoped, would sound convincing to Father Kellen.

"That is very unfortunate, but I understand," replied Father Kellen as he stood to usher the faith healer out of his office. "If you have any open appointments, would you please be so kind as to run them by Michael, my assistant? That way he can re-schedule them."

"Of course," Pastor Faith answered. "I would like to say goodbye to everyone before I go, and I want to make sure that you and your assistant are both aware that my appointment with Eli Taylor tomorrow afternoon will have to be filled in by someone else. I last saw Mr. Taylor yesterday and he was feeling much better. I dare say he seemed to almost be completely healed." He added a wide bright smile to solidify the lie.

Pastor Faith left Father Kellen's office feeling accomplished with the groundwork he had laid in securing his alibi. He relayed the message about his reason to leave town and his most recent visits to Mr. Taylor to Father Kellen's assistant Michael before he made his way through the hospital, saying goodbye to the patients and staff. After satisfactorily letting every staff member that he spoke to in the hospital know that he was leaving for Chicago, he went to the cafeteria to have lunch before he executed his plan to retrieve the necklace.

"What's your poison, Pastor?" Lydia asked as she saw Pastor Faith coming toward the service line with a tray in hand.

Pastor Faith froze in surprise. Beads of sweat instantly appeared on his forehead as he felt the heat from anxiety flush his face. His stomach turned as acid shot into his throat. He stared at Lydia for a moment in shock. *How could she know about my plan?* he thought to himself. *She couldn't.* He must remain calm and not give away his intentions. He noticed that he had been standing staring for what seemed an eternity. He finally spoke, "I beg your pardon?"

"What will you be having today?" Lydia asked as she tilted her head slightly to the side, noticing the Pastor's unusual behavior. "Are you alright today Pastor? You look a little green."

"I'm fine," Faith said as he blotted the sweat beads from his forehead with the white silk handkerchief he pulled from the breast pocket of his suit jacket. "I'm just a little emotional, that's all. I have to go back to Chicago today."

"Oh, that's a shame," Lydia said while feigning disappointment at the news. "The big wigs here seemed to like having you around." There was something about the man that didn't sit right with Lydia, but she couldn't put her finger on it. She just didn't care for the man, and the news of his departure brought her a slight sense of joy. "So what will your last meal with us be?" she asked.

"I do believe I will just have a bowl of soup."

"One bowl of cabbage and polenta soup coming up."

"I was referring to the potato soup."

"Oh, I'm sorry Pastor, the potato soup is too fatty with the real butter and cream that I use for the base. It may aggravate your ulcers. Besides, were fresh out. The cabbage and polenta is all I have for soup right now." Lydia smiled a large toothy smile at the man in the all-white suit.

Pastor Faith returned her smile. "Cabbage and polenta sounds scrumptious," he said.

He ate his soup, left Hope Hospital for the last time, and drove to Eli Taylor's house. He parked, got out of the car, and retrieved the bag with the wrapped pie slices from the trunk. He knocked on the door and was surprised when Eli answered the door and not his hospice nurse Terry Santos.

*This is God's grace smiling on me*, Pastor Faith thought to himself. *It will be easier to get the necklace from Eli without having to deal with that annoying nurse. Everyone will assume that Mr. Taylor would have died from his cancer and with his nurse not being here, no one will be the wiser.*

"Good afternoon and God bless you Mr. Taylor!" Faith announced as Eli opened the screen door to let him in.

"Good afternoon, Pastor," Eli said as he led the visitor to his kitchen. "It's good to see you. I wasn't expecting any visitors today. Please excuse my appearance." Eli gestured with his hands, referring to the blue and white stripped pajamas he was wearing.

"I see you're up and walking around."

"Yes, I can't tell you how good it feels to be out of that bed." Eli poured hot water from a kettle into a cup, then placed a single bag of tea in the cup to steep. "Can I get you some tea?"

"Some tea would be wonderful, thank you," Pastor Faith said. As Eli got a cup from a cabinet to make the tea, Pastor Faith listened for any sounds throughout the house that would indicate another presence in the home. There were none. "I hope I'm not intruding. I'm just so filled with the joy of our Lord concerning your miraculous recovery that I had to bring you and your nurse some pie."

"Oh, that's very nice of you." Eli said as he passed the cup to Pastor Faith.

"Where is your nurse, by the way?" Faith asked as he set the three slices of pie onto the kitchen table, making sure the one he marked with the small tear in the paper plate was for him. "Does she have the day off or have you dismissed her now that you have no need of her?"

"She was grocery shopping," Terry Santos said from the doorway of the kitchen. Pastor Faith turned in surprise as Terry carried two canvas tote bags of groceries into the kitchen and set them on the counter.

"Nurse Terry, the pastor has brought us pie to celebrate my feeling better," Eli said as he sat at the table across from the pastor. "Come and have a slice."

"No thank you," Terry said. "I have to put the groceries away and then do the laundry while you see if you're feeling up to sitting on the back porch today."

"Oh, please," Pastor Faith pleaded. "Please come and have a slice of pie with us. Just a few bites while we thank the Lord God our savoir for the good fortune he has bestowed upon us." Faith smiled his famous white smile as he pushed a slice of poison-laced pie toward the empty chair at the table closest to where the woman was standing.

Terry got a glass and filled it with milk before she joined the two men at the table. "Okay," she said. "One quick snack then back to work."

Eli took a large bite of the pie and wrinkled his nose as he chewed. "What kind of pie is this?" he asked.

"Rhubarb," Pastor Faith answered.

"Oh," Eli said. "I thought it might be cherry. It doesn't taste like cherry."

"It smells a little off," Terry added.

Pastor Faith took a large bite of pie and chewed. "It tastes fine to me," he said, trying to convince Terry and Eli to both eat the pie.

Terry and Eli looked at each other. They exchanged glances of silent communication. They both decided to eat the pie as quickly as they could just to get the unpleasantness over with.

Several minutes later, Terry was putting the

groceries away in the kitchen while Pastor Faith put the paper plates and other remains of their snack back in the bag he had brought them in.

"We have a trash can," Eli said as he watched the pastor place the bag near the front door.

"I don't want to burden you," Faith replied. "I'll take my garbage with me when I go. In the meantime, your nurse mentioned something about you sitting outside for a while. Mind if I join you? Only for a few moments, then I must be on my way."

Eli and Pastor Faith went out to the back porch and sat in white painted metal lawn chairs while gazing into Eli's poorly manicured backyard. They could hear the sound of Terry inside the house doing laundry and general cleaning of the home. They heard her cough and then she came out onto the porch.

"Are either of you feeling funny?" she asked.

"What do you mean?" Pastor Faith asked in response.

"My throat's kind of scratchy and I'm getting a headache," she said.

"Maybe you need to lie down for a bit," Eli suggested.

"Maybe," Terry said as she placed her hand on the door jamb, steadying herself. "I'm schtarting to feel dissy," she slurred.

"Terry, are you okay?" Eli asked. He was beginning to

feel a little dizzy himself.

Pastor Faith looked at Eli and noticed his pupils were enlarged and that he was slumping in his chair, too weak to sit up on his own.

"I'll help you," Pastor Faith said as he took Terry by the arm and led her to the laundry room. Terry was visibly weakened and was not walking well on her own. She looked at Pastor Faith with a perplexed look on her face. She couldn't understand why he would take her into the laundry room. Just then, Terry vomited a pool of blood into the basket of dirty laundry, collapsed, and died. Pastor Faith jumped out of the way quick enough to not get any of the dead nurse's fluids on his bright white clothing. Now he could turn his attention on Eli and the crucifix necklace.

"She's resting peacefully," Pastor Faith said as he walked back to Eli on the porch. He could see the poison slowly taking its toll on him. *The nurse died from the poison rather quickly. Hopefully I'll be on my way to Chicago with the necklace in my hands soon*, he thought to himself.

He sat back onto the metal chair and looked Eli in the eye. He saw that Eli had begun to shiver and lightly convulse from the poison. "Where's the necklace?" he asked as he padded Eli's neck and chest, searching for the crucifix pendant. Eli tried to stand and flee but he collapsed onto the floor of the porch.


When Hiro arrived at the Calhoun Estate, he was met by Sean, who led him into the den where Helen was situated at the desk reading old papers she had found in a drawer.

"Welcome, Hiro!" Helen jubilantly called out. "I'm so glad you've decided to join us. I'm going through some of my grandfather's old documents."

"I'm afraid that I will have to decline your offer, Mrs. Morales," Hiro interrupted.

"But why?" Helen asked. She became increasingly angry with every word. "You know what we're up against. I'm trying to save the world here!"

"I am sorry to disappoint you, but my work as a homicide detective is important. I thank you for your more than generous offer, but I simply cannot accept it at this time."

"I see. Well, Hiro, the offer still stands. If you ever change your mind and decide to join me, you are welcome to." Helen took a deep breath and stared blankly at the papers she had been looking at. Then she reached for her cup of tea to take a sip and noticed the cup was empty. "Out of tea," she said to herself.

"I will tell Sean that you would like more tea on my way out," Hiro said as he headed toward the door.

"Thank you," Helen replied. Her voice sounded as defeated as Hiro had ever heard.

Pastor Faith went into Eli's bedroom and searched the entire room for the crucifix necklace. It was nowhere to be found. He began to panic as his search of every room in the house, including the laundry room with the dead nurse Terry on the floor, yielded no results.

Hiro went to the kitchen to ask Sean if he could make more tea for his mother. He found Sean sitting on a stool, eating an apple while watching a television program about survivalists trekking through the jungle surviving only on their wits and what nature had to offer.

"Your mother would like more tea," Hiro said.

"My mother always wants more tea," Sean replied as he immediately stood and turned the stove on to heat the water in the kettle. "So I take it you're not joining her on her quest for the antichrist," he continued as he turned back to Hiro.

"I am not," Hiro replied. Just then Hiro's attention was drawn to the television. A commercial for a book called *Living With Healing Hands* was being advertised.

On the cover of the book was a face Hiro was familiar with. The bright red hair atop of the bright white smile of the pastor that had been visiting Eli Taylor caught the detective's attention. Then the following words written in bold black ink underneath: *Living With Healing Hands By: Pastor Faith*, let something within him connect. He ran back to the den and asked Helen if she remembered the initials they had found in the call history of the dead thug's phone days earlier.

"Yes, S.S. was one set," Helen replied. "We called it and the number belonged to Salvador International. Another one was P.F. All I know is that it belongs to a cellular phone. It's a Chicago number, but the phone itself could be anywhere."

"P.F." Hiro said. "P.F. stands for Pastor Faith!" He yelled as he ran out of the den toward his car.

Eli lay on the floor of his porch. He felt weak and fatigued. He was cold, and he couldn't keep his body from shaking. He realized that he and Terry had both been poisoned just as Pastor Faith came back out onto the porch and sat down beside Eli, who was grasping to life.

Hiro drove as quickly as he could to Eli's home. He wanted to question Eli and Terry both about everything

Pastor Faith had said and done during his visits. The man who kidnapped Dr. Rose Powell had been calling a large corporation in Chicago and a pastor that just happened to be doing home visits with a friend of Dr. Calhoun.

"How do a pastor, an international corporation, and a possible Russian spy fit in to Dr. Powell's kidnapping and the murders of the Grey brothers, Peter Calhoun-Mitchell and Jordy Morales?" Hiro asked himself as he drove toward Eli's home. The more pieces of the puzzle he tried to put together, the more confusing the case became.

Pastor Faith turned towards Eli and took a kneeling position as he ran his hands through the pants pockets in Eli's pajamas, returning empty. Then he rolled Eli over onto his back and screamed at Eli, "Where's the cross?!" As Eli rolled onto his back, the crucifix necklace that had been lying in his pajama top breast pocket fell out onto the porch.

Pastor Faith grabbed the cross and ran through the house. He grabbed the bag of trash by the front door on his way out. He threw the bag into the front passenger seat of his car and drove off, not noticing that Hiro Tarsus had just parked his black Crown Victoria across the street.

As he parked his car, Hiro saw the visibly flustered

Pastor Faith run out of Eli's house carrying a paper bag. Hiro called out for the man to stop as he got out of his car, but the tall red-haired pastor had leapt into his car and sped away in a fury.

Hiro ran to the house and let himself in. "Hello?" Hiro called out as he stepped inside. He waited a moment. After not hearing a reply, he called out again. "Eli? Terry? Is anyone here?"

Hiro un-holstered his sidearm and carefully walked through the home, checking rooms as he went. After checking Eli's bedroom, he saw that the back door of the home was open. He went through the open door and saw Eli lying on the porch.

Hiro knelt down and checked Eli's pulse. It was weak, but he could feel it. "Terry?" Hiro shouted at the top of his voice. "Terry are you here?" He was now concerned. Maybe it was her day off, he thought. Maybe the pastor was praying with Eli and panicked when he collapsed.

Eli reached up and, with a very weak grip, he grabbed at Hiro's sleeve. "He took the necklace," Eli said in a whisper. "The cross necklace; he stole it."

"What necklace?" Hiro asked. Then suddenly he remembered the conversation he had with Helen Morales where she revealed the secret of the crucifix necklace to him. Adam had used the necklace to heal his aunt, and

246

then he must have given the necklace to his friend Eli to cure his disease. He now understood why Dr. Adam Calhoun had asked him to keep an eye on Eli.

He picked Eli up from off the floor of the back porch and carried him to his room and laid him on his bed. Then he took his cell phone from his pocket and dialed 911. He would get Eli the help he needed, then retrieve the necklace from the pastor. He reported the shallow breathing and weakened pulse of his friend to the emergency services operator while he walked back to the back door to close it. He turned back to return to Eli's room when something from the corner of his eye caught his attention. The laundry room door was partially open and Hiro saw the body of Terry Santos lying on the floor in a pool of blood and clothes.

"Oh God!" Hiro exclaimed as he dove to Terry's aid, dropping his phone onto the floor. He rolled her body over onto her back and checked her pulse. There was none. She was dead. Tears poured down his face from his bloodshot eyes as he lifted her body and held her blood-soaked head against his chest. Hiro had seen many dead bodies in his career as a homicide detective, but he was not prepared for the emotional heart-wrenching that was holding the body of the woman he loved.

"Sir?" The emergency services operator's voice

brought Hiro back to the present moment. "Sir, I have dispatched an ambulance. Help is on the way."

"I also want to report a murder," Hiro announced to the operator. "Send the police."

In a rage, Hiro ran to his car and sped away. He turned the siren on then turned it back off. He didn't want to alert the pastor of his pursuit. Hiro considered the pastor's retreat and assumed that the murderer would want to flee to Chicago. That would put him on the highway heading west.

Hiro took the onramp to the highway and sped along the straightaway, pushing the Ford as fast as it would go. It wasn't long before he saw what looked to be the white Cadillac he was pursuing.

Pastor Faith held onto the crucifix necklace tightly in his right hand as he drove his convertible toward Chicago. He looked at his speedometer and saw that he was going eighty miles an hour. He backed off the gas a bit and allowed the car to slow to seventy miles an hour to match the speed limit. He didn't want to get a ticket for speeding. He failed to notice the black 2013 Ford Crown Victoria rapidly gaining ground from behind him.

Hiro wiped the tears from his face with his sleeve as he approached the Cadillac convertible. Once he positioned himself directly behind the large white car, he thumbed the two red rocker switches to activate the lights and sirens. He saw Pastor Faith's head spin at the sound of the police sirens behind him, his bright red hair streaming in the wind.

The Cadillac pulled away as Pastor Faith floored the gas pedal, causing the 325 horsepower eight-cylinder engine to roar, catapulting the car from seventy to one hundred twenty-five miles an hour.

Hiro saw the Cadillac begin to pull away and answered with mashing the gas pedal on his own car. The Ford engine roared into action and propelled the detective to a smooth one hundred forty miles an hour. Hiro changed lanes and pulled next to the pastor's car. When the two men were side by side, Hiro un-holstered his weapon and aimed the gun at Pastor Faith. He wanted to pull the trigger, but something within him prevented the detective from doing it.

Pastor Faith never saw the weapon that was trained on to the side of his head. His focus was on the road before him and the off ramp that was soon to be on his right. He cut the wheel to the right in an attempt to quickly take the exit while leaving the pursuing car on the highway, only Pastor Faith misjudged the speed of his car and the effect that cutting the steering wheel sharply to the right would have on it.

The Cadillac swerved to the right, the tires squealed as they left black rubber trails on the asphalt. The car passed the beginning of the off ramp while it was still in the second lane. In the blink of an eye, the front end of the long white convertible dipped into the grassy wedge that formed between the highway and the retreating off ramp. The front driver's side tire sank into a ditch and the car rolled along the grassy wedge several times before coming to a rest on its side. Pastor Faith was thrown from the rolling car and landed on the shoulder of the off ramp, breaking almost every bone in his body. The crucifix necklace slipped from his fingers as he slid along the gravel.

Hiro slammed on the breaks and skidded to a stop on the highway. He threw the car into reverse and backed to the place where the Cadillac lay. He got out of his car and ran to the body of Pastor Faith. The pastor was gasping for breath, his right hand sprawled out grasping for the necklace that lay mere inches beyond his reach. His eyes were wide and focused only on the necklace.

Hiro grabbed the necklace and put it in his pocket, and as he did, Pastor Faith heaved his last breath. Hiro reached into the dead man's pants pocket and took his cell phone. He accessed the call history and saw a recent call to a Steven. The number had a Chicago area code. Then he scrolled up through the history far enough to see several other calls from a Mr. Grey.

Hiro had all the confirmation he needed. The Grey brothers had been working either with or for Pastor Faith in an effort to steal the necklace that lay in his pocket that could heal injuries and possibly even cure diseases. Hiro made two calls from his cell. The first call was to 911 to report the wreck and death of Pastor Faith. The second was to Helen Morales to tell her that he would be joining her on her quest as soon as he made his reports and resigned from the police force later that day.

Hiro stayed on the scene of Pastor Faith's accident until the first responders arrived. He gave his statement then went to the precinct. He filed an initial report for the murder of Terry Santos, then he marched into Captain Conrad's office, turned in his badge and weapon and resigned. He collected the last of his personal items from his desk and went to Hope Hospital to spend the night where, he had been told by Captain Conrad, Eli Taylor had been taken and was in critical condition.

# Chapter 21.

"Don't be a stranger," Biddy said to Adam as he packed up the rental car with the last suitcase. The morning sunlight glowed across the dewy Irish landscape.

"I promise I won't be," Adam replied. "I have a feeling our meeting wasn't a chance encounter."

"That's because Henry raised you. And I have a feeling you are right." Biddy hugged him tightly. "By the way, I happened to notice that pretty lass of yours is missing a band around the finger to her heart."

Adam blushed.

"The good ones leave us too soon, my boy. Hold on to the ones with a kind heart like your Rose. A kind heart will always shine even in the darkest times." She hugged him again and kissed his cheek. "Go before I get all puffy."

From the hillside, a pair of grey wool-gloved hands gripped a pair of binoculars. The binoculars watched

Biddy and Rose as Biddy kissed Rose on the cheek.

Adam opened the car door for Rose, who climbed in, before he walked around to the driver's side. Adam smiled one last smile at his cousin and drove off down the country road, destined for the convent of the Merciful Sisters of Charity.

Less than an hour later, Adam sat down in a hard, weathered wooden chair in the dull grey office of Sister Maria Gabriel at the dilapidated aged convent of the Merciful Sisters of Charity. The round-faced nun appeared much younger than her seventy-plus years, but perhaps it was the stark lighting and encompassing habit she wore.

She had an energized tempo to her voice and spoke in a business casual way, as if she was acquainted with the young doctor. "Dr. Calhoun, I am surprised you came all this way in person, but I am assuming your visit is in regards to the check your late grandfather's trust sent us?"

"Check? No, I was not aware of any check?" Adam replied, shocked.

The nun presented Adam with an opened envelope containing an uncashed check from the Trust of Henry Calhoun. "Upon his death, your grandfather's trust sent us a check for quite a large sum of money. Unfortunately, due to the stipulations he set forth associated to the generous donation, we are not in a position to cash it at this time."

"What sort of stipulations?" Adam asked, trying to make sense of the mysterious check. "I've never once heard of him placing any kind of restrictions over his charitable giving?"

"A request to exhume bodies from the premises."

"I'm sorry. I'm…this is very odd. Why would he want to exhume bodies from these grounds? He was a God-fearing Catholic that in no way would want to disturb the remains of anyone." Adam was at a loss for words. This was a curve ball he didn't expect and would require his attention when he returned to Ohio. "As the head of his foundation I am more than happy to review the stipulations and see what can be done, but I am not here over a check."

Sister Maria Gabriel sat back in her chair and watched the doctor intently.

"Before Papa Henry passed, he gave me a name: Alroy Byrne. I was given a record that led me here."

The sister's body language suddenly became tense and closed off. "I'm sorry, but I cannot be of any more help. This is a matter for the archdiocese." The tone in her voice heightened and cracked. "The extent of my authority extends only so far."

"Sister—please. I don't mean to make you uncomfortable. I am just trying to put the pieces of my family together."

Rose wandered the hallways of the old convent. Historical photographs of facility lined the walls, some in color, others in black and white. Rose neared a section of wall that contained the early history of the place. She froze in her tracks. There it was: a framed old black and white photograph, the same photograph Nathaniel had printed out for them.

Her memory was instantly jogged and images along with bits of conversation raced through her mind. She recalled Henry's conversation regarding the series of Magdalene Laundries that he wanted to convert to schools, clinics, and orphanages. The clue that had plagued her at the National Library became clear. This particular site was the only one that was unwilling to take his generous offer, but he wouldn't say why. He had simply pointed to a wall of photographs. Rose hurried back to the office where Adam and Sister Maria Gabriel were meeting to find them seated in silence.

"This was a Magdalene Laundry, Adam," Rose said, standing in the doorway to the sister's office. "Henry had a photograph of this place on a wall in his library."

"He seems to have had a deeper connection to this place than just the name Alroy Byrne," Adam said to Rose.

The aging sister sat tight-lipped, staring off towards the corner of the room. She had a deep compassion in her heart for Adam's situation but struggled to reveal the dark past of the hallowed halls of the convent. She had carried the burden of guilt and shame from what had occurred on these grounds upon her shoulders even though she had not even been alive when they took place. She finally wavered and proceeded to divulge the past to Adam.

"Mother Maureen. She was Reverend Mother when I first arrived here—a beautiful, compassionate soul. She was responsible for converting this property from a workhouse to an orphanage and school for the lost in the 1950s. Then the convent fell on hard times and the orphanage was closed, but she believed God would provide and refused to retire from service. She had a deep desire to help the babies, and I was one of the children she raised. She also knew your grandfather, Henry Calhoun."

"Why would she refuse Henry's financial assistance?" Rose asked.

"There are only so many decisions that fall within our power. Back then Henry had wanted to purchase the property outright. That was simply not possible," the sister recounted. "She had a deep fondness for Henry. He seemed to have the cure for senescence. Mother Maureen on the other hand suffered a stroke at seventy-nine years old. Our order is small, with only handful of sisters still onsite."

"My great-grandfather needed me to find answers, and all questions point here. Please, find it in your heart to help us."

She closed her eyes for several seconds. Then a tenderness cloaked the sister's face as she slowly opened her eyes and spoke. "Please wait here." She rose from her seat and left the office.

After several minutes, the sister returned holding a dark brown, heavily weathered leather ledger. The pages were yellow with age and had damage along the edges. She carefully placed the book down in front of Adam and began to thumb through the entries until she came upon the one he was after.

"Mother Maureen truly was a wonderful woman. She tried to help right the past as best she could and do God's work to serve the helpless, the innocent. Like so many young women, she too was sent here against her will as a teenager." Sister Maria Gabriel shook her head slightly. "She left this ledger in my care, and I have felt the weight of its secrets for over fifty years," she disclosed with a sigh. "Here it is."

Adam stood up and leaned forward beside the sister to read the entry scribbled in faded black ink. His eyes scanned the first name column. As he passed the names James, Shannon, Henry, he came to the entry. "Alroy. Alroy Byrne." Adam took a deep breath and exhaled. "Deceased November 22, 1896. Cause rheumatic fever." Adam tried to decipher the ledger in his mind. He turned to Rose. "Alroy died of rheumatic fever. Is that all I was meant to find? Did Papa Henry want to exhume the remains of Alroy? If so, why?"

The sister touched Adam gently on the forearm. "Alroy didn't pass away here." She said softly, a sense of remorse in her tone. "None of these children died here."


Aberdeen, Scotland. 1916


In spring 1916, for the first time in what felt like years, Henry felt the weight of world lift off his shoulders as the ship he was aboard neared the coast of Scotland. The lush green hills behind the tan beach of Aberdeen may not have been his homeland but ran a wonderful second as he walked off the ship and onto solid ground. Henry fell to his knees, smelled the crisp clean fragrance of the grass, and thanked God he was alive. The smell of sulfur, sage, and rotten, bloated flesh was cleansed from his senses, and the dew from the grass moistened his lips. With one hand, he held the nail, and with the other, he held his mother's locket and breathed a long, glorious breath. After taking some time to simply meditate on his ordeal, he stood up and turned his attention to two pressing items: one, contacting his parents in Dublin, and two, finding a way back to his regiment.

There was a tiny telegraph office located near the shipyard. Henry compiled a telegraph and had the telegraph operator, an older gentleman, send the message off to the post office in Dublin, where his mother worked as a telegraph operator. Henry walked outside, found a comfortable bench that overlooked the North Sea, and sat down to wait for a reply. A few hours passed as he anxiously waited. He had hoped for a quicker reply, but perhaps his mother was not at work today. Then suddenly, Henry felt a tap on his shoulder.

"For you, mate," the older gentleman said, handing Henry the reply telegraph.

"Thank you," Henry said as he zealously opened the message. Henry's eyes darted back and forth as he read the message from his mother.

Words cannot express how overjoyed I am, my son, to learn that you are alive. We received a telegraph from the army last August informing us that you had died a decorated hero in battle. Your father was very proud of you and stricken with grief upon hearing the news.

His mood suddenly turned from joy to sorrow as he read on.

It pains me to tell you that your father was killed this past April 26th during a terrible week-long riot. I have taken lodging with my sister. Please come home soon. I miss you dearly.

A little over a week later, Henry's footsteps crunched the ground outside the family farmhouse, cared for by his mother's younger sister, his aunt Anna. Henry hurried inside the stone structure to find his aunt in the foyer. He acknowledged her with a quick kiss on the cheek and turned his attention to the stairs leading to the second floor.

Anna touched his forearm and implored him not to enter his mother's bedroom for his own health. "Dear Henry, do not go in there, lad. She has consumption."

"Aunt Anna...she is my mother," Henry replied. His

eyes were swollen from despair. The painful loss of his father was still fresh in his mind and now his mother was on her way to meet him in Heaven. Henry dropped his sack and rushed up the staircase.

Loud, raw coughing was heard from behind the upstairs bedroom door. Henry gently opened the door and saw his mother, lying in a white nightgown with a blood-stained cloth in her hand. Her hair flowed over her pillow and across the upper portion of the bed like a golden sea surrounding her ashen face. *If angels could die, this is what they would look like*, he thought to himself.

"Henry, my beloved boy. My Henr—" She heaved another violent cough. Tears of joy filled her eyes, and with that, a tiny hue of pink returned to her cheeks.

"Rest mother. I'm here with you now, forever. I am going to take care of you."

She shook her head. "Your life is yours to live now my son. I am so proud of you. And so was your father—more than you can ever imagine."

"I am going to make you well," he promised. As he stood to rise, she grabbed him by the hand and pulled him towards her with all of her strength.

"Listen to me, Henry. I am not long for this world. I am sorry for that, but you are strong and will persevere. You have many great adventures ahead of you."

"I am able to help you."

"Please. There is something I must share with you: my failing as a mother—my one regret. But the one act that I regret is also the one act that I have cherished more than this world."

Henry had tears again in his eyes as he gave her a questioning look.

"It was becoming your mother."

"You're speaking nonsense. We are going to get you well," he promised, clasping her delicate hand in his.

"Henry." She took a deep breath. "Your father and I took you from your true mother, twenty years ago."

"This is...this is your illness speaking."

She shook her head. "The Merciful Sisters of Charity."

"That's a..a...."

"Yes, son. You and your mother were taken there, I imagine, when you were just a babe."

"This isn't true." Anger and sadness stirred within Henry's belly. He diverted his eyes away from Catherine.

"Look at me. Please. Anger is the devil's needlework, my dear Henry. Please forgive...." She wheezed heavily, causing her chest to tighten. The tears that fell from her eyes had left dried streaks of sorrow upon her waxen skin. The grim reaper was tightening her thread of life, preparing it to be cut.

Henry clenched his jaw and released Catherine's hand. He rose to his feet without a word, rubbed his face with his hands, turned, and walked away. Catherine felt in her heart that she had made peace at last and whispered the Lord's Prayer.

Henry charged down the staircase towards the front door. His feet hit the first floor landing with a thud and he quickly lifted his sack up to his chest. Mucus streamed from his nose, and tears clouded his sight. He unlatched the flap to his sack and opened the bag. He reached deep inside and balled his hand into a fist, then removed his hand from the bag. Henry tossed the sack back onto the floor and rushed up the stairs towards Catherine's bedroom. He leapt the steps two at a time and ran swiftly into the bedroom, but he was too late.

"No!" Henry rushed to her side. He opened his balled fist and placed the Holy Nail onto her chest before draping his arms across her body and rested his head upon her bosom. Henry feverishly prayed for the Lord to show him mercy and bring Catherine back to him. He prayed through the night and into the early morning, but the angel who raised him was now in Heaven. God's light streamed through the window with the waking sun and bathed Henry and his mother. Henry slowly composed himself and gazed upon the woman he had called mother since his earliest memories. She still felt warm to the touch. Her cheeks shone like pearls and her hair blazed with beauty.

"Mother, you never required my forgiveness. It is I who am in need of yours." He exhaled a long steady stream of air and picked the nail up from off her bosom. His body tingled and fell numb and calm. "I will see you and father again," he continued as he placed the nail in his pocket. Then Henry slowly leaned down to Catherine's delicate face and placed a kiss upon her forehead. "May you rest in peace," he said softly.

As if ushered off by the last vowel of Henry's goodbye, the ray of sunlight that blanketed them softened into a dusky hue flecked with the tiny white stars of dust and all was silent.

***

Henry was met with resistance at the workhouse run by the Order of the Merciful Sisters of Charity. The Reverend Mother, Mother Mary Frances, hacked with sickness through her wrinkled and worn sandpapered veneer as she threatened to have the local constable arrest Henry if he didn't leave immediately. Henry refused to leave without answers and stood his ground, forcing the gruff woman to hobble off to obtain assistance to remove the man.

Once the old woman disappeared from view, a nun who carried herself with the stature of a ballerina stepped out from the shadows of a nearby office room. She had heard Henry's thundering claim as he gave the names of his adoptive parents, Matthew and Catherine Calhoun. The sister knew these names and had spoken them to a friend two years before. The sister moved quickly to Henry.

"Please, follow me. Hurry," she said.

Henry didn't have time to be apprehensive, so he complied and followed her through the building and into an alcove out of sight.

"My name is Sister Maureen. I don't have much time, nor do you." She gazed at him with her crystal blue eyes. "I remember your eyes," she said wistfully.

"Do we know each other?" he said, trying to recall the freckled and pretty mousey face of the middle-aged woman.

"I helped care for you when you were just a babe. Your mother was my friend."

"Where is she? I have to get her out of this place."

Maureen's head fell in sorrow. "Follow me."

The sister led Henry into an unkempt courtyard with a stone and brick walled water well that had dried up long ago. "Your mother is here," Maureen cried. "Her remains." Maureen pointed at the well.

"When? Why does she not have a proper gravesite?"

"On the 2nd of September, two years ago. I am terribly sorry." Maureen took a deep breath to calm herself. "I was placed in charge of record keeping and uncovered the names of your adoptive parents. I had given the names to your mother. She was determined to flee and find you, but there was a fire in the laundry and she...didn't make it out. Her remains where laid to rest there. I am so sorry Alroy."

"Alroy?"

"Yes, that's your name: Alroy Byrne."

Henry touched the bricks that encircled the dried-up water well. "Why would someone have her sent here?"

"Humans are flawed. We sin when we think we are saving." Maureen paused. "I remember the first day I laid eyes on you both. You had the most darling ruddy little cheeks."

Henry tilted his head, listening to Maureen. Then he removed his father's field knife from his satchel, knelt before the well and etched a small cross and a series of words into the brick. He chiseled the stone with such fervor and emotion that by the time he had finished, the tip of the blade was a rounded dull stump.

Henry dropped the knife on the ground and wept. His forehead fell and rested on the gritty stone façade of the well. He placed his palms upon the brick, kissed it softly, and said a prayer for both of his mothers. As Henry finished praying, he pulled his hands away from the well.

"She is coming. You have to go," Sister Maureen pleaded. "There will come a day when we can make things right. I promise. God is merciful." Maureen's eyes sparkled at Henry.

Her gentle words and clear eyes gave him a sense of peace. She gave Henry one last smile as he nodded and she hurried off.

Henry glanced one final time at the inscription he had carved and then left, leaving the words to speak for themselves.

*MAEVE, SEPTEMBER 1913, RIP MY ANGEL. LOVE ALROY*

Adam stood in front of the weathered and moss-covered well, reading the inscription. Sister Maria Gabriel had been kind enough to show them the way to the courtyard garden and grant them free access to roam the property while she went to the onsite adoration chapel for prayer. He traced the carved words with his fingertips and imagined his papa Henry chiseling them into the stone nearly one hundred years earlier. The sister's voice went over and over in his head. *None of these children died here. They were only reported to have died. The dates in this ledger were the dates the children were taken from their mothers and adopted out.* Then the sister revealed a second set of entries that corresponded with the death records for the children, only these entries listed the names of married couples. The entry for A.B. or Alroy Byrne, listed the names of Matthew and Catherine Calhoun.

Heartache burst from Adam's eyes as he picked moss out of letters spelling Alroy. "Maeve was his real mother." Adam's face went flush and he dropped to his knees as if he had been kicked in the stomach. "I know what he wanted me to do."

Rose knelt down beside him and took his hand in hers. They held each other's hands as the gravity of the situation sank in. Adam found himself in such as state of shock and revelation that his mind shut off temporarily and suppressed the flurry of questions that would normally flood his mind during a discovery of any magnitude. But he felt strangely centered. He wasn't living in the past or thinking of the future; only this one moment existed and it was silent.

"Everything in life has an antithesis," a croaky voice said, startling Adam and Rose.

The couple turned to find Pavel Volkov looming a car length behind them. His hand was in his coat pocket.

"Agent Rukovsky," Pavel addressed Rose. His eyes were bleak with emotion. "Kyra Rukovsky."

Chills splintered down Rose's spine at the sound of her real name.

The tiger had cornered his prey. Pavel revealed a small handgun from his pocket and aimed it at Rose.

"She has nothing to do with the necklace if that's what you are after. Just let her leave," Adam pleaded.

"You are mistaken, Doctor. Kyra has everything to do with the necklace. She is part of my life's work."

"You have the wrong person," Adam insisted.

"We are of the same flesh, Kyra and I. Mother Russia." Pavel clicked his jagged, scarred jaw to and fro as he glared with vengeance at Rose.

"No one has to get hurt," Adam pleaded. "My grandfather wouldn't have wanted anyone to die over this relic."

"Of course not. He wanted us to live and face judgment on earth. I know this all too well." Pavel turned his scarred jaw towards Adam. "I had the misfortune of Henry Calhoun saving my life. I'm not a polite man, so please hand it...." Pavel's eyes widened, his pupils burst, turning his eyes into a pool of black as his face convulsed before he fell suddenly to the ground.

Behind the man stood David Mosin; a needle was in his hand. He had injected Volkov in the spine with a deadly toxin, causing immediate paralysis and heart failure. When the caretaker of a nearby bed and breakfast located Pavel Volkov's body lying in bed and called emergency services, the coroner would conclude he died of natural causes, but David had to move quickly. He glanced at Adam and Rose for moment as he capped the needle, securing it. Then David placed the man's arm around his neck and swooped Volkov up like a toddler that had fallen asleep on a playground. As quickly as David had appeared, he disappeared from view. His service was done.

Adam glanced over at Rose, frightened and confused. Rose stood speechless, ashamed and scared, but not from the near death experience. She was scared of what Adam's reaction would be and how that would impact their love.

"Are you, trying to...to kill me?" Adam spit out.

Rose bit her lip tightly, diverted her eyes, and shook her head.

"Well that's a plus," Adam joked nervously. Rose

didn't respond. "Is all of...are you and me...are we a lie?" he mumbled.

"No. I was a mistake."

"Rose."

"You don't have to say anything, Adam. I will find a way back to Dublin."

"Don't. I don't frickin' care. I must be nuts, but considering all that I—that we—have been through, I guess this is my new normal."

"Adam. You can be in danger if you stay with me."

"I'm in danger if I'm not with you."

Adam took Rose by the hands as she lowered her head. He knelt in front of her and glanced up at her face. "Please. Don't let this be a moment we will both regret for the rest of our lives."

"It's beyond complicated, Adam."

"Everything is complicated. I'm sticking with you. So if you don't like it then you're just going to have to kill me yourself."

Rose laughed slightly. "Don't joke like that."

"There's only one thing I have to get cleared up."

"What's that," Rose said, warming to Adam.

"What do I call you? Kyra or Rose?"

"Rose. Only Rose. Kyra Rukovsky was never me. Just a name should I ever return to Russia. Once the mission was over."

"Is it over?"

"For me, it was over back in Ohio. I love you, Adam, and I would give my life for you. That is real."

Adam kissed Rose and held her like there would be no tomorrow for them.

"What do you say we get out of here? We have some work to do."

Rose nodded to him, nuzzling his nose with hers.

# Chapter 22.

That evening Adam and Rose returned to the farmhouse to check on his cousin Biddy and ensure she wasn't in any danger. The elderly woman seemed to simply shrug off any thought that she would be in danger and didn't quite understand what all the fuss was about. She expressed that she was happy they were safe and then ventured off to bed.

After having a late supper, Adam's cell phone rang. The phone call was from Tarsus.

"Hello Detective," Adam said as he answered the phone call. "Is everything alright?

"No, Dr. Calhoun, everything is not alright," Hiro replied.

"What's the matter? Did something happen to Eli? Is he okay?"

"I am with him now, here at the hospital. He is recovering from being poisoned."

"Poisoned, how?"

"Someone tried to steal the necklace you hid with him. I wish you would have been more honest with me about the necklace, Dr. Calhoun. It may have saved a young woman's life."

"What do you mean?"

"Eli's nurse, Terry Santos, was also poisoned," Hiro said, choking back tears as he spoke. "She did not survive. Had I known about the necklace and the real reason you wanted me to keep an eye on Eli, I would have done things differently, and Terry would not have had to die."

"I'm sorry, Detective," Adam replied somberly. Then he asked, "Detective, I hate to ask, but the necklace?"

"I retrieved it from the thief and placed it around Eli's neck as soon as we had a moment alone. You do know that your aunt Helen wants to send the necklace to the Vatican and have it housed there for safe keeping."

"I know. The cross is my responsibility. My great-grandfather gave it to me, not Aunt Helen. I don't think that burying the cross in a relic room in the Vatican is the right thing to do just yet. It can heal Eli. Please keep it with him, and please keep its location a secret. Don't even tell Aunt Helen that you know where it is. I will decide what to do with the cross once I've returned. Detective Tarsus, thank you for keeping Eli safe."

"I am no longer a detective, Dr. Calhoun. You may call me Hiro, and you are welcome. I will continue to watch over Eli and the necklace until you return."

"Thank you," Adam said just before Hiro ended the call. Adam would not sleep well that night, but he knew what had to be done before anyone else was hurt or killed.

The next morning, Adam woke early and began ticking off the individuals he needed to make appointments with. The first name on his list was Father Vigano with the Vatican. Adam removed the business card Father Vigano had provided him back in Ohio and dialed.

Adam spoke into the phone. "Father Vigano, this is Adam Calhoun. I would like to meet with you regarding my grandfather's necklace." Adam listened as the father replied. "I am in Ireland at the moment, but I would be happy to come meet with you in Rome."

Father Vigano respectfully asked if the necklace was the full nature of the upcoming meeting request. Adam took a moment and then relayed the discoveries he had made regarding his great-great grandmother Maeve Byrne and that he would be requesting the assistance of the Vatican on the matter. Father Vigano made note of it, scheduled a meeting to take place in two days' time, then thanked the doctor for his phone call and hung up.

Before the morning was over, Adam had checked on Eli and made preparations to travel to Rome, purchasing a single ticket much to the dismay of Rose. She had been adamant that she should accompany him, but Adam insisted she stay in Ireland to keep an eye on his cousin Biddy.

***

In Ohio, Hiro Tarsus followed Sean Morales through the large Tudor revival mansion and to a large rose garden behind the vast building. The two men walked along the winding stone walkway through the beautiful garden full of blooming flowers and impeccably manicured shrubs. At the end of the walkway was a white wooden gazebo that rested along the edge of a pond, where Helen Morales sat on a stone bench, tossing fish food pellets into the water, feeding a group of colorful butterfly koi fish.

"Eat up," Helen said to the fish as she tossed another handful of pellets. "Winter is coming, and you need to fatten up for your long nap."

"Excuse me mother," Sean said, interrupting Helen's focus on the yellow, black, and white fish that had captured her attention. "Hiro is here to see you."

"What changed your mind?" Helen asked, tossing more fish food into the pond. "Don't get me wrong, I'm glad that you have decided to work with Sean and me, I'm just curious as to why the sudden change of heart."

"There was an incident the other day," Hiro said. He paused for a moment. He wasn't certain that giving Helen all of the details of the events of the last couple of days would be the right thing to do. If he did, then he would be revealing to her that he was aware of the location of the necklace. He would have to reveal to her that he held it in his hands and gave it to Adam's friend, Eli, per Adam's request. Hiro knew that Helen would demand that the necklace be given to her to be turned over to the Vatican. He also was keenly aware of her temper and did not want to cross her at this moment. He also knew that he would have to describe the death of Terry Santos, and Hiro did not feel that he was able to without losing his composure. Hiro chose to tell Helen the minimum of the day's events.

"Go on," Helen said as she turned to face Hiro.

"I assume you heard of the man that rolled his car on the highway yesterday?" Hiro began.

"Yes," Helen said. "I understand that he was a televangelist that was volunteering at Hope Hospital."

"Yes," Hiro said, confirming Helen's information. "I believe he was the P.F. that was on Hiram Grey's call history. I also believe that he came to town in an effort to locate the necklace and possibly even steal it from Adam."

"It's a good thing then that Adam's out of town," Helen said.

"Yes it is," Hiro replied. He paused again in thought. Hiro did not feel good about deceiving Helen, but he was determined to uphold his agreement with Adam.

"Is there anything else?" Helen asked.

"The pastor's cell phone records confirmed that he had been receiving calls from Hiram Grey. He also made calls to a number with a 312 area code that looked familiar. I believe it may be the number to Salvador International."

Helen looked at Hiro for a moment then said to her son, "Sean, Hiro and I are going to the den. Would you be so kind as to make a pot of tea, then join us? I have the feeling we may have some work to do."

"Yes mother," Sean replied as he led the others along the winding walkway back toward the house.

Helen stopped in front of the door that led into the den. "Sean, would you be a dear and show Hiro what you've done to the big room at the end of the East Wing? It's going to take me a moment to get the computer up and running, and I need to organize my desk so that we can efficiently look into Hiro's new information."

"Of course, Mother," Sean replied. "Hiro, if you would follow me," he said as the two men walked down the long corridor that led to the East Wing of the house.

Helen went into the den and turned on the desktop computer. The large tower hard drive lit up and made a whirring noise as it came to life. She then cleared off an area on the corner of the desk and placed the contents on a table near the window. She reached down and opened a cabinet drawer attached to the right side of the desk. Inside the cabinet was a recently installed fire safe with a digital key pad. Helen swiftly punched in the passcode and opened the safe to reveal a single item: the codex scroll protected in its leather case. She carefully removed the scroll from its cocoon and rolled it out on the desk.

Hiro stood in the wide double doorway of what Helen called the big room in the East Wing. It was most certainly a big room. Almost the length and width of a basketball gymnasium, and two stories in height, the room that Sean had converted into an exercise and sparring gym looked more like it belonged in a YMCA, not a family home. Hiro saw that the room had been equipped with what looked to be every piece of equipment a professional fighter would need to train regardless of the discipline or style of fighting.

"They used to hold dances here," Sean told Hiro as he walked to an electronic striking machine. The machine was roughly six feet tall and had seven striking pads and a monitor screen at the top. When Sean kicked and punched the machine's pads, Hiro knew by his form that Sean was not a novice at the workout.

Sean then climbed into the sparring ring and motioned for Hiro to join him. As Hiro ducked his head under the top rope, he asked Sean, "What style do you fight in?"

"I fight in the style of winning," Sean said as he handed Hiro protective sparring gear, which consisted of headgear, shin guards, hand and forearm guards, and a mouth guard. "Spar with me, just for fun."

"But your mother is waiting for us in the den."

"We won't be long." Sean replied as he strapped on his protective equipment.

The two men approached the center of the ring. Hiro bowed to his opponent. Sean grinned and returned Hiro's bow. Hiro examined his opponent. Sean was a couple of inches taller than Hiro, which would give him a greater reach. He was as broad shouldered and obviously equally as lean and physically fit as Hiro.

Sean struck first with a Taekwondo attack called an axe kick. Hiro quickly pivoted out of the way of Sean's attack and countered with a back kick.

Sean's next move, Hiro recognized as a Bajiquan style attack that he successfully countered as well. For the next several minutes, the sparring continued. Sean sent Hiro several attacks from an impressive variety of fighting techniques. Hiro countered every attack successfully. Both men had a wealth of fighting knowledge and were equally matched opponents.

After their light sparring match, the two men shook hands, toweled off their sweat, and went back to the den where Helen had been waiting. Hiro went into the den while Sean walked off to the kitchen to make tea. Helen had a file with information about Salvador International pulled up on her computer when Hiro walked in.

"Let's get a look at that phone number," she said to Hiro, holding out her hand.

Hiro took the small black notebook from his left breast pocket and opened it to the place where he had written the phone number from Pastor Faith's cell phone call history. He read off the number to Helen. She looked at the graphite-covered piece of notebook paper she had kept from Hiro's earlier visit when he had Hiram Grey's call history open. The numbers were the same.

"I called this number," Helen said to remind Hiro. "The number goes to the main switchboard operator at

Salvador International. So both of these men were calling this number."

"That much we know," Hiro said. "But who were they being transferred to? Who were they in communication with? That, we don't know."

"Right," Helen replied. "After your first visit, I started looking into Salvador International itself. Salvador International is a huge company that specializes in drilling. They tunnel for subway systems, mining operations, transit projects and government contracts."

"You said that the man that owned Salvador International knew your grandfather. And your grandfather would have been in possession of the cross necklace at the time."

"Yes, Salvador International was founded and operated by Thomas Salvador," Helen said. "But it was a long time ago. Thomas Salvador no longer runs the company. He would be too old to head up a large corporation. I haven't come across an obituary for the man, so I assume he's still alive, but if he is, he would have to be in his eighties or nineties."

"Perhaps someone at the company wants to use the necklace to keep the man alive like it helped keep your grandfather alive for one hundred nineteen years."

"Maybe, maybe that's it. But I've run Thomas

Salvador's name and information through the codex, and he's not the antichrist."

"There is a possibility that this particular case has nothing to do with the antichrist. Perhaps it is a mere case of selfishness where someone wants to use the relic to extend the life of someone they care about, if not themselves."

"You're probably right. It may just be a coincidence that Thomas Salvador started the company that these two men who came here to steal the necklace were in contact with. But I don't think it is. I remember Thomas Salvador being in this house. I remember him being in this room. He and my grandfather had an argument...." Helen paused mid-sentence as she tried to recall more details about the memory.

"I have your tea," Sean said as he came into the room with a silver tray and set it on a small table near the back corner of the room.

"Thank you Sean," Helen said as she glanced up and looked at the tea set on the table. Then her eyes locked onto the empty clay jar that stood next to the table. The empty clay jar that at one time held scrolls that Henry had retrieved from a cave in Turkey, the same scrolls that someone stole from the house one week after the argument between Henry and Thomas Salvador.

"Join us in the Slaughtered Lamb," Helen muttered to herself as she recalled the words she heard Mr. Salvador say to her grandfather that day many years ago.

"Excuse me?" Sean asked, abruptly stopping the pour of the tea.

"Join us in the Slaughtered Lamb," Helen repeated, louder and with more confidence. "That's what he said. I remember, when Thomas Salvador was here and he and my grandfather were arguing. He asked my grandfather to join him and some group called the Slaughtered Lamb. Grandpa Henry threw the man out of the house. I'd never seen him so angry. They had been looking at a scroll that came from that jar over there. A week later, someone stole the scrolls from it."

"You think Thomas Salvador stole the scrolls?" Hiro asked.

"It's too much of a coincidence," Helen said. "Someone at Salvador International must have the scrolls. They probably translated them. And now they're after the crucifix necklace. We have to find out who it is."

Hiro looked at his notebook and saw the name Steven next to the number on the page. "What were the initials in Hiram Grey's call history that coincided with the phone number?" He asked Helen.

"S.S." Helen replied. "Why?"

"Because, according to Pastor Faith's call history, the number belongs to someone named Steven."

"Steven?" Helen asked as she scrolled through the file that was pulled up on her computer. She found the page that she was looking for and highlighted the name Steven Salvador that was under the label "Current CEO."

"Steven Salvador is the son of Thomas, and he also just happens to be the current CEO of Salvador International," Helen said as she stood and walked around the desk to the scroll she had laid out earlier. Carefully, with a pencil and a notepad, she wrote out Steven Salvador and some numbers. Then she carefully referenced the scroll, making marks on the notepad. After a few moments, Helen gasped. She dropped the pencil and pad. Hiro caught her as she lost her balance due to the faint she fell into.

"Mother!" Sean yelled as he ran to her aid. He and Hiro helped her to her chair behind the desk.

"Steven Salvador fits the codex," Helen said softly as she caught her breath.

"Would it be possible for Thomas to manipulate his son's name to make it fit the codex?" Hiro asked.

"He would have had to have had his son born on a specific date. He would have had to have known the code to break the cipher and then named his son to fit."

"But is it possible to reverse engineer the results?" Hiro asked. "He did have access to the scrolls."

"But not the codex." Helen said. "The codex never left this room."

"So what now?" Sean asked his mother.

"We have Steven Salvador arrested," Helen answered.

"We have no actual proof that he had anything to do with the murders," Hiro said. "And we can't have him arrested because an artifact suggests that he may be the antichrist."

"What about the stolen scrolls? Could you get a warrant to search his and his father's properties for the stolen scrolls?"

"I'm not a police officer anymore. I cannot obtain search warrants. Besides, did your grandfather even report the theft of the scrolls when it happened?"

Helen stared at Hiro in angry silence.

"Did he take any photographs of them? Were they insured?"

Helen continued her silent stare.

"The police will not arrest a man without evidence of a crime."

"The codex is the key," Helen said, breaking her silence. "I believe, and I think my grandfather did too, that Steven Salvador's father stole the scrolls. Grandpa

Henry believed that those scrolls were potentially dangerous. He said that they never should have been found. He called them false scripture. And now they're in the hands of the antichrist."

"We can't go to the police with that information," Hiro said. "They won't believe you."

"Do you believe me?" Helen asked Hiro.

Hiro met Helen's gaze. It was his turn to be silent.

"Do you believe?" Helen asked. "Do you believe in all I have imparted onto you? Because if you do, believe me when I tell you that the knowledge Steven Salvador possesses has the power to bring about the rapture. But not how the Bible describes it. A man-made rapture. A civil war of humanity. Our society, the world is already wrapped in religious intolerance. There is great evil in this world bearing the face of an innocent lamb, Mr. Tarsus. And the devil is conducting its heart strings."

"That's a bit dramatic," Hiro replied.

"That's the devil's greatest trick," Helen said. "He's convinced men like you that he doesn't exist."

"Wasn't that in a movie or something?"

"So that people would laugh and doubt his existence even more," Helen said as she got up and went back to the codex scroll. She held the scroll's leather case in her hands. She rotated the leather case, showing Hiro an inscription on the back. The inscription was faint but visible. יהיה לליצן לשמש כמלך ומי שצחק, יצחק בדם.

"I don't understand what you're showing me," Hiro said as he studied the casing.

"For the jester shall serve as king, and he who laughed shall laugh in blood." Helen said, translating the message written in Hebrew.

"I will stay with you on this," Hiro said, "but we can't go making accusations and pushing for arrests without evidence. If Steven Salvador has been involved in this web of crime, he will make another go for the necklace. When he does, he will slip up and I will be there to catch him."

"We will be there," Helen added, taking the man's hand and squeezing it tightly. "And then we will retrieve the stolen scrolls and stop the antichrist."

# Chapter 23.

The days passed quickly, and Adam finally found himself within the Vatican gardens taking a leisurely walk with Father Vigano. The gardens were quiet, much to his surprise, as thousands of tourists roamed Vatican City.

"I want my great-great grandmother to receive a proper burial. She came from a Catholic family. They would have baptized her and it was their shameful actions that committed her to this despicable workhouse," Adam stated as Father Vigano listened quietly. "In fact, all of these women and children deserve a proper Christian burial. And I know now that my grandfather's dying wish was to bring her soul to rest next to his."

Father Vigano gave a slight nod, but an impartial expression remained on his face.

"When he said to me, we all are in need of healing, he was referring to himself as much as he was referring to me. Perhaps he was even referring to the Church itself, Father."

"Perhaps," Father Vigano said simply. He then continued, "Dr. Calhoun, there is no need to convince the Holy See. It has already been discussed. The Holy Father will be declaring this coming year 'The Year of Mercy.' These women deserve God's mercy and love and to be properly laid to rest. I will help you see it done. Regarding the matter of the necklace, that is a decision for you alone to make, Adam."

Adam was not sure how to respond, so he simply thanked Father Vigano for his time and assistance.

\*\*\*

Several news crews were situated on the grounds of the convent of the Merciful Sisters of Charity. Adam stood beside Sister Mary Gabriel, presenting her with a large, symbolic, poster-board check. The act was met with applause from the small gathering of locals, clergy, and members of the media.

After the check presentation, Adam took to a podium to give a short speech. "The Calhoun Family Foundation, working closely and with the permission of the

government of Ireland, the Vatican, and the local
Archdiocese, has taken out a twenty-year lease on the
property to excavate the premises. The hope of my
family's foundation is to exhume and identify the remains
of the many unidentified women and children, in order to
finally provide them with the proper burial their souls
deserve and erect a lasting memorial acknowledging their
identities. A grant in the amount of twenty million euros
will be gifted to Sister Mary Gabriel and her order to
carry out the memory of Mother Maureen and reopen the
school."

Back in Chicago, a flat screen television set was tuned
to the news broadcast showing Adam Calhoun's press
conference. Adam's voice slowly faded out and his body
fell into the background as the television camera zoomed
out to focus on Jonathon Coyne, a senior international
correspondent for CNN who stepped into frame. Jonathon
spoke with an Irish accent and talked directly into the
camera.

"The government has issued a formal apology to those
affected by the Magdalene Laundries. Meanwhile, church
leaders have offered their full support to the efforts of the
Calhoun Family Foundation. Adam Calhoun is the great-
grandson and one of the heirs to the estate of billionaire

philanthropist Henry Calhoun, who passed away this year. I am Jonathon Coyne reporting live from—"

The television screen clicked off. The reflection of Steven Salvador, seated at the desk of his high rise office, holding a television remote in his hand became visible as the television screen faded to a glossy black. Steven sat with a pensive look on his face. His thumb spun his golden ring around his finger.

# Chapter 24.

The sanctuary hall of the Slaughtered Lamb lodge was dimly lit from half a dozen black and gold gilded Baroque style gondola lanterns hanging from the high, plaster ceiling. Painted across the ceiling and bathed from the light of the lanterns in an ethereal haze of orange and yellow was a mural. The mural was a replica of Michelangelo's *The Last Judgment*. Black rails attached to the ceiling framed the fresco and hung fifteen masterly crafted tapestries depicting the Via Crucis, the day of the crucifixion of Jesus. The embroidered canvases were draped in a rectangular fashion throughout the room creating a walled in central area. The fifteenth tapestry was placed at the north end of the hall and depicted the resurrection of Jesus Christ. Below and directly in front of that fifteenth tapestry was a polished altar made of Dark

Emperador marble from Spain. A book stand adorned with gold leaf rested atop the rich brown and grey colored altar.

Steven Salvador knelt ceremoniously on the floor on top of a mosaic emblem of the Order of the Slaughtered Lamb. He was barefoot and wore a simple, white cloak. The backside of his cloak appeared to have a streak of blood as if from a lash. Steven gripped the heavy manuscript he had transcribed as the other twelve members of the Slaughtered Lamb encircled him.

Each member wore a white cloak with either a silver, red or light blue braided cord necklace depending on their rank and tenure with the exception of Steven who wore nothing around his neck and another man who stood directly behind Steven. This man wore a dark purple cord necklace and held his arms outstretched with his palms facing the ceiling. Resting across his palms was a special cord twisted from two separate colors, red and gold. To the side of this man was another man wearing a light blue cord and holding a crown of thorns.

The members chanted a low Gregorian chant as the member with the crown of thorns stepped towards Steven to begin the initiation. He placed the crown atop Steven's head and applied a slight amount of pressure causing several thorns to pierce Steven's flesh. Steven closed his eyes as he continued to welcome the mortification of his flesh with the purpose of overcoming his psychological and physical weaknesses on his path to sanctity. The man released the crown of thorns on Steven's head and backed away.

The member wearing the purple cord stepped forward, raised the red and gold cord above his head and then ceremoniously draped the necklace around Steven's neck. Steven felt the slight weight of the cord fall upon his trapezoid area.

The man then knelt down beside Steven, and said, "You have been purified through water and fire. Your blood has been shed in remembrance of him. Now rise and take your place amongst us as your father did before you." He kissed Steven's hand and aided him to his feet.

Blood trickled down Steven's temples and brow as he turned to face the marble altar. Each member synchronously followed suit as they chanted, "Compassion. Order. Mercy. Sacrifice."

Steven took his place behind the altar and presented the manuscript to the men. "I have transcribed the ancient scrolls." Steven announced with authority. "Bound within these pages is the *Gospel of Salvation*." He opened the manuscript and placed it down upon the golden book stand. The title on the cover of the manuscript was visible through the golden slats of the stand, *The Revelations of Jesus Christ.*

The false knowledge Henry had spoken of was on the cusp of being given a voice and either Helen's fear would prove to be only superstition or that fear would become a reality. The wheels were now in motion and pressure to acquire the iron relic would surely grow tenfold. There was extreme wealth and power within the walls of this lodge and unified, their resources could prove to be endless.

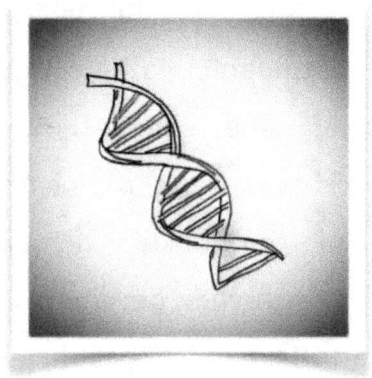

# Chapter 25.

Within a week of Adam's press conference in Ireland a team of top-notch forensic archeologists hired by the Calhoun Foundation descended on the convent of the Merciful Sisters of Charity and went to work excavating the area inside and around the dry water well. The international group of men and women were tasked with evidence recovery and evidence recording in hopes of identifying as many as possible of the lost that were buried there. Any human remains unearthed were mapped, photographed and carefully placed into paper bags to help prevent mold and absorb any moisture before being sealed inside acid-free boxes for transportation to Genecestry Labs for DNA analysis.

The laboratory conducted a number of DNA tests on the evidence collected including mitochondrial DNA testing used to trace a person's mother-line ancestry. The results were then catalogued to be compared against the DNA of potential relatives. The Calhoun Foundation had undertaken the arduous task of locating any possible living relatives but thanks to the amount of media coverage Adam had received combined with the ledger of names provided by Sister Maria Gabriel, the foundation staff received family leads on almost a daily basis. Once the lengthy process was completed, the foundation intended on constructing a beautiful sandstone remembrance wall on the site listing the names of the once lost who were buried on the grounds.

For several weeks, archeologists worked around the clock. They wore masks, body suits and gloves to protect themselves and any skeletal remains from contamination. The entire area was staked out into one enormous grid constructed of pegs and strong cord that were sectioned off into squares of one meter by one meter. A back-hoe was utilized to clear larger debris and rigging was constructed above the dried-up water well. Several persons had been identified through the recovery process but the one Adam had hoped to uncover was still missing.

Years of debris and dirt had clogged the old water well more than half the way up the shaft. The team worked feverishly to remove the debris and carefully sift through it all. After weeks of clearing out and recording more than fifteen feet of debris, the team finally reached the bottom of the well.

"Prepare the rigging." One of the archeologists, Leo, a slender man in his late forties said to the crew around the well. "I want to clear as much as possible before dark."

Leo walked off to a tent set up in the courtyard to put on his gear and prepare to descend into the well. He fitted himself with a harness and attached a shovel, a small trowel and other tools to his belt. After about a half-hour, Leo found himself being lowered down into the well. A light and camera attached to his yellow hard hat documented the descent. The rope swayed to and fro but Leo did his best to balance his body in the center of the shaft. One rough bump against the ancient mudstone walls could cause the shaft to collapse in on him. The beam of light from his helmet revealed just how badly the structure had been damaged from the years of debris.

Leo's cold forehead beaded with an icy, sweat. He could not wait to have his feet firmly placed on the bottom. The temperatures had plummeted over the past few weeks with the onset of winter and what moisture had gathered on the filthy walls inside the well were frozen solid making them dangerously slick.

At last, his boots crunched down onto the stony sand

floor. "I'm on the bottom," Leo shouted. His voice echoed its way up the walls to the crew above.

"We are lowering the bucket down, mate." One of the crew members shouted back.

Leo went to work using his shovel to break through the tough, compacted topsoil. He loaded each shovel full of dirt into a five-gallon bucket attached to a thick rope. Bucket load after bucket load, he dug until he had removed over a foot of soil without any signs of human remains.

He thrust his shovel into the ground and a ding rang out from striking an object that caused his shovel to vibrate. Leo knelt down and carefully dusted around the area. He found a series of stones each around the size of a baseball and there were quite a number of them.

"I'm going to need more buckets." Leo hollered. He removed the stones and placed them into the bucket to be hauled out. "Pull this one out. But be careful, its full of stones."

"Right mate. Here goes." A voice boomed down into the hole.

The bucket rose foot by foot towards the surface. The weight of the stones caused it to sway and collide with the sides of the well. Leo heard the bucket scrape and the stones knock against each other.

"Be gentle." Leo warned. Then he focused back on the earth below him. He used his trowel to scrape away a sharp object just beneath the surface. He knew immediately what it was. "Another bucket! Quickly!" He worked hurriedly but carefully to clear the bone from the ground.

As the men topside prepared to lower a second bucket into the well, the stone-filled pail inside the well struck a loosened mudstone brick. The pail shook side to side out of control as marble-sized bits of stone rained down on Leo. A piece of rock struck him in the shoulder causing a minor laceration.

"Ouch." Leo winced in pain. He glanced up in time to see several fist-sized pieces of brick come crashing down. Leo hurled his body against the wall in a defensive position. The shards crashed around him. His pulse pounded as he waited for the entire well to collapse in on him. After several moments, Leo pulled his hands and arms from off of his face and chest to survey the situation.

"Are you okay, mate?" His teammate yelled from above with panic in his voice.

Leo rose to his feet and dusted off taking note of several minor scrapes. "Fine. Now get me that second bucket!"

Leo and his team worked quickly and efficiently to

remove the skeletal remains before sunset. They catalogued their findings and then had the bones boxed up and shipped off to Genecestry Labs. There the laboratory would compare any testable DNA against the DNA taken from the Calhoun family including Helen and Adam.

***

In Ohio, Adam awaited the results from the DNA test at the home of his best pal, Eli Taylor who had made a full recovery from the ordeal with Pastor Faith. The two men bantered playfully over a hotly contested game of chess.

"I have to say, Hiro is a far superior chess player to you, bud." Eli razzed Adam, as he studied his next move. "At least I felt like I was playing an equal."

"Just move already." Adam sniped back.

Eli moved his bishop into position.

"Have you given any thoughts to your next move?" Adam queried.

"You mean life? Or putting away this game?"

"Life, dude."

"To be honest, I hadn't exactly planned this far ahead." Eli smirked. "I have you to thank for that."

"I'm not the one to thank." Adam said humbly. "I was

just a vessel."

"And so we all are my friend. But thank you nonetheless." Eli watched Adam use his knight to take Eli's bishop. "Nicely played."

"A compliment? Wow. Thank you."

"I was thinking of going to spend a few months with my dad and then apply to a few firms. See who needs a decent architect."

"I know of one." Adam removed an envelope from his pocket and placed it down beside the chessboard.

"I'm not taking any handouts, Adam."

"Who said it's a handout? It's a job offer from the Calhoun Foundation. We just happen to be looking for an experienced, bright, talented architect to design some new—"

Eli cut him off. "Let me think about it."

"Hey, I have to hire someone. Might as well be you. Are you really going to leave me hanging?"

Eli glanced off considering the offer.

"If you are playing hard to get just stop because I already doubled the salary any other place will offer you. Besides, think of all the kids you'd be helping."

Eli looked back at Adam and then opened the envelope. His eyes widened as he read the offer. "Wow."

"I can pay you less if that will make you feel better?"

"I don't know if I'm going to be able to handle taking orders from you."

"You won't be. Just say yes."

"Okay. You actually had me at job offer. But only after I spend some time with my dad."

"I wouldn't want it any other way."

The two reached across the chessboard and hugged. During their embrace, a vibration was felt.

"This is awkward." Eli joked. "Is that you or me?"

Adam reached inside his coat pocket. "Me." He removed his cell phone and looked down at the caller id. The incoming call was from Genecestry Labs. "I have to take this." Adam pressed the green answer spot on the screen. "Hello, Dr. Calhoun speaking." He listened intently waiting for the laboratory technician to relay the results of the DNA test. When the technician spoke, Adam suddenly seemed to zone out, stunned from the first three words he heard.

"We found her."

\*\*\*

The remains of Henry Calhoun's biological mother, Maeve Byrne, were respectfully placed inside of a solid cherry wood casket that was lined in plush, green velvet. The coffin was then boarded onto a plane and flown to

Ohio where Maeve would finally be laid to rest beside Henry.

The empty gravesite of Henry Calhoun at the Heavenly Acres Cemetery was blanketed in fresh snow. A single red rose rested against his headstone. Beside the headstone was a trail of deep footprints that led away from the decoy grave to a plot three sites over. The footprints were recent and had begun to fill with snowfall. The tracks travelled past the resting place of Henry's wife Florence, who was buried directly to Henry's left and continued past a previously unmarked grave. This plot was the true final resting place of Henry Calhoun. The unmarked grave was now adorned with a green flecked granite headstone that read simply:

*HERE RESTS ALROY BYRNE*

The plot to the left of Alroy's site was a freshly dug grave that was surrounded by Adam, Rose, Helen, Sean, Hiro Tarsus and Father Vigano from Rome, who was presiding over the funeral services. Their heads were bowed in prayer as the cherry colored casket was lowered into the earth by a member of the cemetery staff.

A rosy pink granite headstone lay flat at the head of the plot. Etched into the headstone was the following:

## MAEVE BYRNE, LOVING MOTHER TO ALROY. CALLED UP TO GOD IN SEPTEMBER OF 1913

Father Vigano blessed each of the gravesites one last time. His nose was running from the chilly air. Helen stepped over and handed him a handkerchief as she took his arm in hers. She gently patted the man's hand while he dabbed his nose with the hanky.

"Thank you." He said.

"No. Thank you." She replied. Then she removed her arm from his and walked back towards Sean and Hiro, who were admiring the beauty of the snowy landscape.

Adam knelt down beside Henry's true grave and leaned over the dark green headstone. He whispered to the grave. "I hope I made you proud, Papa. And that you and your angel are reunited." He felt a slight sting as he forced back the tears that caused the inside of his nose to swell and his eyes to gloss. A soothing waft of lavender soon entered his nostrils and allowed him to close his eyes. The smell was the silky skin of Rose's hand as she caressed his face.

"He is proud of you. Very proud of you." She assured Adam.

He sucked in a burst of cold air through his nose,

nodded his head and stood up. Rose wrapped her arms around him and kissed him on the side of his mouth. Held within that moist touch of her lips was the healing that Adam's heart had so desperately longed for. The healing that Henry had prayed for Adam in his dying wish: the gift of unconditional love.

*Now it was time to stop putting lives at risk*, Adam thought to himself. He stepped away from Rose and wandered over to Father Vigano.

"I must be getting back to Rome." Father Vigano said as he rubbed his cheeks to warm them up.

"I will have a car take you to the airport." Adam replied. "Thank you for everything you have done for my family."

Father Vigano tilted his head down in acknowledgment. Adam took the man's gloved hand in his own, then removed the glove from the priest's right hand. As Father Vigano started to furrow his brow and give Adam a questionable look, the priest felt the warm sensation of silver in his palm.

"I believe you have the gravitas to bear this." Adam said sincerely. "Papa Henry had his reasons for not giving this necklace to the Vatican but I believe it's time for a new chapter in my family's history. Do God's will with it."

Father Vigano stood in awe, overwhelmed by the

moment. The energy of the relic seemed to flow into his body. His runny nose dried up, warmth flowed into his cheeks and all sensation of cold disappeared from his body.

"Adam." Helen said, startled. There was a tinge of fright in her voice.

Tarsus quickly turned in Helen's direction to protect her. He reached for the pistol concealed under his heavy overcoat.

"No." Helen uttered to Tarsus.

A figure that had been watching them from the shadows of the cemetery emerged and stood within several yards of the group. Adam and Rose recognized the man and glanced at each other. It was the man, David Mosin, who had saved them at the convent from Pavel Volkov.

*Had he saved us or was he just waiting for the appropriate time to kill us?* Adam thought as he reached for Rose and pulled her near him.

"What do you want from us?" Adam demanded. "Enough people have died."

"Do you know this man, Adam?" Tarsus asked, his fingers still wrapped around the handle of his revolver.

"A man tried to kill us in Ireland. He was there." Adam replied.

"Adam." Helen said calmly to the doctor but Adam kept his eyes focused on the man. She took on a motherly tone to her voice. "Adam? Adam?"

Adam broke his gaze and turned his eyes towards his aunt.

"Adam, I know this man." Helen said to ease the tension. She turned her attention back to David. "It's been a very long time, David. We all thought you were dead."

"There were many days I wish I had been. Then I would recall her eyes and start to daydream that you all were safe. And happy." David replied. The man's piercing blue eyes were fixed upon Adam. "I felt like a man without a soul until I saw you standing next to that well in Ireland." David took a step towards Adam causing the young doctor to take a counter step backwards.

"Adam." Helen said. "Don't be afraid. This is your father."

Adam felt as if a tornado had landed inside his stomach. His hands began to fidget from his side to his face back to his side. He breathed in and out so fast that the cloud of air exhaling from his mouth looked like smoke bursting from a cannon. His head tingled and his arms felt numb.

"Breathe, baby. Breathe." Rose said in a slow and steady voice.

Adam turned to Rose. His eyes rapidly shot left and right.

Rose placed her hands on either side of his face. "You're hyperventilating. Breathe a long, deep breath." Rose breathed with him.

For thirty-six years David had carried the guilt he felt for the pain he had caused the family and now he certainly had no desire to bring more hurt upon his only son. The heartbroken father turned to trod away back into the shadows of the snowy property. Step by step he crunched through the snow. *I should have stayed out of his life,* he thought. *How could I have been so dumb to dream that Adam would ever think of me as his –*

"Dad?"

The word went straight to his heart like a sniper's bullet stopping David dead in his tracks. David bit into his lip, lowered his head and slowly turned around coming face to face with Adam. The two stared at one another in a long silence.

"Please forgive me, son. Henry showed me what God's kindness and mercy looked like. He helped me turn to God. And then I was blessed with the greatest gift in this world. You." David's voice cracked. "I thought I knew all there was to know about love with your mom. But I didn't. I didn't. Not until the first time I held you just minutes after you were born and I heard your little cry. It spoke to my soul. And I knew my sole job as a father was to keep you safe even if that meant sacrificing everything. I probably don't deserve your love and understand if don't wish to see me again."

"You're my dad. You're in front of me." Adam said, stopping David from continuing his monologue. "And up until several minutes ago, that was only the sad dream of a little boy who would lie on his back on his birthday and wish to the clouds. You're my dad." Adam wrapped his arms around David embracing him tightly.

The two men wept with gratitude as they hugged one another. Adam felt transported back into his two-year-old self. The longing for a connection to his past, for answers to the questions of his childhood, that seemed to fade into his subconscious, came rushing to the forefront with one slight difference. He knew now that all of this was within his grasp. *All because of this gift, this miraculous iron relic, from Papa Henry*, he thought. He would see the world through changed eyes no longer partially hidden within the cave of his heart and his mind. Life would be full of wondrous revelations and he was eager to submit himself to God's will.

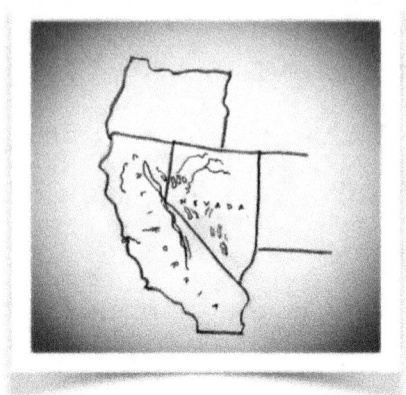

# Chapter 26.

Steven Salvador stood at a heavily marked-up whiteboard in the secure conference room located on the grounds of Naval Station Great Lakes. The sides of his sweaty palms were black from using his hands as a dry eraser. Usually succinct and to the point, he felt disconnected and off his game. His presentation had carried on a good hour over his intended time and he feared that the high level persons in attendance could sense his mind wandering as the words jetted out of his mouth. These stake holders included Defense Secretary Kenneth Ivory, Admiral J.D. Hodkins and two other government suits who sat quietly around a dark, mahogany conference table.

Steven was no stranger to the world of government contracting. As CEO of the company his father built,

Salvador International, he had negotiated a number of contracts for various construction projects. Now, he was tasked with presenting a bid to construct a classified tunnel connecting a secret lake in Nevada to the Pacific Ocean. The underwater pathway would give the navy the ability to launch submarines hundreds of miles inland to the Pacific Ocean completely undetected.

A series of flip chart style maps were mounted on a tripod near the whiteboard. The top map was a semi-transparent map outlining the western United States. Directly behind this map was a topographical map using lines to reveal rivers, lakes and mountain ranges. This map covered a physical map that used colors to indicate variations in the Earth's crust and the continental shelf. The final map was one normally associated with myth and conspiracy theories. It was a bathymetric map featuring a series of 'undocumented' ocean waterways and caverns, from California into parts of western Nevada, directly below the continental shelf.

Steven neared the end of his exhausting, almost two-hour long presentation as he rolled up the first two maps to reveal the third map displaying the continental shelf. "As you can see from the map, parts of California and western Nevada are, for lack of a better word, floating above the Pacific Ocean." Steven flipped the map to reveal the bathymetric map.

The usually upright admiral let out a groan at the sight of the map, slumped down in his seat and began massaging his forehead and temples.

"A pressurized face at the front of the mole will maintain ground stability and the use of ground penetrating radar and advanced sensors on the cutting head will—"

"The sophistication of your robotic worms is impressive," said the secretary, interrupting Steven's presentation, "but we need to know where the rubber meets the road. My primary concerns are the timetable and the cost."

"Are you able to provide us with any examples of recent tunneling projects for cost comparisons?" Admiral Hodkins interjected.

"That's a complicated process. This will be the largest tunneling project that the world will never know about. We will be passing through many different ground conditions including sections prone to earthquakes."

"So you can't?" The admiral said, giving Steven an icy glare.

"No two tunnels are exactly alike. If you want comparisons, I have provided examples as reported by the companies involved in the successful completion of the

Shanghai River Crossing, which is one of the largest diameter tunnels in the world. There's also another project underway in Turkey. In that project moveable joints are being utilized in case of earthquakes. Feel free to cherry-pick but there's no one size fits all, Admiral."

The admiral fumed inside. He had a healthy amount of disdain for private contractors who he felt lacked a sense of patriotism and were simply profiteers who bellowed smoke for higher fees. "A waste of time," he mumbled under his breath.

"We have a secret ace in our pocket, gentlemen. Mother Nature. She's done most of the work for us already." Steven took a deep breath and smiled before continuing. "If you would please focus on the fourth map, you will notice my company has spent a considerable amount of time and money mapping below the continental shelf using sonar technology that the navy could only dream of possessing."

The admiral sat upright and fired back at Steven. "Conspiracies. We have had scientists combing over those areas for decades."

"Yes, you have. And some of those scientists just so happened to have worked for the company my father founded, where we have kept their discoveries locked away until now. This map is a complete illustration of the oceanic waterways from Fort Ord in Monterey Bay to western Nevada. Our project doesn't have to tunnel three hundred miles to the Pacific. We only have to tunnel the short distance from Walker Lake to the largest passage…. Forty-two miles away. Your fast moving attack subs would be able to leave Walker Lake and reach Monterey Bay in a matter of hours, completely unseen."

"I have three booklets in front of me that rival the girth of *War and Peace*, if you will, Steven. I need the abridged version." Secretary Ivory stated casually.

"Some tunneling projects have a cost that's upwards of two hundred million dollars per mile. But combined with these natural passageways and my company's technology, I can bring the project in at a cost of forty-one million per mile."

The admiral clicked his pen and began to calculate the math on the booklet in front of him.

"I'll save you the trouble of doing the math. That's 1.72 billion, dollars, Admiral." Steven stated.

Admiral Hodkins scowled at Steven and slowly placed his pen back down on the table.

"Gentlemen, if you turn to page one hundred and seventeen in the booklet with the grey cover, I have provided a complete work breakdown structure of phase one to Project Groundhog, justifying the costs. We estimate a timetable of eighteen to twenty-two months. You should find the chart easy to digest."

Secretary Ivory picked up his gold-rimmed reading glasses and balanced them on the bridge of his nose. He flipped open the booklet, thumbed to page one hundred seventeen and scanned the chart that broke the project down into bite-sized pieces. The room fell unnervingly silent as the rest of the men followed his lead and scrutinized the chart.

During this interlude, Steven's mind seemed to splinter like a puzzle breaking apart sending his thoughts into fragmented pieces. The thoughts of his dying father, Calhoun's necklace, the nightmares, the translated scrolls and the future of his company all raced around fighting for top position in his head. He felt overwhelmed at the notion that the future of so many things important to him were no longer within his control. He focused back on the task at hand. He was certain of one thing. *I am done jumping through hoops with these men*, he thought. Steven was prepared to throw in the towel on Project Groundhog when the secretary peered up from the booklet and shocked him.

"Gentlemen, it appears that we are about to buy some very expensive hammers and toilet seats," Secretary Ivory said closing the booklet. The sixty-seven-year-old man removed his reading glasses and fixed his eyes directly on Salvador. "Steven, your father's company has a long standing history with us and has always delivered. You have my full confidence."

"Thank you, Secretary." Steven replied.

"When can your company start?" The secretary asked, rising to his feet.

"As soon as we receive the first deposit."

The admiral coughed, clearing his throat before he interjected. "I suppose someone has to play the devil's advocate. Mr. Salvador, necessity dictates a high degree of stealth during construction. What assurances can your company provide us that someone is not going to feel the ground tremble under their feet or that some rancher won't have his home collapse into a sink hole in the middle of the Nevada desert? These areas are growing in population. It is not 1956 anymore."

"There are dozens of tunnel-boring projects going on all over the world in highly populated areas, urban areas and the public has no clue that there are machines digging hundreds of feet below them. As you said, it's not 1956 anymore, technology has come a long way."

"I believe this concludes our business here. Steven, we will be in touch." Secretary Ivory said, shaking Steven's hand as the other men exited the room. "On a personal note," Ivory continued with a doleful expression on his face, "please give your old man my best and let him know Pamela and I are praying for him."

"I will. Thank you."

The secretary gripped Steven's left shoulder momentarily with his right hand. On the secretary's right ring finger was a golden ring bearing the emblem of the Slaughtered Lamb. The secretary released Steven's shoulder and continued after the admiral who was hovering just outside the doorway.

Steven left the Naval Station driving out through the guarded gate. He casually drove around the shoreline towards an industrial section containing a number of abandoned warehouse buildings tucked away behind a high, galvanized steel chain-linked fence topped with razor wire. When he reached a locked gate, he stopped his car, got out and unlocked the gate. He then slowly drove through the gate, stopped, got out again and locked the gate behind him. He returned to his vehicle and drove using a hand sketched map of the area as his guide. He ended up in a secluded area in between two warehouse buildings with one having a steel garage door and a keypad located in front of it. Steven peered back at his map and read the 12-digit key code written at the top of the paper. He rolled his window down and punched the code into the key pad. Suddenly the old garage door creaked and rolled open. As Steven drove inside the parking area a sensor triggered the garage door to close behind his vehicle securing the building.

Steven parked his car and stepped out. He was in a large open area with twenty-foot high ceilings. The vast area was empty with concrete floors. Steven walked towards an elevator at the far end of the room. Once he reached the elevator he found a dust and grime covered security pad. He used his sleeve to wipe the pad clean and expose the numbers. He then entered a second security code causing the pad the light up and the elevator door to open. He cautiously walked inside the freight elevator and removed a key from his pocket. He inserted the override key into the elevator panel and pressed the "5". But instead of going up to the fifth floor, the elevator began to descend ten stories down. When the doors opened, Steven found himself stepping into an elaborate Cold War bunker only it was large enough to house hundreds of people. Steven flipped up a lever on the wall that turned on a series of generators lighting up the facility and activating the ventilation and water systems.

The air was musky and thick as Steven slowly walked down a corridor leading further into the mini underground city that extended directly beneath Lake

Michigan. He heard the clacking of pumps and valves as the water filtration system booted up. The series of pumps and valves extended from the bunker up through the earth and exited a small opening at the bottom of Lake Michigan where a burst of tiny bubbles bellowed out until the pressure in the pipes stabilized. The tiny bubbles floated gently to the surface of the massive lake and popped with the Chicago city skyline in the backdrop.

***

Vatican City State

The sharp clacking of heels echoed down the halls of the Palace of Sixtus V. The footsteps travelled with such military precision that one would be hard pressed to decipher if they belonged to one person or multiple if not for the off cadence sounds of Father Vigano's feet plopping behind the Swiss Guard. The two guards, dressed in their traditional blue, red, yellow and orange uniforms, accompanied Father Vigano to a closed, doorway in a small alcove. The door had the appearance of a simple hallway closet however the faux wood door was made of solid steel. Vigano removed a set of keys and unlocked the door.

The two soldiers took their positions and flanked the

sides of the door as Vigano stepped through the doorway and entered another corridor. Once inside, he closed the door behind him. The automatic lock snapped into position and motion sensors triggered a series of fluorescent lights. The corridor extended for approximately ten feet ending at another locked door.

Father Vigano walked briskly to the next entrance and placed his index finger on the finger scan pad. After several seconds the pad turned green and a set of locks clicked open.

The father opened the door and disclosed a narrow chamber with a velvet drapery in the back covering another entrance. He slid the curtain to one side and then stepped inside a climate controlled museum that was no more than four hundred square feet. The walls of the tiny museum were covered from floor to ceiling with glass display cases housing some of the most historically significant and sacred artifacts in history.

In the center of the room was a stainless steel laboratory table with cabinets underneath. On top of the table were a number of scientific instruments such as a microscope, glass petri dishes, tweezers and various cutting tools including a laser scalpel. The laser scalpel was the size and shape of a fountain pen. Father Vigano walked over to the workbench and then carefully removed

Henry Calhoun's necklace and crucifix pendant from around his neck and set the pendant face down inside one of the petri dishes. The backside of the pendant was exposed showing the small clasp attached to the turquoise stone that covered the secret chamber. He took a pair of tweezers and tried to pry open the small clasp but the chamber was soldered shut. Father Vigano opened one of the cabinets, removed a pair of magnifying surgical loupes and placed them over his eyes in order to better examine the secret chamber. Through the loupes he was able to see a thin metallic sealant surrounding the casing that enclosed the turquoise stone. He picked up the laser scalpel and pressed the sensor activating a small beam at the tip. Vigano carefully sliced through the metallic seal around the casing. The stone wiggled slightly as he finished cutting open the chamber. Using tweezers, he removed the turquoise stone exposing the secret chamber within the pendant.

Father Vigano slid a second petri dish beside the first and delicately lifted the pendant out of the glass dish using his fingertips. He held the crucifix pendant face down over the second dish and with a quick roll of his fingertips, he spun the pendant over. There was no sound, no tick of a lead tip falling into the glass container but when Father Vigano moved the pendant away from the dish, there it was. He saw the tip to the Holy Nail magnified three times its size through the loupes he was wearing.

"Magnifico." Father Vigano said as he admired the relic. He then placed the pendant and necklace inside the first petri dish and covered it with a glass lid before doing the same to the second petri dish. He stacked the dishes on top of each other, grabbed the tweezers and carried the items over to one of the glass display cases against the back wall.

Resting on the shelves were a number of sculptures designed to house relics such as thorns believed to be from the Crown of Thorns and the bones and dried blood of saints. On one of the glass shelves was the original Titulus Crucis, not the medieval replica that was on display at the Basilica di Santa Croce in Gerusalemme. Beside the piece of wood, in a silver box lined with felt, rested the Holy Nail. Father Vigano opened the glass cabinet and placed the glass dish containing the necklace and crucifix pendant on the shelf next to the silver box.

He peered through his magnifying loupes as he used a pair of tweezers to carefully lift the iron tip out of the petri dish. The tip hovered above the blunt nail until Father Vigano slowly lowered the tip down onto the end of the Holy Nail. The micro-sized ridges of the two pieces fit together perfectly.

Vigano removed the glass dish with the crucifix pendant from the shelf and closed the glass cabinet door, sealing the iron relic inside.

## THE END

# ABOUT THE AUTHORS

## James Stevenson

James Stevenson was born and raised in Hannibal, Missouri. He was catholic schooled from the first through the seventh grades. James joined the U.S. Navy in 1988 and served until 1992. He now resides in Los Angeles, California where he works as an actor under the stage name Dallas James. James' has a children's book *Walter The Earthworm* coming out later this year.

## Bobby Hundley

Bobby Hundley has always had a fascination with history, archeology and medicine which made The Iron Relic Book Series a true passion piece for him. As a child, he grew up hearing stories of miraculous healings from his own Papa, who was a strong man of faith. He now resides in Los Angeles, California where he works as a producer, writer and actor. Bobby serves as the Producing Artistic Director of the San Gabriel Valley Music Theatre. He has a children's book series: *The Adventures of Princess Lainey* coming out soon.

Thank you for reading *The Iron Relic Book II: Revelations*, we'd love to hear what you thought of the book. Please consider writing a review and/or rating our book online under the book's page at: Amazon, Barnes and Noble or Goodreads.

To learn more about The Iron Relic Book Series, please like us on Facebook: The Iron Relic Book Series, follow us on Twitter @TheIronRelic or visit us on the World Wide Web at

# www.theironrelicbook.com

www.ingramcontent.com/pod-product-compliance
Lightning Source LLC
Chambersburg PA
CBHW060358260626
47160CB00006B/2358